the
Devil
in
Beauty

the Devil in Beauty

A Lord Trevelin Mystery

HEIDI ASHWORTH

Interior design by Heather Justesen
Edited by Kim Huther
Formatting by Heather Justesen

Cover design by An Author's Art
Cover image photo credit: Christopher Bissell
Published by Dunhaven Place Publishing

This book is dedicated to my very own Willy and his young brother.

Please Note:

The events in this book take place eight years prior to those of the novella, *The Lord Who Sneered*, and five years prior to *Ghosts in the Graveyard*, both of which are found in *The Lord Who Sneered and Other Tales: A Regency Holiday Anthology*.

Señyor Juliol Rey speaks the Catalan version of Spanish, which accounts for the differences in spelling and pronunciation.

Number 50 Berkeley Square was occupied in 1811 by the former Secretary of State for Foreign Affairs George Canning and his family. The house is considered to be the most haunted in England.

Prologue

"Dead!" was the cry heard to ring through the air of a pale dawn. Behind it a young man made his labored way into the carriage drive of Berkeley Square. He dragged his lame foot through the mud and the knife in his hand dripped with blood. "M'brudder…he'sh dead!" he wailed. The leaves of the plane trees that lined the square barely quivered at the news.

Chapter One

England, October 1811

I recall it as if it were yesterday; the moment I learned of the tragedy that changed my life. I had chosen to attend a soiree to which I was not invited...

I scanned the room for a cordial face. The urbane smile I was in the habit of offering in exchange for icy glares did naught to solve my dilemma; I wished to dance. Recent events had taught me that a young lady was far more likely to accept my invitation if she did not first turn from me in distaste. Despite months of such encounters, they still had the power to take me aback; the scar that bites into the right corner of my mouth hasn't the power to disturb my equanimity. In point of fact, coupled with the ice blue eyes and chestnut curls with which my Maker graced me, I feel the scar to be rather dashing. Society, however, are of a different opinion.

If I were honest, (a perplexing conundrum, at best,) I would have willingly entertained the truth: 'twas the months-past scandal that created the scar that prompted others to view me with distaste. Unwilling to accept my fate, I stifled a sigh and turned 'round to take up my usual stance in the corner of the room. From this universal vantage point, I had recently observed a good deal of life's pleasures pass beyond my nose. However, my way was barred by the presence of a young lady whose dearth of height had put her, quite literally, beneath my notice. As I gazed down at her, I could not help but be filled with curiosity at her lack of temerity in my presence.

"I beg your pardon," I began as I studied her face for a reaction.

"The fault is mine entirely," she demurred, but her eyes flashed with good humor. "I ought certainly to have learned how to afford comfort to those around me by now. As it is, I have sustained unintentional blows to the head from more than one stray elbow."

"Pray, say it was not I who has done such a thing!" I begged.

"Very nearly but, as I have said, I ought to have taken better care. It is not as if this is my first season," she murmured into the glass she brought to her lips. Having taken a sip, she squarely met my gaze. "Or my second."

Curious, I stepped back to get the measure of she who seemed not in the least hesitant to address me. I turned the scar away from her in the case her composure signified that she had not yet been availed of it, and studied her from the corner of my eye. She was indeed rather small, and wore a simple gown of gold silk that made the most of what little height she had. However, its deep color established her claim that she was no debutante. In fact, she looked to be close to my own age of twenty-three. I thought that if I took care not to alarm her, perhaps I would dance after all.

"How any could overlook such an enchanting lady is a notion of which I cannot conceive." I knew that I exaggerated more than a little, but liked the lady better for her knowledge of the same.

"Perhaps," she said with a tilt of her head, "but not so captivating that any has asked me to dance."

"I shall ask the moment someone makes us properly known to one another," I insisted, though, I surmised I might wait forever for such a courtesy. I intended to dance with her anyway. "People appear to be a good deal occupied," I prompted as I looked about. "Would you deem me uncivil if I were to offer my name in exchange for a set?"

Her sudden smile produced a pair of bewitching dimples. They added an unanticipated charm to what was a somewhat plain face crowned by a coiffure of glorious golden tresses. The whole of it was arranged so artfully that it distracted one from imagining her to be not much taller than she was wide. The result was wholly pleasing and I thought her quite the most elegantly-styled lady in the room.

"I shall take courage and assume your smile conveys your willingness," I said with a bow. "I am Julian Silvester, the Marquis of Trevelin."

I fervently hoped for a positive reaction despite the actions of the Duke of Rutherford. The previous season he had successfully put a period to my reputation as good *ton*. Since then, I had often thought of myself as a ghost; a spook; a shade; one that flitted about in an attempt to converse with the living. Before I could congratulate myself on such a judicious comparison, I was gripped by the elbow and whirled round.

"How dare you importune this lady?" demanded the man before me in a nearly imperceptible Spanish accent. No words accented or otherwise were needed to convey his taut anger.

"We were merely conversing," I replied with fabricated mildness. I knew it essential to withhold my outrage, at least until I took the measure of this foreigner. As he was all of five feet tall, it was short work. "I cannot say that I have ever known it to be considered a crime," I drawled.

"Maybe yes; maybe no," the Spaniard allowed. "It is your name that fuels my rage. You are not fit to be in the presence of such a lady."

I swallowed my laughter, but allowed myself a sigh. "Shall we not grant the lady the courtesy to decide with whom she dances?" I longed to ascertain her feelings on the subject but I thought it prudent to keep the tight-ground fist at his side within my purview.

"Perhaps the lady has not yet heard tell of your reputation," the man suggested.

I quelled my disappointment; dancing with unnamed lady was now out of the question. I favored him with what I hoped to be a perfectly poised smile. "If not, I hardly think it gentlemanly to apprise her of it at my lord's and lady's ball," I said lightly.

"And yet you think it gentlemanly to speak to her?" The man ground his fist tighter.

"Please," the lady in question begged as she stepped from behind me to engage her champion. "At least he has given me his name whilst I am in utter ignorance of yours, sir."

Promptly, the man executed a deep bow. "I, Señyor Juliol Rey of Barcelona, am at your service, *señyoreta*."

5

"And now you are as guilty of an improper introduction as Lord Trevelin," the lady pointed out.

Gratified, I gave her a bow of my own. "I applaud your good sense. Have I your permission, Señyor Rey, to inquire after the lady's name?" I felt my obvious scorn sufficient to convey my opinion on the matter, but in this I was mistaken.

"No!" he began, but the lady was having none of it.

"I have heard your name, my lord, from my parents. It was in connection to unknown but beyond-the-pale behavior, or so they would have me believe." Her tone implied her mama and papa were awash with disapproval for their fellow men. "However, I have found that there are those who cannot afford such equivocating." She held out her hand for my grasp. "I, Miss Desdemona Woodmansey, am such a one."

"No! I will not allow it!" Señyor Rey insisted as he took her hand in my stead. "You are not meant for such a man!"

"Oh?" I looked down my nose at the Spaniard. "I suppose by that you mean she is meant for none but you?" It mattered not that Señyor Rey was struck temporarily dumb as anyone with a pair of eyes could not fail to discern the truth: Miss Woodmansey was the only female in the room whose lack of height equaled the Spaniard's.

"Why should I be meant for only Señyor Rey?" Miss Woodmansey asked in genuine bewilderment.

It would seem she had little perspective from where she stood. I turned my head hastily away so as to hide my amusement.

Señyor Rey behaved as if he had not heard her query. "This man lacks honor! It is said that he. . .he bets on the horses!"

"As does my father," Miss Woodmansey riposted as she removed her hand from his. "Come Señyor. You must do better than that."

I considered slinking away, but there was a sparkle in the lady's eye I could not help but admire. "If it shall raise me in your esteem, I shall most humbly resolve to refrain from betting on the horses," I said meekly. "That is, all but for the very fast ones."

Somewhat mollified, Señyor Rey continued. "He is said to go about with Mr. Rogers-Reimann, a man whose reputation is so vile it has crossed the sea."

I gave Miss Woodmansey a sidelong glance; one which I hoped would allow the cursed scar to remain unnoticed. "It's true, he and I have been known to sally forth together; it pleases his mother, also known as my aunt." I refrained from adding that I had only just dropped all social connections with my cousin, despite our mutual grandparents. I had had quite enough of pulling his tongs from the fire.

"I do not see that these accusations should preclude one from speaking with his lordship," Miss Woodmansey said pleasantly enough, but it was clear that her good opinion of me had begun its decline.

"Very well, then; there is more. The Marquis of Trevelin is said to have fought a duel over a woman; a married one. It resulted in an injury most serious."

It was with great difficulty that I restrained a finger from making its way to the relic of said duel. Instead, I pondered my choices. Miss Woodmansey's crestfallen demeanor indicated that it was pointless to explain. Indeed, who would have believed the truth, even if I had bothered to speak it aloud? Rutherford had seen to that. Neither was it the time or place to invite scrutiny on the subject. With a carefully crafted air of nonchalance, I did my worst. "I confess I hardly know the woman."

Señyor Rey's mouth fell open in horror. "You are a rapscallion and a knave! Miss Woodmansey, allow me to take you away," he insisted as he held out his hand.

Her only response was to favor me with a canny look.

"I do believe he is inviting you to dance, Miss Woodmansey. As for myself," I said with a shrug, "I should have gone about it much differently."

She bit her lip as if to quell incipient laughter, and allowed Señyor Rey to draw her away. With a sigh, I took up my place in the corner and watched as Miss Woodmansey smiled prettily at the passionate Spaniard. I knew that to approach her again was to invite a scene of the sort undeserved by my host and hostess. Determined to attend the next ball in disguise I quit the room, bound for the front door.

It was only after I had thanked my hostess, a habit that never fails to prompt a perplexed reply, as I am rarely invited, that I overheard a startling disclosure. It would seem that a man had killed his young brother. As I waited for the butler to produce my greatcoat and hat I heard it again, but with names attached, ones most untenable. Willy Gilbert! I could hardly believe it. He could not have done such a thing. I had known the man since my school days. Hastily, I returned to the ballroom to eavesdrop on more reliable gossip-mongers. To my consternation, the news was being tossed about the room like confetti.

"Trevelin, have you heard?" Robert Manwaring

demanded exactly as if he had not given me the cut direct each of the last three times we had met. Rutherford had much for which to answer. I was heartily glad that he was not present.

"I do believe I have, but I can hardly credit it."

"What? Do you suppose it impossible for young Gilbert to kill?"

I regarded the man, his dimpled chin, and the golden curls along his brow, with equal loathing. "I do not suppose it impossible for anyone to kill another, should the circumstances warrant it. However, for Willy Gilbert to have killed his young brother is inconceivable."

"He has not been right in the head ever since that horse threw him nearly to Scotland." Manwaring lifted his glass to his lips and tossed back its contents. "Perhaps he feared he should be made ineligible to inherit, and thought it best to get his brother out of the way."

"He did not do it," I said shortly. "I have known him this age, since long before his riding accident. I tell you, he is not capable of such." He had not the temperament, the character or, due to the fall on his head, the skill required of a killer.

"It is difficult to predict what a man will do when he is desperate, eh?" Manwaring said with a wink, one that implied a wealth of insults.

"I beg to differ." How little surprised I should have been in that moment to learn there were those who had reason to put an end to Manwaring. "I find that it is the desperate man whose actions are most predictable." Deceit, betrayal, treachery: had I not learned it all at the hands of desperate men?

Manwaring narrowed his sapphire-blue eyes and turned away without a word of reprisal. No other approached me as I moved around the room, hoping for a more satisfactory version of the story. None was forthcoming. All were only too eager to condemn poor Willy. Indeed, the very air seemed to crackle as would a barn full of hay set instantly alight by a falling taper. I envisioned great plumes of smoke as they rose towards the ornate ceiling, imagined how they obscured every means of escape…felt Willy's doom crash down upon my shoulders.

My emotions were so like those at the first ball I attended after my own accident that it nearly undid me. Five months prior, I had not realized Society would condemn me for an injury at the hand of a cuckolded husband. In truth, I had no reason to suppose the Duke of Rutherford would attempt to dignify the sordid affair by making his revenge so public. This man who had torn into my lip with his sword took steps to ensure that I was not invited anywhere. The sole exception was the ball at which I learned my fate, so as to make Society witnesses to my shame. My stomach churned at the memory. It prompted gratitude that the Gilberts were not in attendance to hear their betters discuss the murder of their younger son at the hand of his brother.

My melancholy was further exacerbated by a vision of Willy in a dank gaol, falsely accused, his brother dead and his mother and father bereft of both their sons. I confessed to myself (there is no better confessor) that Willy's pain must surely surpass the heartache I experienced every day. Suddenly, I knew that I must intervene. I returned to the vestibule and once again bespoke my hat and coat. In the end, I hardly had need of either as I strode home in the heat of my growing fury.

By the time I mounted the steps of number 50 Berkeley Square, my anger had all but burned out. Indeed, I was relieved to feel some of my usual pleasure when entering my sole oasis in a desert of disdain. My room in the house of George Canning, former Secretary of State for Foreign Affairs, had placed me in the center of family life. I never failed to delight in the company of his wife, Joan, and their three young children. Their presence always lent me a respite from the continual rejection I received due to my imprecise reputation and the oh-so-revealing scar. It also had provided a reprieve from the company of my cousin, who has been barred from the house by its owner.

"Is that you, Trevelin?" Canning called to me from his study two doors down the hall. "You are home rather early."

"Were you expecting someone else?" I called back as I removed my hat and greatcoat and handed them off to Hughes, the butler.

Canning, his pate gleaming amidst its ring of light brown hair, appeared at the door of his study. "Yes; Joan. She is still out. I wish to speak with her before I retire."

I crossed the hall to shake his hand. "You did not accompany her to whatever rout she attends this evening?"

"I had business, and have just arrived home." I followed Canning as he returned to the study and took his seat behind his massive desk. "What of you?" he asked with a kindly smile. "You are far too young to retire at such an hour."

As I lowered myself into the chair opposite him, I treated my landlord to a sardonic look. "If you mean that I am too wicked to sleep in the dark of night, I wonder that you have welcomed me into your home."

Canning's smile deepened. "You know the answer to that well enough. If it weren't for my own unfortunate circumstances," he mused as he rubbed the spot where Lord Castlereagh's bullet had bit into his thigh two years prior, "I might not have taken pity on you. One day, however, you must ensconce yourself in your own residence. You shall never persuade a woman to buckle herself to your side if she is not to be mistress of her own establishment."

"You know very well that I cannot abide Silvester House. In addition, I would thank you to refrain from speaking of my highly unlikely nuptials," I said ruefully. "My spirits are low enough as it is."

"May I ask if your present gloom is on account of William Gilbert having been carted off by the constable?"

I nodded. "I am far more troubled by Willy's state of affairs than my own. At least I am not imprisoned for my crime." I rose and went to the mantel before the woe, heavy as lead, settled into my feet. "Surely you realize that Willy and I are not so different from one another. He was gravely injured," I said as I flicked a mote of dust from the woodwork, "and has been more ostracized than even I. He is now denied his freedom and the association of those he loves. It is intolerable." Indeed, I had not realized just how similar were our circumstances until I spoke the words. The tragedy of it hit me so hard, it forced the air from my lungs.

Canning gave me a keen look, one that perceived all, and still he chose to add to my distress. "You are so certain he does not deserve his fate?"

I turned to him in surprise. "Are you not?"

He frowned, and threw a hand into the air. "I have no means of discerning the truth, but it seems as if the authorities are satisfied of his guilt. Who am I to assume them to be mistaken?"

I was not sure I had heard aright. "You have known Willy and his family for decades. They are good *ton*. I cannot perceive how you can doubt. And to think I supposed you might help me to prove Willy's innocence." I went again to my chair into which I collapsed.

"I wish to believe that he did not do it," Canning said with an emphatic nod. "If not, my next wish should be that he not be held accountable for his brother's death. If he can be proved innocent, I should do everything in my power to save him."

The knot about my heart loosened a trifle and I sat up in my chair. "In that case, you have my word that I shall do all that I might to uncover the truth. I assume they have taken him directly to Newgate?"

"Do you intend to visit him there? Perhaps you should leave that much to the authorities, at least."

"If the authorities had known what they were about when they arrived at Gilbert House this morning, they would never have taken Willy away!"

"Yes, indeed. Well, I am for bed," Canning said as he rose to his feet. "I suppose I shall have to speak with Joan later. And, Trevelin," he added with a sharp look, "I should like to know what you learn from your visit to Newgate."

"Rest assured, you shall know all," I replied shortly. In truth, I was delighted that he had conceded the point. I stared into the fire and thought of the unfortunate Willy, who doubtless suffered from the cold and hunger, as well. What other ills he most likely felt, I hardly dared to think. To my chagrin, I soon resorted to pitying myself, instead. As painful as were my misfortunes, they had been somewhat dulled by time and association. I lay my head back and closed my eyes.

I lay in the damp grass, staring up into the frenzied eyes of my attacker. I had never seen anyone so demented with rage, and yet the razor-sharp blow to my face came as a shock. The blood that covered the fingers I put to my mouth was equally extraordinary. Soon the gash in my lip filled me with unrelenting pain, and still I could make no sense of it. I knew my cousin was by my side but his voice seemed to come from far away, as did the clang of steel when Evelyn's sword was joined in battle. Reassured, my field of vision narrowed and faded into black until, finally, I knew no more.

I awoke with a start. All was quiet; even the crackling of the flames in the fireplace had fallen silent. The tapers had all but burnt out. I rose to my feet; it was past time to retire. As I made my way to the stairs, I heard a faint rap at the front door. "I shall see to it," I called to Hughes, though he had most likely already gone to bed. Upon pulling open the door, I was surprised to find Señyor Rey on the other side. "You are certainly a persistent fellow," I remarked when I had recovered from my astonishment. "Have you come to further harangue me?"

Señyor Rey scowled. "No. But, *si*, it is you I have come to see. I wish to beg your pardon. However, I believe my intentions would be better understood if you were to let me into the house."

I did not for a moment believe it was an apology that had prompted a call so deep in the night. Fatigued as I was I felt more deprived of companionship, so I waved him into the house, shut the door on the cold, and led him to the warmth of the study. As I coaxed the flames with a poker, Señyor Rey took a seat and held his hands out to the fire. Once the flames were sufficiently flickering, I poured two glasses of refreshment and offered him one.

"*Gràcies.*" Señyor Rey took the glass, and sipped at his drink so long I heartily regretted that I had not gone upstairs and to bed an hour past. When I finally took up the other chair by the fire, he raised his bright black eyes from his glass and began to speak. "Miss Woodmansey is a remarkable young lady."

"I imagine she is but, as you are aware, she and I have just met." I waited for a reply, but he said nothing. "I believe you made reference to an apology," I prompted.

"Yes. It is Miss Woodmansey who has driven me to this point."

"Has she?" I asked. "It would seem she is far more remarkable than I had supposed."

"Why do you say this? Do you doubt she has the power to persuade a man such as me?"

"Not in the least. And, might I add, persuasion is a more practical means of going about matters than tooling the carriage in which you arrived."

"Of course she has done no such thing! She is a lady and does not drive the carriages. No, she has brought me to the point of apology—to you!—when I had thought such a thing not in the least required."

"Is that so?" I said in tones I knew sounded strained.

He gave me a sharp look. "She deems you a noble man despite what is said of you. She insists that I beg your pardon. I am new to this country but I am not new to the ways of women."

I pushed aside a stab of envy and allowed myself a chuckle. "I see which way the wind blows."

"What does this blowing wind mean?" he queried, his brow furrowed in frustration.

"It means that I understand you. Your purpose in being here is to please Miss Woodmansey, is it not?"

"Yes, but only on account of my respect for her. I believe her to be wise for her years, do you not? And so, I beg your pardon for my behavior."

I nodded. "I shall accept your apology, if only to please Miss Woodmansey, who is not," I suggested, "as young as you might suppose. Yet, I think it a matter that might safely have waited for a more convenient time. Are you not really here for some other reason?"

Señyor Rey's eyes widened in surprise. "Why, yes. I am a guest of Lady Vawdrey who lives at Hampton House in this same square. When I arrived at her home after the ball at which you and I met, she was most distraught over the death of a neighboring gentleman. I believe she called him Johnny Gilbert. She says his brother, who is lame, was taken away and shall hang for the crime of murder. She finds it difficult to believe him capable of such an act. She has also asked that I speak with you in hopes that you might be of some assistance. Is she right to expect as much, my lord?"

"Lady Vawdrey has asked for my assistance?" I said in

faint surprise. In truth, I was amazed. I had been acquainted with Lady Vawdrey for a number of years. A somewhat foolish woman dedicated to rescuing strays from the streets of London, she had taken it amiss when I had refused to pay court to a young woman whom I, at the time, thought unworthy of me. In retaliation, she had assiduously applied herself to bolstering Rutherford's efforts to ostracize me from society. She was more capable than Manwaring in making me feel the lowliest peasant whenever we met. "How have you come to know her?"

Señyor Rey straightened his spine. "We met by chance in Switzerland last July."

"Ah," I said, the light dawning. Surely, this was how he came to learn of my reputation and that of my cousin. It did not take much of a leap to suppose she had most likely invited Rey to England in pursuit of the petite Miss Woodmansey, as well. I was gratified to see that Rey had divined my thoughts and had the grace to look discomfited. "I should think Lady Vawdrey would wish the aid of any before mine," I insisted.

"*Si*, she supposed you would say as much. This explains the apology, yes? You would not have listened if I had begun by revealing Lady Vawdrey's request."

I was dismayed at how much this revelation vexed me. The notion that Miss Woodmansey found me noble enough to warrant an apology had been a balm to my wounds. I rose and went to the door with every intention of showing him out. "You speak in riddles. It is my fondest wish to spare my friend the noose, but I find I cannot believe one word of your story."

Agitated, Rey also stood. "It is my wish to please Lady Vawdrey. She has given me a home in London at a time most convenient. She is fond of the Gilberts, and knows the older son could not have killed the younger. She also knows that you are fond of Mister William. She fears there is no one else who shall care to save the life of a man who is lame."

As it turned out, I heartily agreed. As I looked down into Rey's eyes, I saw my opportunity. If I agreed to make myself available to Lady Vawdrey, perhaps she would assist in bringing about my former good standing in Society. Perhaps I could find a lady who was not ashamed to share my name. Perhaps that lady should even turn out to be Miss Woodmansey. I had tried and failed to dismiss the canny look she had given me. I felt certain she had realized there was more to my story than she had heard from Rey. If so, she was the first. I thought myself half in love already.

"Very well, then," I said with a slight bow of my head. "You may inform your hostess that I shall call on her before the morning is long gone. I pay a visit to Newgate Prison after that. I should be pleased if you were to join me, Seynor Rey." It would afford me a chance to learn more of the Spaniard and what else he might know about the Brothers Gilbert.

He smiled and held out his hand. "*Fins doma*; until tomorrow then."

Chapter Two

I peered at myself in the glass and frowned. With a nod, I dismissed Canning's valet and executed a well-placed tug to a fold in my cravat. Satisfied that it was the last blemish in my apparel, I turned from my reflection and pondered the matter of Lady Vawdrey. That she expected me, I had no doubt; it was that she had felt it her duty to read me a catalogue of my faults not many months past that troubled me. That not one of her accusations was based in fact had nothing to say to it; she had made herself the keeper of my conscience and I had avoided her assiduously ever since. How I was to conduct a proper conversation with her was a difficult riddle to solve. Why she should desire to converse with a man 'so without ethics, morals, or lofty ambitions' long enough to discuss the means to Willy's rescue was one a good deal more difficult.

I endured no small amount of apprehension as I crossed the square. I also dared to hope Lady Vawdrey was in possession of resources to aid in Willy's release. I rapped on the door and was unhesitatingly admitted into the house by Hoagland, the butler. His expression of neutrality was startling in light of the scornful looks he cast upon me whenever the two of us met in the square. It would seem I had risen in his esteem.

"Ah! There you are at last," Lady Vawdrey cried in delight as Hoagland ushered me into her luxurious salon.

As I recovered from my bewilderment at her approbation, I allowed my gaze to sweep the occupants of the room. Lady Vawdrey I knew well enough. She was a typical graying, horse-faced, ladder-tall Englishwoman, whose family dated back to the era of William the Conqueror. Her secretary-cum-housekeeper, an elegant young man whose peculiar status doubtless contributed to his churlish expression, stood just to her left. Señyor Rey sat on a sofa to her right.

"I beg your pardon; it seems I have kept you waiting. Not for long, I hope?"

"It is only that we are most anxious," Señyor Rey hastened to explain, "to begin the business of proving the innocence of the crippled young man."

"Then, let us be on our way to Newgate." I suspected that my wish to depart in such haste was impertinent. However, my desire to sit and make polite conversation with Lady Vawdrey was decreasing with every moment I spent pinned in the hostile glare of her singular housekeeper.

"Before you depart, my lord, I should like to wish you the greatest of fortune in this endeavor," Lady Vawdrey claimed. "How anyone could suppose a young man with a withered arm and foot could have done such a thing is troubling in the extreme. And to think that it was agents of our government who have taken him away!"

Her words pierced me to the core. "If you knew him as I do, you would be affronted for the sake of his character alone. He is not a man who could do this, not to his brother, of whom he was most fond and who was one of his few companions."

Lady Vawdrey's mouth fell open. "Indeed! Have I not just said so?"

It was with difficulty that I restrained my desire to point out the disparity in our assertions. I turned instead to Señyor Rey. "The sooner we set out, the sooner we shall have in our possession the facts that shall prove key to Mr. Gilbert's freedom."

"But you mustn't take your leave yet!" Lady Vawdrey insisted. "I have just rung the bell for refreshments."

"Lady Vawdrey," I said with a bow that made it possible for me to avoid her gaze, "I believe you shall agree that our task is most imperative. But, pray, if you have anything of import to convey I am anxious for you to disclose such."

"As you are in such haste," Lady Vawdrey said, "perhaps we ought to postpone further discourse for another day. I know that Señyor Rey is at *aux anges* to absolve young Gilbert."

He was indeed. Why this should be so, I could not say. It was a question that warranted further examination. For now, it was enough that it pleased Lady Vawdrey and that she had the power to influence Rutherford. My desire to be regarded as suitable for Society was outweighed only by my desire to see Willy free. Grateful that Lady Vawdrey saw fit to send us speedily on our way I sketched a bow, quit the room, and was halfway across the square before Rey joined me.

"*El meu señyor*, it is with pleasure that I attend you, but I am doubtful of my ability to keep up with your long strides all the way to the side of this *lamentable*."

I gave the Spaniard a sharp look. "Lamentable? It almost sounds that you believe he has earned his plight."

"No, not at all. I only believe him to be unfortunate."

"Indeed, he is," I said grudgingly. "Naturally, we shall take the carriage. It waits for us, even now." I gestured across the square to Number 50, its address placard in the transom window over the door obscured by the driver on his perch. My curricle was faster, but I had no wish to announce my presence at Newgate Prison by arriving in an open carriage; my reputation had been damaged by association once too often.

"But, tell me, my lord, how do you plan to prove Mr. Gilbert's *innocencia*?"

"It depends entirely on what, in reality, occurred." We dashed up the carriage steps and took our seats across from one another. "We must first pay a visit to Mansion House to acquire a permit from the Lord Mayor. It will take us a bit out of our way, but the turnoff to Newgate is on the way back again so it shall not prove too inconvenient."

"I am not in any great hurry to arrive again at the establishment of Lady Vawdrey," Rey said doubtfully. "She is kind to serve as my hostess during my sojourn in London, but that Throckmorton is most disagreeable."

"Is that what her housekeeper is called?"

"Yes," Rey replied, his expression grave. "He is such an odd-looking fellow—those violet eyes!—and his position in the household odder still."

"I have thought much the same."

"Then it is not only I who quails under his gaze?"

I burned to insist that I did not 'quail,' but restrained

myself. "There is something distasteful about him, there is no question. And yet, I thought his appearance today to be a sight more doleful than usual." When Throckmorton's expression lightened enough for a smile it was the simpering sort, far too smug for a servant. He was another mystery that warranted scrutiny. "What is it that Lady Vawdrey values in such a fellow?"

"This I cannot ascertain," Rey replied with a shrug.

"Perhaps someone ought to," I said quietly. "He is a servant in the dwelling across the square from where poor Johnny was killed. It is possible that he knows something useful. You, Señyor Rey, are in a position to discover what that is."

"Me?" Rey asked in disbelief. "What am I to do? Accost him in his sitting room below stairs? I am not allowed into that portion of the house."

"I am confident you shall arrive at a suitable solution," I said briskly as I straightened the seams of my gloves.

"As I do wish to be of service, I shall endeavor to succeed."

I studied Rey's face, and wondered again at his enthusiasm for a cause not his own. I did, however, admire his determination. My opinion of Rey rose accordingly. "For how long do you intend to sojourn in London?"

"I am of the means to do exactly as I please," he replied, his expression unaccountably defensive. "My invitation from Lady Vawdrey is for an indeterminate length of time. I am entirely at her disposal and thereby yours."

"And what of Miss Woodmansey?"

Rey looked surprised. "What of her?"

I directed my gaze out the window so as not to observe my companion's expression; it was too guileless for comfort. "Do you intend to call on her during the course of your stay?"

"I...cannot say," Rey demurred. "May I ask how it is any concern of yours?"

"It isn't," I admitted, but my thoughts lingered on Miss Woodmansey until the carriage arrived at Mansion House and I was obliged to disembark. "No need to stir," I instructed the Spaniard as he rose. "I shan't be long."

My business took only a few minutes, and we were once again on our way to Newgate Street and the prison. I inspected the permit I had acquired and, satisfied that all was as it should be, tucked it into a pocket of my waistcoat.

"What is that odor?" Rey asked in dismay.

"I daresay you refer to the scent in which I doused my handkerchief."

"But why?" Rey asked with a frown. "It is most disagreeably strong!"

"Yes, I suppose it is. And yet, when you enter the prison you shall wish you had brought the same."

"Does this prison, then, smell so *desagradable*?"

"It is a prison, which is to say, yes, far more disagreeable than you can imagine." I retrieved the handkerchief from my pocket, tore it in two, and offered half to my companion.

"You are a man with much experience of prisons?" The tone in Rey's voice indicated that he, in part, regretted the question.

"I know of which I speak," I replied in arctic tones designed to discourage such queries. That I had only been inside a prison the once, and that for the sole purpose of

24

visiting my cousin Evelyn to arrange for his release, was more than I wished to divulge. "However, you may remain in the carriage should you prefer."

"No! I do not prefer," Rey said with a lift of his chin. "I wish to learn what I might from Señyor Gilbert, and offer him my condolences on the death of his brother."

I inclined my head in respect for Rey's intentions. "Willy shall surely be grateful for your belief in his innocence, as am I."

"But of course! Should I be on my way to this prison most notorious if I did not?"

Despite my dubiousness as to the depth of his interest, I was grateful for it. "I have not called at Gilbert House for several months. As my reputation is not news to you, you can comprehend my desire to spare them any…unpleasantness. However, Willy and I have been associates since we were boys at school. The accident that led to his lame arm and leg happened only a few years ago. Since then I have spent some time in his company. It occurs to me that there are a few details pertaining to his condition you shall find useful to know."

"Please continue," Rey said with a wave of his arm.

"It is actually rather peculiar. The injury that has affected the muscles of his arm, leg, and tongue has done nothing to damage his mind. His intelligence is in no way affected; only his ability to express it."

"I see," Rey mused. "Then he knows well enough the fate that awaits him. We must hurry to his side, my lord!"

I could not restrain a smile in response. Though I had reason to envy Rey, I found his anxiety for Willy endearing.

To have a companion, someone of an age to mine, with whom I could share my concerns, was pure delight. "There is more."

Rey nodded. "If I am to be of assistance, I should be made acquainted with all the facts. Let us start at the beginning."

"I only know of the gossip and what I have read in the papers," I said regretfully. "Yesterday morning, rather early . . ."

"Which is to say," Rey interjected, "prior to the rising of a gentleman such as yourself."

I inclined my head. "Not to put too fine a point on it, but yes. Therefore, though the events I am about to describe occurred only a few doors down from where I live, I witnessed nothing firsthand."

"That you were not a witness firsthand is all I wished to know," Rey said with an echoing inclination of his own head. "Thank you."

"Not at all," I replied, refusing to be provoked. "However, those who did hear or see what happened all agree on certain facts. One, it was early. Two, it was Willy they saw out on the carriage drive. They also agree that he was distressed and calling out to alert others to the death of his brother."

"I wonder that he did not go immediately to his parents," Rey mused.

"Yes, that has been a troubling question of mine, one I intend to pose tomorrow when we call on them. I dislike imposing on their grief, but perhaps Lady Vawdrey ought to send 'round a note explaining my reason for calling on them so soon after their loss."

Rey nodded his approval. "Is there no more?"

I nodded. "He was seen with a bloody knife in his hand. The authorities are satisfied it is the same knife that killed Johnny," I said, the words sticking in my throat. I kept my own counsel for the remainder of the journey, but found that I was full of admonitions once we entered the prison.

"Do not cast about such looks of pity," I quietly advised. The air echoed with the commotion of gallows construction as we followed the gaoler across the open yard. "Also, refrain from placing your hands in your pockets, do not look directly into the eyes of the prisoners, and do have your handkerchief at the ready," I added as we entered a door that led into the dank hallways of the old prison.

Scented scraps of cloth to our noses we were led along several lengthy corridors, past chambers filled with miserable humanity.

"*El meu* señyor," Rey moaned, "there are too many men in each *habitacio*. How do they sleep? There are not beds enough for all."

"I couldn't say," I said, sick at heart with the thought of Willy in such a circumstance.

"You do not know? But you are a man most experienced, is that not so?"

I ignored the question as memories of my last visit to the prison flooded my mind. My cousin had been taken into custody because of a brawl at White's over a lost bet. I recalled with ease the horror I knew when I read Evelyn's missive requesting that I pay the blunt for a private cell rather than one into which petty thieves and cutthroats were thrown together. I had brought the funds myself and saw to it that my cousin was placed in the wing of those more privileged. It seemed as if the path the gaoler now took led in the same direction. If I proved incorrect and Willy was not in a cell of his own, I resolved to see to it before the day was out.

The main corridor echoed with the cries of the incarcerated and I was relieved to depart from it. We made a sharp turn and headed deeper into the prison via a pair of narrow steps. They were slippery with condensation and something else I dared not contemplate. What mattered was that they led to the private cells I wished for Willy, and when we came to a halt in front of a heavy door set in a brick wall I realized we had arrived.

The gaoler fitted the key and pulled wide the door. It creaked in protest; I paused on the threshold so as to give my eyes time to adjust to the murky light. Gradually, I was able to make out the outline of a man curled up on a narrow cot. Beside it was a small table that bore a washbasin and a bible. There was a chair pulled up to the table, but the room was bare of any other content save the privy.

My instinct was to run to his side, but I had no wish to humiliate him. "Willy," I said, "it's Trev."

He slowly raised himself onto his elbow and turned his head. Through the dim light, I saw his eyes widen in recognition when he gazed upon me.

I stepped into the room and stood upon the barred square of sunshine that fell from the window to the stone floor below. "We are here to learn if we can be of any use to you."

As he turned his gaze on Rey Willy's expression darkened, and his features settled into a decided frown.

"I beg your pardon, Willy. This is Señyor Rey," I

explained as I reached out to take my companion by the arm and draw him forward. "He also hopes to be of some assistance." I should have liked to shake Willy's hand, the one that was whole and healthy, but it was the one upon which he braced himself.

"May I sit?" I asked, indicating the chair. Willy grunted, and I disposed myself in as much comfort as could be had on a hard, damp chair. Rey, his scented handkerchief still held firmly to his nose, moved to stand behind me.

"What has happened, Willy?" I asked gently. "The newspapers state that you were found in the carriage drive with a bloody knife. Is that true?"

Willy nodded. His expression was arrested; wary.

"This was the first thing in the morning? Right after you woke?"

Again Willy nodded and, quite suddenly, fell onto his back. His strong hand now free, he began to pluck at his clothing. "Not nashty; clean!" he cried, greatly agitated, his speech more impaired than the last time I had spoken with him.

"Yes, it is a nasty business," I offered, "but we are here to help sort it out."

Willy suddenly left off thrashing about to stare at me. "Hel' me!"

"Yes, of course! But first we must find out what exactly happened."

"M' brudder," Willy wailed as he began to once again pluck at his shirt. "Clean!"

"It would seem," Rey said as he leaned over to speak into my ear, "he would like us to pay heed to his clothing."

"But to what purpose?" I stared through the shadows at Willy's shirt and breeches as closely as I was able. "Is this what you were wearing when you found Johnny?"

"Yesh!" Willy murmured over and over as he plucked at his shirt. His chant turned to "No!" as his hand moved down to rest on his breeches.

"It was the first thing in the morning that you found him?" I asked again.

Willy frenziedly nodded his head up and down against the thin pillow on his cot. "Yesh!"

"Then you were in your shirt alone?" I prompted.

"Yesh!"

"And you want us to know that your shirt is clean? After two days in this place?" I pointed out.

"Clean!" Willy cried in a long, agonized wail.

"I do not understand," Rey said. "His shirt is not clean. Nor are his breeches, stockings, or shoes."

"However, they were clean when you entered the prison, is that not right, Willy?" I gently prodded. "Is that what you wish us to know?"

"Yesh!" he repeated.

"There; you see, Rey? Willy has provided us with the means to prove his innocence!"

"I do not understand," Rey said with a small frown.

"We know that Willy was seen on the carriage drive with a bloody knife. That his shirt remained free of that blood is pure good fortune. However, it would be akin to a miracle for it to be bloodless if it were he who wielded the knife."

Willy raised himself again on his strong arm, looked intently into my eyes, and nodded vigorously.

A lump rose into my throat. When I could again speak, I posed him a question. "I am soon to call on your mother and father. Do you think they will receive me?"

"Yesh." His eyes filled with tears.

Mine did as well and I quickly looked away. "Whilst I am there I shall arrange for clean clothing to be sent to you. Is there a message you would have me convey to them?"

"Yesh! Clean!" Willy insisted.

"Yes, of course," I assured him as I rose from my chair and took him by the shoulders. "They know you are innocent, as do I, but I shall not neglect to point out the fact to them. Now," I said, seating myself on the edge of his cot. "It is cold. I shall have additional blankets brought as well. Is the food sufficient?"

Willy shrugged and looked away.

"I suppose you haven't had much of an appetite. That is likely to change now that your release is imminent."

Willy gave me an uneven smile. With a jolt, I realized it was the first time I had seen him smile since his accident some years back. In repose he looked quite like his old self, whilst I only looked like my old self when I smiled widely. It was a self that had been taken from me.

I lay on the ground and looked up into the sky. All I knew was its endless blue, a loud buzzing in my ears, and pain; endless pain. Suddenly, a blob of white loomed over me. It moved closer until I realized it was a face: Evelyn's. Why was he looking at me in such alarm? "It's all right, old fellow," he said as he and the surgeon we had brought along gathered me into their arms. Their uneven gait prompted such agony, and yet I was startled when I realized that the groaning I heard was my own. I knew well enough from whence came the tang of metal in my mouth and the flaming pain on the right side of my face. Evelyn and the surgeon deposited me, somewhat unceremoniously, onto the bench of the carriage. My face collided with the leather squabs, and all was throbbing anguish until I plunged into unconsciousness.

I shook my head as if to clear the memory, knowing full well that it would never depart. "Willy, is there anything else you can tell us about what has happened to poor Johnny? Did you see anyone? Do you know who has done this?"

"Nooooooo," Willy crooned, tears streaming down his face.

I caught Rey's eye and turned my gaze to the door. I turned again to Willy. "You are tired. I think perhaps we ought to be on our way."

Rey stepped up to take Willy's good hand in his, and shook it warmly. I did the same, and then quickly fled before my tears undid me. It wasn't until we had made our way out of the prison, back through the yard, and nearly to the carriage before either of us spoke. I was not in the least surprised that Rey should be the first to break the silence, which he did in a voice thick with emotion.

"I cannot believe Mr. Willy killed his brother. But what shall the authorities say to it? Won't they believe he merely changed his shirt for another?"

"Whatever for? So as to be more convincing when he limped out of the house with the murder weapon?" I snapped as we climbed into our conveyance. I should have been giddy with relief, but something restrained me.

"*Exactament*! He is certainly clever enough to have thought of it. But is he able to change his shirt on his own?"

I knocked on the ceiling and the coach lurched into movement. "I haven't any idea," I said, troubled by his questions.

"One would think the changing of the clothing would be very difficult for a man with his weakness. Is this why he goes about in only a shirt?"

"Of course he does not!" I could not say why the notion affronted me so. "As I said, Willy is a gentleman, born into a family of gentility and raised as such. We were at school together. Before the accident, he was my equal at mathematics, riding, and shooting; certainly my superior in Latin. Naturally, under normal circumstances, he would be fully clothed before venturing out into the front hall." However, for some reason, on the day in question he was not.

"It is fortunate, then, that they allowed him to don his breeches before they took him away, is it not?" Rey allowed.

I agreed, but could not be troubled to reply; something about Rey's comment triggered a notion. If the constable who took him away could be counted on to tell the truth of what happened once he arrived at the scene, perhaps there was hope.

"You have many questions, then, for the *pare* and the *mare*?" Rey asked.

"Yes, I do believe so," I said slowly. "Certainly, we shall be able to hold a more suitable conversation with his parents than with Willy."

"We? Do you invite me to attend you in this?" Rey asked, his dark eyes glowing with anticipation.

"I do not see why you should not come along. It shall afford you the opportunity to learn for yourself the qualities of the man we are attempting to save."

"If you think I shall be of use to you then, yes, I shall accompany you with pleasure."

I was not persuaded that it should be pleasurable, but I had begun to like the man nevertheless.

Chapter Three

Early the following afternoon, when Señyor Rey and I stepped into the Gilberts' salon, I was surprised to be in the presence of both of Willy's parents.

Even though Rey was a stranger, he went directly to greet them. "Mr. and Mrs. Gilbert, please allow me to express my regret for your sorrow," he said as he took Mrs. Gilbert's hand and bowed deeply over it. "It is a circumstance most tragic," he said with a nod for Mr. Gilbert.

"Naturally, I add my most sincere condolences to those of Seynor Rey of Barcelona," I said by way of introduction. "As for myself, I pray that you will not allow my sins to stand in the way of my being of use to you in this matter."

Mrs. Gilbert looked up from her lap for the first time since our arrival, gratitude shining through the tears in her eyes. They were gray and very fine, her hair a burnished brown under her cap. She looked entirely too young to have a son of three and twenty years. "We owe you many thanks for your kindness, my lord. To have lost both of our sons in one foul stroke is more than we can bear." She put her handkerchief to her trembling lips and turned her gaze again to her lap.

"Surely all is not lost," I insisted. "You cannot believe Willy capable of such a deed."

"The idea is simply preposterous," Mr. Gilbert expostulated, the veins in his thick neck purpling. "No son of mine..." he choked out.

A moment of patent silence ensued before Mrs. Gilbert recalled her duties as hostess, inviting us to sit. Rey took up a chair to the side of Mrs. Gilbert whilst I sat across from her husband.

"Mr. and Mrs. Gilbert, you cannot be unaware of my longstanding friendship with your son. I wish to do all that I may to secure his release from prison. We have the support of an individual whose name I am not at liberty to disclose, but who is a near neighbor of yours and an influential man in the government. I assume I need say no more on that score. If I am able to provide him with proof of Willy's innocence, this man has promised to ensure Willy's safe return."

"He is most certainly innocent!" Mr. Gilbert grated. "How they dared to take him away is beyond my comprehension." He twisted his large hands together as if warming them for hand-to-hand battle.

"I am of the same opinion," I hastened to assure the angry man. "He is innocent, but proof shall be needed and may prove difficult to obtain. We must determine who has robbed you of Johnny. Do you know of anyone who might have wished him harm?"

Mrs. Gilbert raised red-rimmed eyes to my face. "That is the very trouble; we can think of no one! He was only fifteen years old, far too young to have been so hated by anyone. Besides, why should they? He is..." Her voice trembled. "He *was* everyone's favorite. He was intelligent, talented, kind, and so very dear. He would have done anything for Willy and they were, naturally, quite close. Johnny would be appalled to learn that Willy was being held responsible for such a horrid act."

"Precisely my thoughts on the matter," I assured her. "And yet, someone has deprived Johnny of his life. Why?"

"That very question runs through my mind every moment of the day and night until I think I shall go mad!" Mrs. Gilbert remonstrated. "There never was a more delightful boy. I do not know how I shall go on without him."

Willy had, once upon a time, been a delightful boy as well. It seemed his mother had forgotten. I could not help but notice the look of helplessness in Mr. Gilbert's eyes. It appeared to signal something more than an inability to restore his son to life. Perhaps he felt the lack of his wife's affection in the face of her grief.

I forced aside a throb of my own grief. My pain was not for Mr. Gilbert, but for Willy, who it seemed had, since the accident, endured his mother's patent preference for her younger son. It was a rejection that might have prompted a lesser man than Willy to murder. "Then we must think of what else might have happened; an intruder, perhaps? A burglary gone awry? Is there any evidence that a stranger was in the house?"

"Yes," Mrs. Gilbert said in a low voice. "A key to the kitchen door has gone missing. The knife," she whispered, "was from the kitchen as well."

"The constable didn't seem the least interested in that information, however," Mr. Gilbert bellowed. "They claim Willy took the key to make it appear as if someone entered the house from outside. But that is ridiculous, as Willy could not have taken the key. He cannot manage the stairs to the kitchen on his own."

"They are most certainly catching at straws," I allowed. "However, someone has taken it. Whoever has it is most likely the person responsible for so much misery. Mr. and Mrs. Gilbert, have I your permission to question your household?"

"Yes, of course. We are grateful for your assistance, as well as that of he you have not named," Mr. Gilbert replied.

We both knew we spoke of George Canning. I acknowledged Mr. Gilbert's words with an inclination of my head. "Tell me more about John. Why was he not away at school?"

Mr. Gilbert *tsked* and turned away. "She could not bear to part with her son, even for the sake of his education," he said scornfully.

I felt Rey's gaze on me and we shared a glance that begged the selfsame question: Was John not as much Mr. Gilbert's son as his wife's?

"Did he have a tutor, then?

"Yes; Mr. Huther," Mrs. Gilbert said so quietly I almost did not catch her words. It made me wonder what it was about Mr. Huther she did not wish us to hear.

"Is Mr. Huther still in the house?"

"Yes," Mr. Gilbert said, with what I thought to be some resentment.

"Very good; I shall wish to speak with him as well. What of Johnny's friends and his other pursuits?"

"He has been very much on his own, as his friends are

all away at school," Mrs. Gilbert replied, her hesitation vanishing. "To think, if I had sent him to Eton or Harrow he would even now be living!"

"Mrs. Gilbert," Rey soothed, "there is one and only one who is responsible for the death of your son: he who wielded the knife. Please do not hold yourself to account for the dreadful deed. It is too awful to contemplate."

"And yet contemplate it I do," she cried as she wrung her handkerchief between her fingers.

It felt as if it were myself she twisted in her hands. I, too, knew regret. I regretted the duel, the time I had spent in the company of my cousin, the consequences of our folly; those were merely the ones I had begun to examine. As such, the pain I now felt was for Willy's mother.

Drawing a deep breath, I pushed on. "Let us assist in discovering who has done this," I urged. "Only then may you know some measure of peace."

"We shall aid you to the best of our ability," Mr. Gilbert assured him. "John might have been all that his brother is not," he said darkly, "but we cannot bear to lose Willy, too."

I did not doubt the sorrow Willy's father felt at such a loss, and turned away from the face of his sorrow. "Then let us begin. We shall start with the keeper of the household keys. It would be best if we were provided a room other than your salon in which to speak with your staff."

"Yes, of course," Mrs. Gilbert agreed. "I shall ring for Bugg. He will arrange everything to your satisfaction."

"Mr. Gilbert, whilst we await the butler I must tell you that Señyor Rey and I have been to Newgate."

Mrs. Gilbert gasped as her husband finally came to life.

"Did you see him?" he demanded. "How is he? Is he all right?"

"Mr. Gilbert, if you are so anxious to learn of his condition why have you not been to see him yourself?"

Mrs. Gilbert gasped again. "To Newgate? It would not do!"

I swallowed an angry response and thought carefully on my reply. "He is very concerned for you both, and wants you to know that he is innocent of this crime."

Mr. Gilbert seemed once again angry. "Of course we know that! To think otherwise would be ridiculous!"

"Of course. He, however, is not in a position to think clearly. He is feeling quite low and suffers from the cold. His clothes have become soiled with the little food he has attempted to feed himself. Better victuals would be appreciated, as well."

"Yes, of course," Mrs. Gilbert said. "I shall arrange for someone to bring him everything he needs. Thank you for calling on him in such a vile place. How you were able to bear it, I cannot imagine."

It was at this moment that the butler answered his summons. He was given instructions by Mrs. Gilbert, and after the appropriate bows for our host and hostess, Señyor Rey and I followed Bugg from the room.

As we walked along the first-floor gallery, I took note of the portraits hung of the Gilbert boys hung on the walls. They were a moving reminder that with the end of John's life came the loss of hope for an heir to carry on the family name. I felt the loss almost as keenly as if it were mine. As an only child, whose father and mother had already gone to their reward, I knew how I would mourn if all hopes of progeny were to be forever extinguished. The paintings of the boys together prior to Willy's accident were the most cutting, and I found I must look hastily away.

Bugg, who was as proficient as promised, showed us into a chamber suitable for our purposes. It was small enough to encourage the intimacy required and gracefully appointed so as to prevent the questioning from feeling like a wearisome interrogation. Rey, disposed on a divan by the mantelpiece, looked nearly average-sized in front of the petite fireplace. He drew up a small table upon which he placed a piece of parchment and a pencil. I further inspected the room and noted the dainty tables and the equally dainty chairs placed in close proximity to a variety of mirrors. Suddenly, I realized the purpose of the space was to allow ladies some privacy to refresh a coiffure or mend a tear in a flounce during the course of a ball or rout.

"I am pleased that the ladies with whom we speak shall feel comfortable," I murmured, "but I am persuaded Mr. Huther shall feel himself an oaf in such a room."

"Is this not a circumstance much to be desired?" Rey queried. "As the only man in the house besides Señyor Bugg, he is the man most suspected for this crime. I shall enjoy watching his discomfort."

"Perhaps, but the butler must not be overlooked," I insisted as I paced to the window and looked down upon the mews. "Nor is he the only man upon the premises. There are the groom, the boot boy, and the coachman." It was then that I was struck with a new thought. "Why is it you are unconvinced that someone other than a man could have perpetrated such a crime?"

Rey frowned. "Perhaps I am mistaken, but I feel a woman would be too soft and of emotions too maternal to have thrust a knife into a boy so young."

"In truth, I have thought the same. If Johnny had been a different sort of young man, it might have been possible. As matters stand, even if a woman were to have reason to dispose of him, I am persuaded she could not do it. His face was too angelic," I added softly, recalling the paintings we had passed in the gallery.

"Yes, but the murder occurred so early in the morning," Rey replied. "Was he asleep when the knife went in? Such circumstances might have made it possible."

"I do believe you have arrived at an important notion. We shall ask each of those we question as to when they were first aware of what had happened, where they were at the time, and where the body was found."

There came a scratch at the door, and I bade whoever stood on the other side to enter. A middle-aged woman, her waist girdled with a chain of keys, appeared. She bobbed a curtsy and quickly took up the chair in which I indicated she should sit.

"I am Trevelin, a friend of the family, and this is Señyor Rey, a…friend of mine," I added with a slight hesitation. That I felt the Spaniard a friend was as astonishing as the fact that I had made the admission aloud. It was a testament to my loneliness that I found pleasure in his company after so short an acquaintance. "Who is it I am addressing?"

"Mrs. Lynne, the housekeeper, my lord," she said, her voice brisk. "Might I ask why it is that I am to be questioned again? Am I thought to ha' done this?"

"Should you be thought to have?" I replied.

"Someone must ha', but 'twas not I!"

"Then you do not agree with the authorities that Mister William is to blame for his brother's death?"

"No, I do not," she stated emphatically. "He ne'er would ha' done what he is said to ha' done. I ha' been hopeful that there would be more questions in search of the truth, but only from those whom the authorities presume to be involved. That is not me."

"All of you who live in the house are involved, Mrs. Lynne, and all shall be questioned again by me and Señyor Rey." I indicated the Spaniard with a wave of my arm. "Though, I confess, there are none to my knowledge who feel you capable of such an act, or that you have any reason to have done so. It is our hope that you might have seen or heard something that could lead us to the killer; that is all."

"Very well, then," she said as she folded her hands tightly in her lap. "I shall be most pleased if there is anythin' I know that might be of use, but I already told the constable everythin'."

"Yes," I readily agreed, "of course you have. And yet, they have Mister William in custody. I imagine you are unaware that he and I were boys together at school. I am most anxious to discover some indisputable fact that shall lead to his release, and as soon as possible."

Tears sprang to Mrs. Lynne's eyes as she looked up at my face. I fancied that she too quickly averted her gaze from my ruined mouth, but I could not be certain. "I shall do all that I can to help, you may be assured o' that, my lord."

"Thank you, Mrs. Lynne. I am persuaded you shall have

much to say that shall throw some light on our comprehension," I began. "Perhaps you might start with when you first learned that Master John had been killed."

"Yes, o' course," she said as tears spilled from her eyes and down her plump cheeks. "It was early yet, too early for the Gilberts to be stirrin'. The exception would be Mister Willy; he does not go out or stay up late. He generally awakens long before the others."

"Yes, I understand. Who else was up and about?"

"The maids were just risin' in order to light the fires in the bed chambers; Cook was below stairs, having already started on breakfast. Bugg was in his pantry. I ha' not been below stairs as of yet and was countin' the linen in the second-floor closet when I heard Mister Willy's shout. It was fearsome, to be sure, but I could not make out the words."

"Why ever not?" I wondered aloud.

"My hearin' is not what it used to be," she said stiffly, "and he was two floors below."

"Willy was on the ground floor? In his nightshirt? How is that?"

"He cannot manage stairs very well, my lord. He sleeps in a small room directly off the library."

"Then," Rey said slowly, "it seems that it would be safe to assume that Mister William found Master John on the same floor. Why was *he* not abed at such an early hour?"

"I can't say," she said with a sniff, "though I ha' also wondered what he was doin' up so early in the morn. And he was dressed as if to go out, which I thought very odd."

I put my finger to my scar as I paused to consider her words. "I suppose a case against Willy could be made," I mused, "by assuming that he, the night prior, had in some way indicated to his brother that he wished him to rise early, dress himself, and appear on the ground floor so that he could be dispatched with more readily."

"He must have arisen very early, then, my lord. No one saw or heard anythin' until Mister William raised the alarm."

I nodded. "Precisely where was Master John's body found?"

"By the front door, my lord."

"And no one saw him there before Mister William found him?"

"My lord, the servants use the back staircase. There ha' been no reason for anyone to ha' crossed over into the front of the house so early in the mornin'."

"Very well, but why was he in the hall? Might Master John have had an assignation with someone? A friend, perhaps, who might have waited for him by the front door?"

"And when the door was opened, he was killed?" Rey suggested.

"We cannot know for certain, unless there was a witness to the events just prior. Mrs. Lynne," I asked, "did you see Mister William before he was taken away?"

"Yes, I did. I ha' never seen him so taken with grief, even after the ridin' accident."

Rey leaned forward in his seat. "What was Mister William wearing, señyora?"

"He was in his nightshirt; that's how early it was to be sure."

"Was there anything amiss?" I pressed. "Anything not as usual?"

Mrs. Lynne cocked her head. "No, nothin' that I noticed. Should there ha' been?"

"No, there should not have," I returned, somewhat in awe of Willy's ability to arrive at the one clue that should certainly exonerate him. "I suppose Mister William soils his shirt on occasion. Does he don a fresh one before he retires?"

"I cannot say; 'tis a duty I don't' see to, my lord," Mrs. Lynne said, her mouth a prim line.

"Forgive me." I gave her an indulgent smile, one I knew would cause the scar at the corner of my mouth to all but disappear. "To whom does that duty fall?"

"I am not entirely certain," she said. "Perhaps you ought to ask Mr. Bugg."

"Very well. Were you present when Mister William was taken away by the constable?"

"Yes, I was. As I said, I ha' never seen him so forlorn. He was devastated that Master John was no more, and I am persuaded he was most anxious for the state of his dear parents."

A wave of sorrow assailed me but I continued. "Were Mr. or Mrs. Gilbert present when the constable took their son away?"

"Yes, of course. They had been fetched to the front hall by none other than myself." Her voice was strong, but the tears coursed down her cheeks.

"Mrs. Lynne, I cannot imagine how difficult this must be for you. Do you feel able to answer one or two more questions?"

She nodded.

"Yesterday Señyor Rey and I called on Mister William.

You say that he was in his nightshirt only, but when we saw him he was fully attired. How was this accomplished?"

"Bugg was sent to acquire clothing from his chamber; the constable, with the boot boy's help, dressed the poor man in the hall like a babe," Mrs. Lynne said as she dabbed at her eyes with her handkerchief.

"Was a clean shirt also procured?" I queried, my heart pounding a bit with anticipation.

"No, my lord; there was no need."

"Then," Señyor Rey interjected, his voice alive with excitement, "the constable, he would have seen that Mister William's shirt was clean, yes?"

"Do you not rise each mornin' in a shirt as clean as it was when you laid your head upon your pillow?" Mrs. Lynne demanded.

"We mean no insult to Mister William or your household, Mrs. Lynne," I soothed. "We only wish to prove his innocence. Tell me, does Mister William require assistance to don a clean shirt each night before he retires?"

"I couldn't say for certain, my lord. If I were to hazard a guess, I would say yes. However, it would be best to ask Mr. Gilbert's valet to be certain."

I did not relish asking my next question, but knew I must. "Was a bloodied shirt found anywhere in the house that morning or since?"

"Not that I am aware, my lord," she replied stiffly.

"Thank you. I shall ask the others of your staff, just so that we can be sure there was not. Do you not see?" I asked Mrs. Lynne, who was still clearly affronted. "Mister William could not have killed his brother without sullying his shirt with blood."

"Oh, yes, I do see," she breathed. She looked up at me, the belligerence in her expression finally vanished. "You are so very clever!"

"You will not be surprised, Mrs. Lynne," I returned, "to learn that it was Mister William himself who alerted us to this fact."

She raised her hand to her mouth as she choked back a sob. "He has changed in very many ways since the accident, but his mind is as sharp as ever."

Indeed, I felt just the same. "Now, we do not wish to distress you any further, but we have some questions as to the disappearance of the key to the door from the area steps into the kitchen. What can you tell us about this?"

Mrs. Lynne seemed to rally, and answered in a firm voice. "I have a set that I wear at all times. That is not the key that has gone missin'. There is an extra set of keys that hangs on a hook in the kitchen. I check them every mornin', at mid-day, and before I retire. One cannot be too careful. It is my duty to ensure that whoever asks for the use of a particular key returns it when agreed. The mornin' prior to that dreadful day, the key to the kitchen door, the one that leads out onto the area steps, was accounted for. It was not there that night, however."

"And at mid-day?" I prompted. To my astonishment, Mrs. Lynne's cheeks glowed bright red.

"I ha' so many people comin' and goin' that day, I cannot recall if I checked at mid-day or not."

I favored Rey with a questioning look. "Who comes to call in the kitchen, Mrs. Lynne? Yours is a world of which we know little."

She pressed her lips together and nodded. "It might be quite a few. For example, the servants who ha' been out, whether on their day off or when they return from executin' a task. The grocer and fish-monger often send a servant of their own to collect payment for their goods. The kitchen girls are known to ha' a caller or two come to the door if they are walkin' out with a boy. It seemed that there was plenty of each on that particular day."

"In other words, nobody out of the ordinary?" I prompted.

"Precisely," she said with confidence.

"Are you quite certain, Mrs. Lynne, that none of them could have been in a position to take the key without your knowledge?"

"Few of them get past the threshold, my lord. However, it could have been any of the servants. They have all been questioned at great length by Bugg and myself, but we have arrived at no conclusions."

"We shall be certain to question each of them, as well," I assured her. "Think carefully: was there anyone else who had access to those keys that day?"

Mrs. Lynne closed her eyes and bowed her head. Just when I feared she knew nothing else of import, she raised her head and smiled in triumph. "Yes, there were several deliveries that day: the girl with the vegetables, and a boy who brought in a box of sundries such as sugar and flour. They both entered the kitchen and stayed for a chat. There was also Throckmorton; he came by to request the recipe for Cook's jugged hare. Lady Vawdrey relishes it so."

"Señyor Rey," I mused. "Please make a note: we needs

must question Mr. Throckmorton as to his memories of that day. Thank you, Mrs. Lynne; you have been most useful. I find I have only one more question for you: who knows when Master John was abed the night before he died and at what time?"

"Mr. Huther sees to it that the young master is abed. His mother generally checks in on him before she departs for whatever entertainment she attends of an evenin'."

"Very good," I said. "That will be all."

As the sound of jangling keys followed Mrs. Lynne from the room, Rey and I shared a pensive glance. There wasn't the time to exchange our views regarding her testimony, as a thin man, his face sharply reminiscent of a rabbit, appeared in the doorway. As his attire was that of a gentleman, I surmised him to be the tutor.

"Please be seated, Mr. Huther. I apologize for the delicacy of the room, but I shall not complain if you do not."

Mr. Huther offered no reply as he entered, but his nose twitched a bit as he sank into the proffered chair under the weight of my insistent stare. I was quite certain I had never clapped eyes on such a timid specimen, and then I noticed the tutor's black armband and recalled that this was a house in mourning.

"Mr. Huther," I said with as much compassion as I dared; I had no wish to induce tears in the man. "I am Trevelin, and this is Señyor Rey of Barcelona. It is my understanding that you serve as the tutor in the household."

"I have done." Mr. Huther twisted his hands together in his lap. "I have been dismissed. Tonight shall be my last in this house."

I turned to take note of Rey's expression on the heels of such a revelation, and was satisfied to find him as surprised as I. Turning again to Mr. Huther, I asked "Do you go far?"

The tutor looked up; his eyes were bloodshot and rimmed with red. "I have no place to go."

"Why is that?" I asked.

He did not immediately reply. "I have not been given a reference," he said slowly.

I refused to allow the jolt of shock that went through me to show on my face. "Pray tell, for what cause?"

"You must inquire of the mistress for I am sure I do not know."

I rather suspected Mr. Huther knew the reason well enough, but refrained from speaking the thought aloud. "Seynor Rey, please write down the question to ensure that I put it accurately to Mrs. Gilbert when next I speak with her."

As Rey bent to his work, I studied the tutor's reaction. He sat frozen in place, staring at the scratching of the pencil against parchment, the sound of which seemed to dwarf every other. When Rey finished, and looked up with a gentle smile, the tutor offered the ghost of one in return. I, however, did not fail to note how Mr. Huther's brow was beaded with sweat and his chin trembled in a manner unbecoming to any but the youngest of maidens.

"Mr. Huther, I have been told that you were always the last to bid goodnight to Master John. Was that the case the night before he died?"

Mr. Huther's face turned white, and he pressed his folded hands against his stomach as if it pained him. "Yes. That is, I believed myself to be the last to see him."

"What can you mean?" I asked in some impatience.

The tutor's face flamed red and he all, but jumped from his seat. "Who are you to pose such questions? Why, you look as if you cannot have quit university more than a twelvemonth past! I am not suspected by those who are in authority, and I cannot imagine why their good opinion of me is not adopted by all in this house."

I could feel Rey's agitation as he rose to his feet. "Do you dare to speak so to a Peer of the Realm? My lord is a man most important, a marquis, and you must treat him with the honor due him!"

This was the most surprising revelation of all. It would seem that Rey's opinion of me had experienced a sea change. "It is quite all right, Señyor Rey. I have been accused of far worse than an abundance of youth," I added with a wry smile. It is true, Mr. Huther, that I came into my marquisate at a tender age, but it is not due to my position in the world that I am here today; it is as Mister William's oldest friend. I have no knowledge of any who suspect you of this vile deed, and question you only in hopes of learning something that will lead to his release. We can only ask for your cooperation and hope that you have the leisure to endure us for a while longer."

"If you insist," Mr. Huther said patiently, though the expression in his eyes revealed his resentment.

"Very good. Again, I ask you to explain your previous remark. Were you or were you not the last to see Master John?"

"His mother usually speaks to him after I have bid him goodnight, before she goes out for the evening," the tutor replied grudgingly.

"At what hour did that occur?"

Mr. Huther took a deep breath and folded his hands once more across his stomach. "She went out somewhat earlier than is her habit when in town. I believe it was near to eight. Master John generally retires; that is," he amended tearfully, "retired just after they have spoken. That occurs most nights about nine. I check on him again perhaps an hour or so later, before I blow out my candle."

"And on this particular night? Did you do as usual?"

"Yes." An unaccountable misery washed over Mr. Huther's face with this admission. "I thought he was asleep...in his bed...I saw him there. Only, it wasn't him."

I jerked in surprise. "It wasn't him? Who was it then, pray tell?"

"It was no one." The tutor's eyes grew moist.

"First you say it was someone," Rey demanded, "and then you say it was no one. Do you mean to say it was a *fantasma* that you saw?

"Of course not," I insisted. "Mr. Huther has far more sense than to believe in ghosts. I suspect Master John was up to some form of chicanery. What was it: a bolster under the blankets and a Punch or Judy puppet on the pillow, perhaps?"

"An old periwig from the attic," Mr. Huther said as he drew a trembling hand across his brow, "draped over a globe from the schoolroom."

Pensive, I ran a finger across my bottom lip. "When did you discover he had deceived you?"

"Not until I learned what had happened to the poor boy. You can just imagine the hue and cry that arose in the household. I dashed below stairs with naught but a coat over my night-shirt."

"And?" I prompted.

"I saw him lying there in a pool of blood," Mr. Huther replied, his voice hollow. "He was dressed as if he had never been to bed. I couldn't believe it, couldn't make sense of it. I ran back upstairs to see if he was not where I had last seen him." He frowned. "I fear it makes me appear quite irrational to say so, but my mind could not accept that he was truly dead. I had seen him fast asleep!"

"And that is when you discovered how he had betrayed your trust?"

"Yes." The tutor nodded. "When I opened the door, I knew I had been right; it wasn't Master John lying dead in the vestibule after all. There he was, right before my eyes, lying in bed just as he had been the night before. I called his name, and when he didn't answer I went to the bed and pulled back the blankets. It was only then that I truly understood that he was gone."

I considered carefully before posing my next question. "Do you suppose that was the first time he had practiced such deceit? Cast your mind over the past: could he have done this before?"

Mr. Huther looked up at me, visibly irritated. "How should I know? If he had, I failed to perceive it. One sees what one expects to, is that not so?"

"Indeed, it is," I concurred. I had certainly seen my villainous cousin as a fine fellow before I learned otherwise. "If you have nothing more to add, you are free to go."

Mr. Huther rose immediately to his feet. "I do not," he said, rising. He went to the door and quit the room, without even the cursory bow that was due a marquis.

"For a man with nowhere to go, he seems most eager to shed himself of this house," Rey observed. "Why did you not press him as to the reason for his dismissal without a reference?"

"I am as eager to know the answer to that question as you are. In the meantime, I am hoping Mr. Bugg shall prove more loquacious on the subject."

Rey's face lit up with approval. "Then, I anticipate his interview with pleasure."

Chapter Four

Next to enter the room, however, was not the butler. Rather it was the upstairs maid, followed by the lesser servants who had nothing illuminating to add, and who answered most questions with a simple yes or no. Even the valet had nothing of value to say, except to verify Mrs. Lynne's account regarding Willy's difficulties in changing his attire. By the time the butler hesitatingly hovered over the indicated chair, I felt weary of the whole business.

"I assure you, Mr. Bugg, it is quite unobjectionable for you to sit in my presence," I insisted. "If it eases your discomfort, I shall sit as well." I couldn't say why I had chosen to stand whilst questioning the other servants; perhaps I fancied it imbued me with an increased superiority, an essential quality in such an endeavor.

"Thank you, my lord," Mr. Bugg intoned as he took his seat.

I sat as well, choosing a teetering over-stuffed stool that added nothing to my consequence. "Mr. Bugg, you have waited on me on any number of occasions, both in town and at the Gilberts' country estate, over the course of many years. You have given your master no reason to dismiss you. In short, you are a man who can be trusted."

"I do hope so, my lord," the butler agreed.

"As such, you are the position to know the answers to many questions, all of which I intend to put to you before the day is done."

"Yes, my lord," Mr. Bugg said, without a flicker of either humor or annoyance.

I put to him first the usual question as to the key, with no new results.

"Very good," I said. "Let us begin with the matter of Mr. Huther. Why is it that he has been dismissed without a reference?"

"He failed utterly in his duty to monitor his charge," the butler said unblinkingly.

"By this statement am I to assume that Mr. and Mrs. Gilbert blame him for Master John's death?"

"Only in the respect that they feel he neglected his duties."

I frowned. "Do you refer to his failure to detect that Master John had placed a bolster in his bed in order to mislead his tutor into believing he was asleep?"

The butler cleared his throat in what proved to be the first sign of his hesitation. "That news was not well received by the master and mistress. However, it is a minor indiscretion compared to others in the past."

"We have come to the heart of the matter at long last," I said with a glance over my shoulder at Rey. "Do proceed, Mr. Bugg."

"I fear that it would be revealing more than Mr. Gilbert should wish."

"I am in awe of your sense of duty, Mr. Bugg. However, if you know something that might serve to prove Mister

William's innocence, should not Mr. Gilbert be naught but grateful?"

The butler's countenance cleared. "Yes. As I most fervently believe in Mister William's innocence, I find that I cannot dismiss the logic of your argument."

"Very well, then," I said with a flourish of my hand. "On the subject of Mr. Huther's indiscretions, do tell."

The butler's shoulders relaxed visibly and he settled more deeply into his seat. "He often left Master John to his own devices. In addition, he was known to leave the house when he was meant to be teaching lessons. It is believed that he frequented a place where his addictions could be sated."

"Indeed! What addictions might those be?" I asked.

"I could not say specifically. I only know that he felt compelled to depart the house when he did not have leave to do so. Whether he went to a house of drink, a gaming house, an opium den, or somewhere worse, I cannot say."

"As head of the staff, was it not your duty to discover what Mr. Huther was about?" I asked, somewhat incredulous.

"My authority does not extend to the tutor. He reports directly to Mr. Gilbert."

"Of course, but did you not feel it your duty to inform Mr. Gilbert of your suspicions?"

"Yes, my lord. I did, indeed, report all that I knew to be fact when it came to Mr. Huther."

"Then how is it that he was not dismissed?"

"I believe it was on Mrs. Gilbert's account that he was allowed to stay."

I felt my eyebrows rise in surprise. "Why should that be

so?" I dared not suggest that Mrs. Gilbert felt anything inappropriate regarding the tutor; Mr. Bugg would never betray his mistress so.

"No exact reason of which I am aware," he began slowly. "Only that the idea of dismissing him caused her some distress."

"Mr. Bugg, I assure you that I am fully cognizant of how improper it would be to air your opinion on this matter. However, I am persuaded you have one. On behalf of Mister William, will you not share it with us now? I swear never to divulge what you have said if it can be helped."

The butler hung his head and nodded. "Very well, my lord. You are correct in that I have puzzled over the matter myself. The only reason of which I could conceive as to her wish to keep him on would be to alleviate her anxiety over her young son. She is…was very protective of him. It is well known in the household that it was the mistress who refused to send him off to school. More recently, I believe she felt that a change in tutor would be too disruptive."

I felt that the butler's observations tallied very well with what I had learned from Mr. Gilbert's own lips, and very nearly spoke my thoughts aloud. However, it would never do to divulge such information to Bugg, in spite of his keen observations of the truth.

"Very well. Señyor Rey, please make a note to question Mrs. Gilbert as to her reasons for keeping Mr. Huther on."

Mr. Bugg's face revealed his alarm at this request.

"Rest assured, Mr. Bugg, we shall not air your opinions on the matter, but rather hope that she reveals the truth without further prompting."

The butler drew a deep breath. "Thank you, my lord."

"Now," I said briskly, "we are interested to know if a bloody shirt, one that would have belonged to Mister William, was found anywhere on the premises the morning of Master John's death."

"No, sir."

"Was there any blood between where Master John lay and the front door? Or a trail of blood leading anywhere else for that matter?"

"Yes. There was what looked to be the result of a light trickle of blood from the. . ." The butler hesitated. With a hard swallow, he continued, "the body, through the hall, out the front door, and out onto the street. That is where Mister William was found holding the knife."

"Indeed, that is to be expected. So, there were no pools of blood or bloody footsteps or any such evidences that Master John had been stabbed anyplace other than where he was found?"

"Precisely, though I fear that I have said something amiss. Mister William was found holding the knife, that much is true. But there is no possibility that he could have killed his brother."

"And why is that, Mr. Bugg?"

"Because he would not. He loved his brother. In addition, he did not possess the coordination of muscles. He still has some strength in the one arm; that is not the trouble. It is his lack of ability to do a proper job of it, what with the tremors he endures."

"Yes, I comprehend you completely. May I enquire as to the state of Mister William's shirt when he was taken away by the constable?"

"It was the same shirt he had donned before retiring the night prior," he said, clearly bewildered. "At least I presumed it to be."

"I understand that the constable and the boot boy helped him to don his breeches and the rest before being led away. Was that your observation?"

"Yes, indeed. I was prepared to do it, but the constable had ordered the boot boy to assist him; though I am persuaded he regretted his choice, he did not alter his course. He looked to be a man who does not enjoy being in the wrong, a circumstance at which he must have had much experience. It was an unpleasant scene, to be sure, as neither had any idea as how to go about it correctly. I believe it caused Mister William no small amount of humiliation."

Several moments passed before I could trust my voice to operate as it should. The disgrace Willy would have felt must have been past bearing. I took a deep breath and forged on. "Indeed. It pains me to even hear of it. Do I assume correctly that it is you who most often assists him with changes of clothing?"

"When he cannot manage on his own, it is either his father or I who aids him. At times, the valet assists as well."

"Am I right to assume that Mister William has as much trouble with a shirt as any other item of apparel?"

"Yes, absolutely. His father generally helps him to change before going out for the evening."

"So, it would be unlikely that Mister William bloodied his shirt, removed it, and successfully disposed of or hid it all on his own?"

"Highly unlikely, and not simply due to his physical

weaknesses. Mister William is not capable of such deceit. I wish I could say it was always thus, but the truth is that there was a change in him after the accident. I do believe he is as intelligent as before, in spite of his inability to express his thoughts at any length. And yet, there is a profound ingenuousness about him that has never before been his constant companion. It is as if the accident wiped away all desire to do ill, and left only the nobility of his soul."

Tears threatened to fill my eyes until the sound of Rey's sniff brought a smile to my lips. "Thank you, Mr. Bugg," I said. "My observation has been thus, as well, though I had not the words. When did you first learn of Master John's death, and what steps did you take?"

"I was below stairs in the pantry, and heard nothing of Mister William's cries. That he managed so many steps from the door down to the street on his own shows well how intent he was on acquiring help. He must have fallen, for there were fresh bruises upon his knees already. No, it was not until one of the maids found me that I heard the news. Naturally, I ran immediately to where the young master lay."

"So, Mr. Huther did not alert you?" I noted the flare of suspicion in the butler's eyes at the question.

"If he claims to have done, I assure you he did not. He was not about at the time. At least, I do not recall seeing him."

"Very well. What did you do next?"

"I attempted to determine for myself if the boy was truly dead."

I feared my next question was too callous, but I would have been unable to speak a word if I had not hardened my heart. "And in what state did you find the body?"

Mr. Bugg blinked as if he had been struck. "He was most certainly dead. The maid brought a mirror to determine if it clouded when held under his nose; it did not. Also, his skin was cold and then, of course, there was so much blood," he said with a slight gasp, "including where the knife had entered his chest."

"I realize these are difficult questions, Mr. Bugg," I said, full of remorse.

"I hope that I have not given any sign that I resent your queries, my lord. It is only that the constable posed none of these questions, nor did the other authorities who came to the house later in the day. I had not thought to expect them."

"They did not?" I asked, surprised. "I can only assume they felt they had their man, and therefore the answers to such questions were not helpful. However, it is my aim to prove that Mister William could not have committed this evil act. As such, I need ask a few more questions, as unpleasant as they are. For example, did the blood still flow or was it congealed? Also, if you attempted to move his limbs were they at all stiff?"

"The bleeding had stopped, though there was quite a large puddle on the marble floor. We did turn him from his side onto his back and managed to place one of his hands over the wound before his mother came upon him. However, when they lifted him up to take him away, it seemed that the body was much stiffer. It was nearly as if he were a plank of wood," the butler added, faintly.

"Thank you, Mr. Bugg. I am very sorry for your loss. Rest assured that your observations are valuable information as to when Master John met his fate."

"I understand, my lord." The butler's eyes filled with tears. "I, as well as the entire staff, wish to thank you for all that you are doing for Mister William as well as for Mr. and Mrs. Gilbert. We are extremely hopeful that you will succeed in your efforts to exonerate their son."

"And many thanks to you," I said, "and the other servants. Please tell them how much I appreciate their candor. I hope to not find it necessary to speak with them again, but it might be best if you warn them that I shall should it prove needful."

"Yes, my lord," Mr. Bugg said as he rose, and executed a bow. "I hope that when we meet next, it is under more favorable circumstances."

I waited until the butler quit the room before I turned to Rey. "What think you? Have you formed any fast opinions as of yet?"

"But of course!" Rey insisted. "This Mr. Huther has much to hide. He seems a most unsavory character, and there is much mystery as to why he was let into the house in the first place."

"Your thoughts echo mine. Come," I said as I rose heavily to my feet, "it has been a long day. Will you join me for dinner at my club?"

"I should like to very much!" Señyor Rey collected his pencil and parchment and readily followed me from the room.

It wasn't until after we had walked to Canning House and were safely ensconced in the carriage before I again spoke. "I believe it would best if I returned on the morrow to question Mrs. Gilbert about Mr. Huther. In the meantime, I should like you to follow him when he is turned out of the house in the morning."

"I?" Rey asked with such vehemence I found it difficult to determine if he felt affronted or greatly pleased.

"Yes, you, should you be amenable. As you are aware, my reputation is not the most robust. Should I be spotted lingering in the vicinity of, for example, an opium den, I shall surely never again dance with a young lady."

"Dance? I do not understand, my lord."

It was incomprehensible that Rey had forgotten his objection to my dancing with Miss Woodmansey. "'Twas nothing," I said, deciding that Rey wished for the both of us to forget the heated exchange we had endured when first we met. "Meanwhile, you are a stranger here and cannot have too much care for these things."

"What is this? I do not care for the good opinion of the peoples of this island? Perhaps not," Rey said with an airy wave of his hand, "but I do care for the generous opinion of some."

Doubtless it was not my opinion he favored so highly, but that of Miss Woodmansey. "I am persuaded that English ladies are quite taken with black curls and eyes," I said lightly.

"But this is not in the least satisfactory, my lord." He lifted his chin and turned his face such that it afforded me a view of his rather regal profile. "It is not for my appearance that I wish to be admired. I wish a lady to admire me for who I am, to see past my face to the heart that beats red for her."

I felt a frown crease my brow, but I was powerless to remove it; I had wished for others to see past my face too often to enumerate. "If wishes were horses," I said.

"Pardon? I do not comprehend."

"It is I who must beg your pardon, Señyor Rey," I said briskly, trusting that my usual quasi-affable expression had returned to my face. "It is merely a piece of nonsense the English utter. We may wish with all of our might, but it won't produce the objects of our desires."

"What? Do you say that you admire this Miss Woodmansey as well?" Rey demanded.

I was taken aback. "I failed to assume Miss Woodmansey to be the lady of whom you spoke," I prevaricated. "She is, however, worthy of admiration by all who encounter her." I most certainly did. She was one of the few women who seemed undeterred by my scar or the rumored means by which I had acquired it. "She is possessed of much charm and intelligence."

"But you have failed to include her uncontestable beauty on your list!"

"Does not any woman worthy of admiration wish to be so admired for her character rather than her face every bit as fervently as does a man?" I riposted. I failed to add that I did not find Miss Woodmansey especially beautiful, or that her lack of it did not matter to me in the least. "Regardless, the benefit of beauty is somewhat puffed up in the eyes of society, wouldn't you agree?"

"Perhaps," Rey conceded, "though, the society in which you associate favors far more than beauty, all of it as undeserved."

"All of it?" I did not attempt to hide the amusement in my voice. "Pray, do share with me your observations. I find I am rather curious to learn what it is about our society you find so offensive."

"Very well," Rey replied with a frown. "The high society of England cares overmuch for money. In my mind, property, land, an ancestral home, is enough to earn the approbation of all."

"I own if one has a place to lay his head at night, the blunt to pay one's bills is hardly urgent. Do go on," I urged.

"Very well! There is the English obsession with titles. Some of these titles are meaningless, given for paltry favors!"

"I agree. It was far more seemly when a man was granted land, title, and monies in exchange for his sword arm and that of his tenants. That being said, there is little need for such defenses in this modern age."

Rey grunted. "*Si*, it is *poc cavallerós*. Where is the chivalry in this?"

"I'm afraid I could not say, though I suspect you are not yet through proving your point. What else, in your eyes, do the English value far more than is sensible?"

There was a slight pause before the impassioned Spaniard revealed his thoughts. "Height! I find that the English are dreadfully concerned with height."

"You don't say!" I gibed. "Perhaps this is why your Miss Woodmansey remains on the shelf despite her less than tender years."

Rey drew himself up as far as he was able whilst seated in a moving carriage. "Miss Woodmansey does not lack in height, my lord. I cannot think why you should believe it to be so."

I began to suspect that my little friend was a financially-embarrassed, title-less man, possessed of a large ancestral home on a lovely bit of land, but I dared not say so. "Ah, we have arrived at our destination. I, for one, am famished."

"I am most pleased to dine with you, my lord, but must insist that we leave off the subject of murder; at least until the morrow."

"Agreed!" I said as I clapped an arm around Rey's shoulders. "Sufficient unto the day is the evil thereof."

The next morning, I walked from my residence and along the square to Gilbert House. I reflected on how little I had seen of Willy since the duel. In truth, the road into Willy's presence had seemed long ever since his riding accident. It was the pity that was the problem; I had never landed on a means to hide it from my friend.

As I took the steps to the grand entrance of the Gilberts' abode, I caught sight of the shadow of a man's hat at the far end of the house. It would seem that Rey still waited for Mr. Huther to quit the premises. I gave my accomplice a grave nod and rapped on the door. It was answered in good time by Bugg, who bowed and held out his hand for my card.

"It seems I haven't one," I murmured, so startled that I could barely get my fingers into my pockets in the case there was a lone bit of printed pasteboard about my person. "You know very well who I am," I prodded, and gave up the search. "I wish to speak to Mrs. Gilbert. Is she in?"

"If you would wait in the anteroom, my lord," he said, indicating a room off the hall, "I shall see if she is at home." He then rolled his eyes in so dramatic a fashion that I concluded that Mrs. Gilbert was most certainly at home and had been the cause of some trouble.

I waited long, and found it difficult not to pass the time in wondering why I had not been immediately ushered into the first-floor salon. Finally the door opened, and Mr. Gilbert appeared at my side.

"Mr. Gilbert; it is a pleasure, but I had expected your good wife."

"Yes, well, there was somewhat of a fracas this morning seeing Mr. Huther out of the house. Naturally, his services are no longer required," Mr. Gilbert said as the veins in his neck purpled. "I cannot fathom why he should think we would feed and house him under the circumstances!"

"It is Mr. Huther I wish to speak of to Mrs. Gilbert. Is she in?"

Her husband regarded me with some suspicion. I had little time to reflect on how unwarranted such an emotion was when he spoke again.

"She is busy," he said shortly. "It seems there is much to do when a member of the household has expired."

"Of course," I said, regretful that I had failed to recall that this was a house in mourning. "Please forgive me for my lapse. It is only that I was persuaded that you wished me to do what I might to prove Willy's innocence. There was a question in the minds of the some of the servants as to certain actions that were taken, and I am wishful of making matters clear as soon as possible."

"What question?" he demanded despite of his softened expression.

"Ah, well…" I hesitated in hopes Mrs. Gilbert would appear, "for one, there was some question as to Mr. Huther's suitability and why he was not dismissed when it was discovered he did not monitor his charge as he should have done."

Mr. Gilbert's face turned red, with shame or anger I could not discern. "You shall have to ask that of my wife. I would have seen the back of him many days since."

"Touché!" I hoped my bow hid what I feared to be a smile too smug.

"Very well. However, I should like to be present when you put your question to her. I yearn to know the answer to that one as well," he replied as he opened the door and motioned to the butler to enter. "Bugg, do have your mistress attend us at once."

The butler's bow was too slow, allowing me to catch his expression of alarm. Again, I wondered what might have happened earlier that morning to cause him such dismay.

"Has Mr. Huther already quit the premises?" I asked. I remembered the distinct impression I had that Rey yet waited in the shadows, and wondered why he had not followed the tutor as directed.

"Yes, and my wife is absolutely mindless with grief." Mr. Gilbert's words belied his stony expression.

"Surely, it is because of her sons that she grieves," I insisted. "What could Mr. Huther have been to her?" My tone was dismissive, but I realized that I wished to know the answer to the question almost as much as, I was beginning to suspect, Mr. Gilbert. "Were you aware he was given no reference upon his dismissal?"

Mr. Gilbert cast me a look of aspersion. "That is most certainly untrue. I wrote one myself. I should not like my friends and associates to learn that Johnny's former tutor was thrown out into the street with no place to go."

"I do beg your pardon. I should have said that it is only rumored that it was so. I wonder where he has gone."

"I cannot think what it is to you," Mr. Gilbert said, his expression sour.

At that moment, Mrs. Gilbert appeared in the doorway. Her eyes were red and swollen. I had not seen her so sorrowful.

"Mrs. Gilbert, how good of you to join us," I said as I gently took her by the elbow and led her to a chair. "This must be difficult for you."

"Indeed it is," she murmured as she sat. I noticed that she did not spare a glance for her husband and kept her eyes downcast. She clearly suffered from some discomfiture, but whether it was due to her disheveled appearance or something else I could not say with any certainty.

"I shall ask my questions straight out so that I may leave you in peace as quickly as may be. Are you aware that there is a belief amongst your servants that Mr. Huther was dismissed without a reference?"

"I am unaware of such talk." Mrs. Gilbert's reply was low and nearly unintelligible.

"Madam, it is not my desire to shame you," I said gently. "I merely wish to know if perhaps Mr. Huther had any reason to put a period to your son's existence."

Her head snapped up and her eyes blazed with anger. "Naturally he had nothing to do with Johnny's death! Mr. Huther was often negligent in his duties; he sometimes left the house when he ought to have been teaching lessons, and I wager he daydreamed during instruction time more often than did Johnny. However, he is not a killer. Of that I am most certain."

Mr. Gilbert's dismay at her words was palpable, but he said nothing.

I decided it wise to alter my course. "Might I ask why you did you not dismiss the tutor before now if he were unsuitable?"

"I do not know," she insisted, as if she had given the answer to this question many times a day. "I suppose," she said slowly, "I wished to keep Johnny happy. He did not endure change well. This is precisely why I kept him home from school and sought the services of Mr. Huther in the first place." She sniffed and put a much-used handkerchief to her nose. "I would give anything I possess to find Johnny safe at Eton or Harrow this very moment," she murmured.

"Naturally, Mrs. Gilbert. No one doubts your love for your son. If I could trouble you to verify one more matter: you are certain you gave him a reference when he departed?"

She flicked a look in my direction and pressed her lips together in what I felt to be apprehension. "Of course I did! It would be wrong to do otherwise. My husband wrote it himself. There is already such a cloud over Mr. Huther's head with the death of his only charge. That is more than enough with which to contend when presenting yourself as a candidate for a new position."

Mr. Gilbert nearly jumped to his feet and paced angrily to the other side of the room. Clearly the tutor was a sore point.

Before I could pose another question, Mrs. Gilbert also rose from her seat. "If that is all," she said stiffly, "I am needed elsewhere."

"Yes, of course."

I rose and proffered a bow far deeper than her due. "Thank you for your tolerance. I pray that I shall have no cause to ask further questions."

She inclined her head and swept from the room, utterly ignoring her husband who sat with his arms crossed against a chest, heaving with indignation.

"Mr. Gilbert, does something trouble you?"

"Other than the fact that Johnny is murdered and Willy wrongfully incarcerated for his death?"

"I, too, find it intolerable," I said quietly. "My sole desire is to see that this wrong is righted, and as soon as may be."

There came a scratch at the door, and Bugg admitted himself. "Sir, there is a missive for my lord, just delivered."

"For me?" I asked, greatly surprised that any should believe me to be anywhere but abed at such an hour. I took the note and skimmed its contents. "Mr. Gilbert, do excuse me, but it seems that I am also needed elsewhere. However, should you learn anything new, anything at all, please send word 'round to Canning House immediately."

He gave a short nod in acknowledgement, whereupon I quit the room. As I departed, I picked up a black armband from a supply on the hall table and drew it over my arm. Then I made my way across the square to the abode of Lady Vawdrey. The armband spoke of despair, just as my brisk stride proclaimed hope for Willy's release and the reformation of my reputation.

Chapter Five

I was admitted to Hampton House by the stony-faced butler, and led directly upstairs to the salon with nary a request for a card to identify myself; it seemed that my arrival was anticipated. Once I stepped into her presence, I quickly ascertained that Lady Vawdrey was distraught despite her valiant effort to hide it from the other occupants of the room, which included Rey. To my distaste, Throckmorton stood in his usual place behind his mistress' chair, his hand on her shoulder. It was a gesture most possessive, and I wondered what it was he feared.

"I am delighted," I said to the room at large, trusting Rey to interpret my words as for him alone.

"And to think I expected to find you more surprised than otherwise," Lady Vawdrey said with a smile broader than I had been accustomed to receiving of late.

"Shall we say that I am equal parts surprised and delighted," I said with a wary glance at Rey.

"Such pretense, my lord! I assure you that you needn't uphold it for my sake," Lady Vawdrey insisted. "The good señyor has kept me apprised of all of your doings."

"All of them?" I could not at that moment identify the emotion that filled me at her words, though I daresay betrayal was at the heart of it. "I should think a lady of your discernment should find such a recital more than a little tedious."

"Well," she said with a lofty air, "he only shared the pertinent events. I should enjoy hearing your impression of them. When we are satisfied that all is being done on that score I shall inform you as to why it is, precisely, that I have requested your presence."

I looked again to Rey. His expression resembled nothing so much as a dog who had watered the carpet for no better reason than that he could not be bothered to do otherwise. I, however, was perversely pleased that he perceived the wrong he had done in apprising Lady Vawdrey of our activities. "I see. Shall we begin with what our good friend here has learned this morning? Or, dear señyor, did you find that your quarry had departed before you arrived?" I hoped I did not sound as bitter as I felt.

"*Sí* and no, my lord. Yes, I did find my quarry and no, he had not left before I arrived. I laid in wait as you requested and followed him a great distance. I have only just returned."

"How is that? I am persuaded that I saw you lurking in the shadows when I arrived at Gilbert House less than a half hour past."

"My lord, if I may speak," Throckmorton intoned. "I believe it must have been me whom you saw." He spoke very precisely, but with what seemed an unaccountable effort. "I was on my way to Canning House with my lady's message for you, but when I saw you on the pavement I knew not what to do."

"Thank you, Mr. Throckmorton," I said with as much approval as I could muster. "You did very well. Now, would you be so good as to leave us?"

Throckmorton turned his disarming violet gaze on his mistress. "Is that your wish as well, my lady?"

"Yes, dear." She threw a claw-like hand over his where it rested on her shoulder. "You may be assured that I shall inform you of whatever I feel is needful."

"Very good, my lady," he murmured, in tones quite at odds with the malevolent glare he cast at me, and quit the room.

"Please do have a seat, Trevelin," Lady Vawdrey insisted, "and let us put aside our differences for the sake of your friend."

"Ours?" I echoed in some disbelief. "The only differences I have with you are the abundance of picked bones you have made of my person in recent months. But, as you say, I am able to let bygones be bygones as well as any."

"And what of me?" Rey ventured. "Are my bones to be picked for my *indiscreció?*"

"Not at all, my friend," I murmured as I took up a chair across from them both. "I find it odious."

"Very well, then," Lady Vawdrey said with a lift of her chin, "I shall take no notice of your insolence. Shall we discover what Señyor Rey has learned from his spying this morning?"

I raised my brow at him. "You have told her much already, I think."

"She rises early, my lord, and it is most difficult to resist her questions, especially when one's stomach is devoid of contents," he explained, his face wan.

"My dear Señyor Rey!" Lady Vawdrey crooned as she very nearly jumped to her feet in her haste to pull the bell. I shall have sustenance brought *immediatamente!*"

"No, no, no!" he said in a voice less kind than I had ever before heard him utter. "That is the Spanish. If you wish to speak Catalan, you must forget that you ever had ears for the Spanish! *Immediatament, immediatament, immediatament!*"

"What is this?" I looked at Rey in astonishment. "You cannot be teaching Lady Vawdrey to speak your native tongue!"

"Why can he not?" she asked as she drew herself fully upright, causing her already-lofty form to take on new heights. "Do you expect me too dull to learn?"

"Not at all," I insisted. I dared not voice aloud the reason for my disapproval. A man such as I suspected Rey to be did not stoop to teaching language lessons. "I merely supposed him to be unencumbered during the course of his visit to England."

"His visit to England, my lord," she said crisply, "has all to do with my lessons in Catalan. He is a language tutor. I am surprised he did not inform you of this at the outset."

Since I suspected Rey was in England to win the heart of a certain petite, large-dowered young lady, I felt her statement to be, at most, partially true. "Perhaps he felt it was not his place to tell such a tale," I suggested. Certainly, he would have no wish for Miss Woodmansey to get wind of how financially distressed a Spanish gentleman must find himself to embark on such a career.

"He is most correct, my lady," Rey agreed. I did not know whether you wished to have such talk bandied about."

"Very correct, señyor. I applaud your good sense. Now! Do tell us what you have learned this morning. Ah! But see;

here is Hoagland now." She turned to the newly-arrived butler and ordered a tray of food for her guest. She took no care to ask if I required anything. I thought I did not, but soon regretted having not requested anything.

"Very well, then! We are finally alone and ready to hear your tale."

Rey looked to be relieved, a circumstance for which I could hardly blame him. If I were he, I should have no wish to share my thoughts on how my profession might fail to impress Miss Woodmansey. I felt grateful I was not in such a position, then recalled the scar that symbolized the earning of my reputation and felt myself humbled.

"As you may have guessed," Rey began, "I went without my breakfast so as to be across the square very early. I wished to be hidden in a spot most secure when the tutor departed. I was surprised to see him emerge from the house with his bag and no carriage to be seen. It was only then that I wondered how I should have followed him had he boarded one."

I was taken aback at my own lack of foresight on the matter, and said as much.

"There is no need to assign blame, my lord. As he did not board a carriage I surmised that he had not far to go, and in that I was most correct."

"And yet you have only just arrived," I pointed out. "What has kept you?"

Rey lifted a finger. "Ah! I have not yet come to that. I waited until he had taken himself a ways ahead, and then I proceeded to follow him. He walked to the end of the street, turned right at the corner, and entered the house a few doors down on that side of the square."

"Could that have been Manwaring House?" Lady Vawdrey mused aloud. "Do you remember anything about the house that was unusual?" she asked.

"How can I say? These houses, they all look very much the same. Tall, narrow, faced with white brick." He shrugged his dissatisfaction.

"Not at all, my good señyor!" Lady Vawdrey exclaimed. "Was there a portico? Railings? A bow front window, perhaps? Of what hue was the door?"

"I believe there were two doors, both black."

"But, of course." Lady Vawdrey made a moue. "I should think it terribly odd if they had not both been painted the same color."

"You are correct, señyora," Rey conceded. "They had brass door knockers. I seem to recall a pair of columns and the top step was set out in black and white check all the way to the threshold."

Lady Vawdrey clapped her hands. "Yes! That is Manwaring House! I wonder what use they have for a tutor. They have no offspring, though he does have children from his first marriage, all of whom are at university. Well! This is a tidy piece of news, indeed!"

"I fail to see what is tidy in it, Lady Vawdrey," I admonished. "For instance, as you so aptly stated we haven't any idea as to why the tutor should have gone there. That is what we would do best to learn. Señyor Rey, did you see him emerge from the house?"

"No. I laid in wait for hours, but did not see his face again."

"And I have paid you for your thoroughness with an

empty belly," I confessed just as the butler entered with a tray. "You have proven yourself worthy of such a repast as Lady Vawdrey has provided." In truth, the tray bore a toothsome assortment of foodstuffs, and my stomach growled in appreciation.

"What shall we do next?" he asked with a marked lack of concern for my longing.

I wished to state the obvious: that I was too distracted by the delicious odors that wafted past my nose to think. However, this would be to remark on the mundane. "I do believe we shall find it needful to inquire as to the happenings at Manwaring House. If only there were a rout or ball we might attend in order to garner gossip."

"Which brings us to my own little drama, my lord," Lady Vawdrey said. "There is to be a ball tonight, one in Bloomsbury Square, on the same side of the street on which that clever Isaac D'Israeli lives."

"I perceive the trouble already," I said dryly.

"How could you?" Lady Vawdrey demanded. "I have not yet told you of it."

"That being my point," I said, with a smile designed to soften the insult.

She gave me an arch look, but she was apparently determined to conduct a harmonious discourse. "The trouble is that I had counted on wearing my diamond necklace, the famous one modeled after that belonging to Marie Antoinette."

Aside from the Gilbert tragedy, it was the first thing the lady had said in months in which I felt the least interest. "You are correct: that does sound rather ominous. Doubtless, La Antoinette thought it such."

Lady Vawdrey smiled her scorn. "As I have said, it is merely modeled after hers and, truth be told, the diamonds, all forty-three of them, are not nearly as large as those of the original. My husband had it made for me shortly before he died, and I treasure it most for its sentimental value."

"I had not thought you old enough to be acquainted with Marie Antoinette, let alone her necklace," I twitted her, "but if you say it is so..." Lady Vawdrey gave me a look as cold as Rey's was alarmed. "The point imperative is that it is gone. Stolen."

"I am indeed sorry that a piece of such beauty and value has been lost," I claimed, for it was the truth, "but for what am I needed?"

"I thought you would be interested to know, so that you might help me to find it."

"But my lord is very occupied, my lady," Rey sputtered around a quantity of jam tart, "in his search for the killer of Johnny Gilbert. You would have it so, would you not?"

"Yes, but as long as he is poking and prodding and asking a good deal many questions, as I imagine he must since he seems to vastly enjoy the sound of own voice, he might as well be asking about my necklace whilst he is at it." The smug smile that put a period to this lengthy discourse was a sight to behold.

I was inclined to tell her she was wrong, a truth I had never bothered with when she harangued me as to my character or, more precisely, the lack of it. However, there was something in what she said. "I suppose it would not hurt. Indeed, one might wonder if perhaps the two crimes are possibly related. It is not often we have such a murder amongst us, and the theft of such a valuable piece is not a common occurrence, either. For it to be a coincidence might be a matter of too much naiveté."

"I heartily agree, my lord," she said, with a deep respect her comments to me generally lacked.

"However," I stated, in a voice that brooked no argument, "you must first tell me everything you know about your man, Throckmorton."

Lady Vawdrey was visibly taken aback. "Throckmorton? Why ever should I? You cannot suspect him of any wrongdoing; I have known him since he was a boy and trust him, body and soul."

"What duties are these which you trust him to perform? He is clearly not the butler."

"Naturally he is not the butler! He is my house-keeper. I know 'tis odd, but it is because I trust him so. He keeps the servants in line, keeps a keen eye on the household funds, that sort of thing," she said with an airy wave of her hand.

I tried to imagine Throckmorton in the linen closet counting, the sheets like Mrs. Lynne, and could not. "And the necklace?"

"Yes, indeed, he is the one who makes certain it is well secured, along with all of my jewels."

"But only the necklace à la Antoinette is missing?"

"Yes, though I fail to see what that has to say to it."

"I seem to recall seeing you at various parties in several lovely pieces. To have taken only the one seems like a missed opportunity for anyone who might be breaking in to steal whatever upon which his eye might fall. As such, it would seem that the thief knew what to look for. And where."

"Well! That is not so mysterious," Lady Vawdrey insisted. "It is quite famous. Everyone knows of it. As I've said, it consists of many diamonds, the one in the center being the largest. It is really quite stunning and well worth the bother for just that jewel alone!"

"It sounds absolutely *meravellós*, Lady Vawdrey," Rey breathed. "A man might live his entire life without laying the eyes upon such a wonder."

I was ashamed of myself for the thought, but I made a mental note to inquire of Lady Vawdrey everything she knew about Rey; his reaction to the description of the necklace struck me as suspect, though I could not say exactly why. "Yes, I see that it would be a worthy piece to own, and better yet, the perfect necklace to break up and sell, here and there, so no one would be the wiser as to its origins."

"My thoughts exactly," she said, in a voice drenched with doom. "I suppose I shall never see it again. It might have been broken up already and there shall be no recovering it."

"We shall see," I soothed, "but we must not forget about Throckmorton. As the keeper of the keys, as you say, he is far from above suspicion."

"I cannot believe it of him for an instant!" she cried. "He owes me his life. He would do nothing to jeopardize his position here."

"In that case, I believe you should tell me about it, Lady Vawdrey. Why does he owe you so much?"

"Well," she began, a tremor in her voice, "as I said, I have known him since he was a young boy. I am a patroness of the foundling hospital in Bloomsbury. I first began to visit often when I finally concluded that my husband and I should never have children. And yet, we had so much to share: this house in town, his enormous pile in the Devonshire countryside, horses, carriages, endless fields to run and ride in, and enough money to clothe and feed an army. I hardly knew what to do with it all. So, when we were in town, I made a habit of visiting the foundling hospital. It was a place where I could do some good. I brought food and clothing, and soon I found that I hungered to see the faces of the children who went to and fro' past the gates."

I began to see Lady Vawdrey in a new light. Perhaps the loss she felt due to her childlessness was the catalyst behind her stray-collecting and match-making. "Do go on."

"Well, Throckmorton, as anyone might perceive, could not be ignored, even at the beginning. He was a vision of beauty from the start; his hair was all thick black curls just as it is now, skin as clear and fair as a sheet of vellum, and those eyes! I have never seen the like, before or since."

"But who were his parents?" Rey asked. "Violet eyes are, as you say, not so commonplace. He must have earned them from either the father or the mother. Is anything known of them aside from the surname?"

"There would have been a committee of inquiry to determine the mother's need. She would have been unmarried but of previous good character, and left with no other option. The father would have refused to marry, and abandoned them. Any records that might have been retained as to his parentage would be sealed and not accessible or even spoken of willingly. His name was given to him by whoever received him, so, as you can see, we cannot know to whom he was born."

"Then tell us what you do know," I prodded.

"I believe," she said with emphasis on the latter word, "that he arrived at a very tender age, days old, perhaps only hours. He was taken to a wet nurse in the country until he was four or five, as is the custom. He returned to the foundling hospital nearly the same month that I first began to visit. I noticed him at once; he was always, as I have said, a beautiful child. I watched him grow, even attended his music lessons. He sings most beautifully! I became attached, and even went so far as to supervise his lessons. By the time he was thirteen, I could not bear to see him go."

"Go where?" I asked, drawn into the story despite my dislike for its protagonist.

"The children are most usually apprenticed out, girls at sixteen, boys at fourteen. They are often treated cruelly by their new masters but, worse than that, I would never see Edmund—that is his Christian name—again," she explained as she put a handkerchief to the corner of her eye.

"So, you took him on here."

"Exactly; I agreed to foster him. I would have done so sooner but my husband had no wish to take on a foundling. I began to entertain the idea after Vawdrey's death, but when I learned of Edmund's eventual fate I was determined to keep him by me."

"But, surely, there was a more suitable position for him than housekeeper," I suggested.

"Of course," she agreed, nodding. "He has always been quite tall, and it was only natural to assign him the role of footman. I was the envy of all my friends, I must say. Only, it didn't matter with whom I paired him, there was never anyone as perfect as Edmund. It is the epitome of elegance to have a matched set of footmen, so I found two other young men, twins I believe, also from the foundling hospital. Many of my servants are from there, or the workhouse. In the interim, Edmund has been tutored and trained as if he were my own son."

"Of what use could that be to him?" I asked, appalled. "He is not of your blood. Even were he gently born or the son of a nobleman, he cannot hope to make a match within our class. He would be a man without a place."

"I confess, you are correct," she said with some reluctance. "He was not slow in coming to the same conclusion. It was he who cobbled together his disparate duties so that we might have some discourse with one another. He has the manners, poise and accent, of a nobleman, which one might expect of the best of secretaries. At the same time he has experience with people from the lowliest of classes, a circumstance that is often useful to a woman who is alone and who spends so much time at charitable work. For example, he accompanies me to the workhouse, always, for which I am most grateful. I feel so safe in his presence."

There was still much I felt I needed to know about Throckmorton but the man himself entered the room without first rapping on the door, and our tête-à-tête came to an end.

"Thank you," I said as I rose quickly to my feet. "You have given me much to think on. Oh! I nearly forgot; when was the last time you saw your necklace?" I watched Throckmorton carefully, but he gave nothing away at the mention of the stolen diamonds.

"It has been since I wore it at the end of the Season; the last of June, I believe."

Señor Rey, if you would be so good as to call on me when you are free," I prompted, whereupon I hastily withdrew in hopes of begging a morsel from the Cannings' kitchen before the servants became too occupied with luncheon preparations.

I spent the balance of the day in accumulative disgrace. It is not often a marquis needs must chase after an invitation to a ball. I bore in mind that it was for better reception in Society that I went about attempting to discover the truth of anything for Lady Vawdrey. If she did not smooth the way to my renewed entre into Society as a reward for my efforts, I intended to be enormously put out.

Once I had learned to whose home to tool my carriage come the evening, I gave up on contriving to arrange for an actual piece of vellum to be delivered to my door. The hostess, Lady Truesdale, had been horrified when she learned of my indiscretions, direct from Lady Vawdrey I wagered, and Lord Truesdale had disliked me for far longer and for less reason. As Lady Vawdrey expected me to attend in order to garner clues I considered that enough of a summons, and put the matter of a formal invitation aside. I would simply present myself at the door, as had become an alarmingly frequent habit of late. It wasn't long before my relief over this pitiful problem was replaced with renewed apprehension: Rey had not come to call as requested.

That I most likely had not been present when he arrived was utterly beside the point; he might have left a card in proof that he had discharged his duty to me. Surely he was better at keeping a supply of cards about his person than was I. The only body with less reason to do so, I thought ruefully, was the one waiting at the churchyard to be buried.

As a whole it seemed that Rey had now given me two reasons to doubt his steadfastness. A curious feeling of melancholy threatened to overwhelm me at the thought. Additionally, I was chagrined that I had not considered him a candidate for suspicion from the outset. A foreigner recently arrived on our shores should have been the first to come to mind when considering the perpetrator of any crime. 'Twas only common sense; a murder, a purloined necklace, and a new person in the proximity made for the perfect triad. It occurred to me that if Rey had stolen the necklace, Johnny, living so near and often unsupervised, might have been out and seen something he should not have done, something that had led to his demise.

Determined to put my misgivings aside, I dressed for the ball and strode across the square. By the time I found myself at Lady Vawdrey's door, I was at low ebb. The door was opened, as usual, by the dour butler whose answering frown alerted me to the fact that I was presently not in his good books.

"Is Señyor Rey dressed for the ball? I thought to transport him there tonight." It was an unequivocal untruth; I had had no such thought until that moment.

"He has gone out with Lady Vawdrey."

"To the ball? So early?" I felt something akin to panic, though I could not say why.

"I believe it was to partake of dinner at the home of a young lady."

"Miss Woodmansey?" I asked, incredulous.

"I could not say," Hoagland replied. "Do you wish to wait for their return?" he asked, opening the door wide.

I gave him a sharp look. "You know well enough that I do not."

"Very well. In that case, do you wish to leave a card?"

"There is no need," I murmured as I turned from the door and drifted down the steps. It seemed pointless to live amongst your peers if you were to be treated as a stranger by their servants. There was no room for doubt in my mind that Hoagland knew precisely where his mistress dined that night, even that I had had Canning's carriage called out in order to attend the ball. From there it was no leap to conclude that Hoagland perhaps knew more about John's murder, the stolen necklace, and Señyor Rey than most.

I turned 'round and dashed back up the steps, nearly silent in my dancing pumps. I peered through the long window along one side of the door and noted the footman standing on the other side, so close that he was surely aware of my presence. I turned to look over my shoulder to determine how likely it was for he or the other footman, the butler, downstairs maid, or any servant for that matter, to see anything that occurred down the street. I finally concluded that it was far too dark, in spite of the street lamps, to see farther than the pavement directly in front of the house. However, matters might prove otherwise come morning.

I returned to Canning House to collect my greatcoat and hat, and stepped into my waiting carriage. I was grateful Canning had allowed me the use of it, as well as his driver, as I had brought only the curricle with me when I came to live at Berkeley Square. By the time I was arrived at the home of Lord and Lady Truesdale, I felt entirely recovered.

Firstly, I intended to dance with Miss Woodmansey, a thought that filled me with delight. What's more, I supposed I might hope for Lady Vawdrey, in exchange for my assistance, to introduce me to each and every one of the Little Season's debutantes, most of whom were doubtless unaware of my reputation. And then there were the questions I should ask of all and sundry in order to determine the truth behind Johnny's death and the missing necklace. All in all, it promised to be the most fruitful event of any Season in recent memory.

Chapter Six

The moment I entered the ballroom, Fate revealed its plans for a singular evening. It began with my gaze being drawn directly to Rey and Miss Woodmansey as they danced. Her face was flushed, with happiness no doubt, and the two of them looked almost regal if one failed to compare them with the others. My heart swelled with envy. I considered letting slip a remark in regard to Rey's impoverished state within Miss Woodmansey's hearing, but my thoughts were immediately stopped short. To disparage the reputation of another, regardless of how warranted, was an act I had recently resolved never to execute. He did not deserve it any more than I had done.

A painful memory of the first ball I attended after the duel came forcibly to mind:

I studied my reflection in the glass for what seemed hours. I had never seen anything less beauteous. The scar that began at the corner of my mouth and curved up towards my cheekbone was puckered and red. To my dismay, unless I produced a wide smile it looked as if I were frowning. Worse; sneering. *The man who stared back at me appeared arrogant, even wicked. It might have been easier had Evelyn been by my side, but he had cried off without cause. By the time I appeared at the ball, I was later even than is fashionable. As I glanced about the room a hush fell over those not occupied with dancing. It seemed as if everyone either markedly turned away from me, or jerked 'round in my direction like puppets on a collective string. Women covered their lower faces with their fans, their eyes round and white, whilst the visages of the men turned to claret. My heart dropped into my stomach and an ineffable weight hung from my shoulders. Such consternation at the very sight of me; for what did I deserve such?*

Forcing the memory aside, I temporarily abandoned thoughts of Miss Woodmansey and wondered on whom I could count to be truly verbose. (To wonder as to the verbosity of Miss Woodmansey was pointless; I was confident Rey would ask her a great many questions, some of which might even have to do with Johnny's death.) As I stood contemplating the refreshment table, Robert Manwaring appeared at my side. I would have preferred to converse with any but he, then remembered that he seemed to have known about the Gilbert tragedy before nearly anyone. I stared at him, casting about for a means to start a conversation.

Perhaps I ogled him a bit too boldly, for he seemed almost to blush. "I hadn't known you to be of that persuasion, Trevelin."

I was now faced with a fresh dilemma. My reputation was of such fragility that I dared not so much as protest too much. "What persuasion might that be?" I asked more frostily than I had intended.

"You needn't be skittish. There are plenty of men who could admire that face."

92

"How can that be, I wonder," I asked as I drew forth my quizzing glass through which I studied the dancers, "when the ladies have proven impervious?"

He took a step closer, perhaps so as not to be overheard. "I believe I can be of some assistance."

As I dared not hazard a guess as to what exactly he referred—the possibilities seemed too numerous—it was difficult to adopt one attitude over another. I settled on *ennui* and hoped for the best. "Is that so?"

Manwaring chuckled. "I can improve your scar. That is all that I meant to imply," he added with a smile of regret.

I took my time in composing a response. If Manwaring were as much of a scandalmonger as I hoped, I knew it to be foolish to give him further fodder. My current reputation had already done much to impede my way to wedded bliss. "I hadn't known you to be a trained surgeon. At any rate, there is no more to be done for my poor face." If I had spoken plainly, I might have indulged in some fault-finding as to the size of the original stitches. They were not anything of which a seamstress could possibly be proud.

"No, not trained, not in any official capacity," he admitted. "I enjoy dabbling, however."

"Dabbling? With a scalpel? Do I wish for you to elaborate?" I asked, genuinely alarmed.

"I've actually become rather proficient. I have restricted my experimentation to inanimate objects, for the most part."

I failed to determine which portion of this horrifying explanation frightened me most. "I confess I am nothing short of bowled over. And yet, I fail to comprehend. You operate on…objects? Even animals? To what purpose?" I quelled an incipient trembling; my mouth had been subjected to more than one blade too many.

He shrugged. "Rarely, but yes, so as to learn how they can be altered. It amuses me."

"Altered, how?" I immediately regretted the question.

"As people do, animals have certain traits that are more attractive to the others. You might be surprised to learn that even animals produce those which are shunned by their own kind."

I began to understand. "And you feel it would benefit me in my quest to find a wife if I were to allow you to somehow improve my scar?" I was astounded. I was aware that the scar marred my face but hadn't thought it a deterrent to matrimony, aside from its tendency to recall my scandalous past.

Manwaring clapped me on the shoulder. "You needn't bellow, my lord. I am not anxious for the world to know of my hobbies."

Quickly, I grasped the proffered straw. "I cannot help but to agree. It is not pleasant to have your business bandied about." Before he could compose a glib reply, I pushed ahead. "Yet, gossip seems to be rife at a ball. I was surprised you had known of the Gilbert boy's death before even I. From whom did you hear it?"

Manwaring frowned. "I believe it was Lady Jersey, though I might be wrong."

"But, of course!" The Jerseys were near neighbor to the Gilberts. Unfortunately, "Silence" Jersey had had very little use for me since the duel. "She is, no doubt, in attendance. I shall attempt to speak with her." I smiled with confidence, though I knew I should be fortunate to get close enough to merely overhear her constant flow of conversation.

Manwaring smiled and walked away. I thought perhaps his wife, Lady Clara, might know more than her husband was willing to divulge, and looked about for her. She was the eldest daughter of an earl, who had retained her title upon her marriage to a commoner. She was a beautiful woman, only slightly older than I; she might successfully have held out for a duke. Why she hadn't was something to wonder at. However, I did not see her.

I saw, instead, Mr. Gilbert as he danced with a charming young lady who was not known to me. I thought it odd that he should be out in Society so soon after his son's death. Surely Mrs. Gilbert remained at home. That he had left his grieving wife to her own devices seemed odder still. Perhaps there was, indeed, trouble between them, something more than their current tragic circumstances. Tragedy, I had learned, has a habit of magnifying the already-existing cracks in connections of all sorts. It had certainly put an end to my friendship with Evelyn.

When I looked about, my eye fell upon Miss Woodmansey deep in conversation with Rey. As I made my way to them, I observed Lady Jersey. She was holding forth near the entrance to the card room, surrounded by others of her stamp; in other words, those who would have little to do with me. I abandoned all thoughts of the missing necklace, as well as poor Johnny's murder, and concentrated on my number one desire—to dance with Miss Woodmansey.

It seemed that she was as aware of me as I was of her, for as I drew near she looked up, as if she waited for me. She smiled prettily and my stomach seemed to pitch, a sensation that was in no way diminished by Rey's less fervent greeting. She curtsied; taking her hand, I very properly kissed the air above it.

"If we are quick, my lord," she said, her eyes twinkling with merriment, "I believe we might lose ourselves amongst the dancers before my mother is aware of the identity of my partner."

I had no wish to hesitate, but I did cast Rey a look of commiseration as we went. To this day, I would swear that my compassion was nearly half-genuine. His misery, as we left him on his own, was such that I actually doubted the wisdom of taking such an action. Miss Woodmansey, however, smiled up at me with such affect that I momentarily forgot about my friend.

Dancing was a pleasure I had not engaged in all Season, and it was bliss to respond to the music as I wished. As it was a *contra danse*, there was little opportunity to converse. However, I had plenty of time to reflect on Miss Woodmansey herself. She was refreshingly intrepid, and clearly enjoyed a mind of her own. If she were to develop a *tendre* for me, perhaps she would have the courage to defy her parents and insist they allow me to court her. In the meantime, I would need to discover who took Johnny's life, as well as Lady Vawdrey's diamonds, in order for Society to smile upon me once again.

These thoughts gave me a very pleasant sense of duty, one that was some reparation when the set was over and I returned Miss Woodmansey to Rey's side. He had been joined by an angry woman, whom I could only presume to be Mrs. Woodmansey. She was taller than her daughter and Rey both, but I still felt a veritable giant amongst them.

"Good evening," I said as a peace offering. I unlinked my arm from Miss Woodmansey's and took a step away from her for good measure.

Mrs. Woodmansey dipped into something resembling a curtsy, never lowering her gaze from mine. She then clapped her hand to her daughter's arm and drew her briskly away. Miss Woodmansey had the good sense to bow her head as she struggled to keep up with her mother. I do, however, believe I saw a quickly repressed smile. I fancied it signaled her pleasure for the absurd, and I thought her nothing short of marvelous.

Rey cleared his throat. "So, we are both to contend for the hand of the remarkable Miss Woodmansey?"

I turned to take in the turmoil in his face. "Perhaps," I admitted. "However, I am not likely to rise in the esteem of Miss Woodmansey's mother. Yours shall be a Christmas wedding," I quipped.

"Pray, do not mock me, my friend," Rey said. "I have no wish to duel."

"Over whose honor should we draw our swords?" I asked in astonishment. "Though, I daresay you should prefer pistols." I restrained a bark of laughter.

"Is it your belief that I cannot wield a sword, my lord?" Rey asked, haughty.

It seemed there was something about a ball that brought out the worst in the señyor. "I haven't the least idea. However, my reach is longer than yours, which should give me quite the advantage."

"Yes, but skill can compensate for the length of your opponent's arm. I have studied under the Spanish masters and I assure you, you should not like to face me in a duel."

I looked into Rey's face and saw how much of his bluster was but pure passion. "In that case, my friend," I said, clapping my hand to his shoulder, "I should choose pistols, for my own sake."

He stared at me for a moment then, together, we burst into laughter.

When we had recovered, I thought to ask questions. "Tell me, Señyor Rey, have you gleaned anything of use to our cause tonight?"

"*No!* No one to whom I have spoken seems to know anything about the necklace or the *llunàtic* who deprived Master John of his life."

Since I suspected he had not spoken to anyone other than Miss Woodmansey and her mother since arriving at the ball, his statement revealed naught. It was then that I spotted Canning bearing down on me. "Perhaps you might attempt to overhear what is being said amongst that gaggle of geese near the card room," I suggested, "whilst I seek answers elsewhere."

As Rey set off without a flicker of hesitation, I felt myself a Judas. How could I suspect and trust him at the same moment? I knew I must choose. Quite suddenly I knew he was simply too ingenuous to doubt. He could speak a lie—of that I was certain—but he was incapable of not being found out. Everything showed in his face. Trust him, then, I would.

It was then that Canning appeared at my side. "Trev, it

was good to see you dancing," he said with a fatherly smile, the sort I had been robbed of when I was the age Johnny had been at his death.

"I enjoyed it excessively," I said with a fond smile for this man who had rescued me somewhat from my loneliness. "I am happy to see you. I have learned something I hope shall exonerate Willy Gilbert."

"Truly?" Canning asked in delight.

I nodded. "He is not able to don or remove a shirt on his own. They are long and cumbersome; therefore, someone helps him each night to don a clean one. He insists that the one he was wearing when he found his brother in the morning was clean; not a drop of blood on it. The person who killed Johnny would have had some amount of blood on his clothing. A man—or woman," I conceded, "with Willy's difficulties would have a sight more."

"Yes, of course," Canning mused. "But can this be proven?"

"It shall require the testimony of the constable, but if he is willing to say that he arrested Willy in a clean shirt it ought to be enough. The servants have all indicated the same."

"Very well, but can they be trusted?" Canning asked with some doubt. "They would naturally be quite protective of Willy. Bad enough to serve in a household where someone has been murdered. Worse for the killer to be one of those whom you serve."

"If you say so." I knew he was most likely correct, but I could not like it. "I shall have to run the constable to ground and see what he has to say to it."

"Excellent!" Canning shook my hand. "I shall see you at home."

I smiled gratefully, and watched as he walked away. No one turned from him in disdain. He was afforded all the respect he was due, despite a duel with one of the most revered men in all of England. The difference was Rutherford—he was the author of my fall.

I looked about for Lady Vawdrey. I wished to dance again, and it was she upon whom I relied to make me known to a suitable young lady. I even had one in mind; the lovely girl I had seen dancing with Mr. Gilbert. I perused the ballroom but did not find her, so I headed to the card room, skirted Lady Jersey and her set where they gossiped near the entrance, and went straight to Lady Vawdrey.

I found her deep in a game of whist, and I stood for some time waiting to be acknowledged. I am a marquis and she only the widow of an earl, but she has always made it much known that she believes age to take precedence over even a superior title. Or perhaps it is merely she, herself, whom she feels to be above her betters.

Finally she lifted her head and addressed me. "Trevelin! What is it?"

"I thought," I said with a patience I did not feel, "that perhaps you would introduce me to the young lady with whom you play." She was a beauty with masses of deep mahogany hair all done up in a variety of curls and braids. I could not recall having ever seen her before, and assumed her to be one of the Little Season's debutantes. As such, she might not yet have been warned away from me.

"I shall do nothing of the sort, you rapscallion! Take yourself off and leave me to my game," Lady Vawdrey added with a sniff.

I fell back a step, as if I had been dealt a physical blow. My face must have reflected my emotions, for the young lady giggled behind her fan, prompting my thoughts to fall on how best to achieve a dignified exit. I considered taking myself off in a huff, but quickly realized Lady Vawdrey's objection had little to do with me. She merely detested being interrupted during a game at which she was winning. So, I bowed to each of the four players, made a show of studying the young beauty through my quizzing glass, presented her with my unblemished profile, offered her a faint smile, and sauntered away as if I had every young lady at the ball from whom to choose.

Once I had regained the ballroom, I began to tremble. It was all I could do to prevent my frame from collapsing in a heap. It was as if the life had been drained from my body through my feet, which seemed to drag along the floor. It hadn't been so difficult to hold my chin high since my first ball after the duel.

I entered the ballroom and began to circulate. For every smile I offered, a head snapped away from me. It was as if choreographed. I knew the scar was not beautiful, but I had been accustomed to being thought of as attractive. It was then that I saw a young lady whom I had met at a Christmas house party prior to the duel. I smiled in relief, and she did not look away from me; neither could she hide the pity in her eyes. She gave me a curtsy every bit as deep as was my due, and I parried with a most elegant bow. And yet, before I had regained my usual stature, she had disappeared into the crowds.

The memory gave strength to my spine. I had endured

much since then. I knew I could endure this as well. Looking about me, I saw that Rey was again dancing with Miss Woodmansey. I wondered if he had overheard anything said by Lady Jersey before he went after his young lady. With regret I realized that I had best forget about finding a bride, and instead attempt to learn something of use.

It was then that I saw Manwaring's wife, Lady Clara. I was struck, as usual, by her effortless beauty: her skin was like cream, her brow perfectly formed, her nose charmingly blunt on the end, and her eyes and hair the exact same shade of deep brown, like a cup of the richest chocolate. I had been yet a schoolboy when she enjoyed her first season, or I might have pursued her myself.

To my surprise, she turned and her gaze locked in mine. I was astonished when she smiled and began to approach me. I told myself that it was someone behind me whom she sought and that, at the last moment, she would merely pass me by. She did not.

"Good evening, Lord Trevelin." She held out her hand, which I dutifully kissed. "I wonder why I have not seen you of late."

As I attended most of the balls, routs, and soirees to which the Cannings were invited, I realized the fault was hers. "I believe it is you who has disappeared from Society."

"That is true," she said with a sweep of her lashes. "You have not heard I suppose, that I have been entertaining at home most evenings." She bit her lip, and gazed up at me expectantly.

I stared at her with no small amount of consternation. A proposition from both Manwarings in the same night hardly seemed possible. Even one was beggaring disbelief. "I beg your pardon," I finally managed. "I am persuaded I did not hear you correctly."

"You needn't look so alarmed," she said, laying her hand on my arm. "It's only a bit of gambling."

The conversation was becoming more and more fantastic. "I do believe I have missed some pertinent piece of information..." I hedged.

"Oh! I thought you knew! I hesitate to say too much with Lady Jersey so near, but I can say that it is more like a *great deal* of gambling. I invite those I wish to see in my salon." She gazed at me with a knowing smile.

I finally understood that the Manwarings were running an illegal gambling hell in their home. This notion tallied very well with what had been reported as to how Mr. Huther spent time in the indulgence of a powerful addiction. That he had gone directly to Manwaring House upon his dismissal from the Gilberts was all of a piece. I was suddenly at *aux anges* to see this gambling den for myself.

"Then for what do we wait?" I gestured towards the door.

She favored me with a tiny smile, revealing a row of perfect white teeth. There was something about it that troubled me, but I could not think what.

"I know of one or two other gentlemen who may wish to join us," she said, raking me from head to toe with her gaze. It was like the old days, when I was admired. Then I realized that it was the emerald stickpin in my cravat, the gold watch fob, and the large silver buttons on my coat that had caught her eye.

"I daresay it shall not be of any use to go there directly, shall it?" Now that I had a clue to work with, I was anxious to follow where it might lead.

"I am afraid not," she said. "No me; no gambling. Should you arrive before I, do not present your card at the door. You need merely say that you are expected." She smiled with her perfectly shaped lips and disappeared into the crowd.

I immediately looked about for Rey. I did not intend to drag him away from the ball, only learn what he knew and inform him as to where I intended to go. I found him collecting a drink for Miss Woodmansey. When he heard about the gambling den at Manwaring House, however, he was eager to join me.

"I should prefer it if you were to remain here and see what else can be learned. Did Lady Jersey say anything of interest?"

"Not within my hearing," Rey said, regretful. "It is almost as if no one has a care for who has killed Johnny!"

I grunted. "The premier offender is Mr. Gilbert. I have seen him here tonight, dancing with a young lady."

Rey's frown was ferocious. "He is a man most callous! This displeases me to the utmost. I shall stay and watch what he does."

"Thank you. I was going to suggest the same." I immediately quit the room, descended to the ground floor, and requested my carriage. I alighted at Canning House and walked the short distance to Manwaring House on the side of the square perpendicular to Hampton House. I made it my business to look around. A glance down each side of the house towards the back availed me nothing—the glow of the street lamps did not reach so far. I noticed that the lamps on the house that bracketed the door were dark. It seemed Lady Clara was scrupulous when it came to the protection of her visitors. I then crept up to the railing that lined the steps down to the basement kitchen. I was surprised to see that a man scurried up the steps.

Quickly, I darted into the shadows and waited for the man to emerge. Once he made it to the lighted walkway, I could see that it was Huther. He had a bottle and was drinking from it quite freely as he set off along the square. Whether he had some destination in mind or simply wished to drink in peace, I did not know. I watched him only briefly before another coach came to a halt in front of the house. Lady Clara alighted. She must have seen Huther, but she gave no sign. I stayed in the shadows until she disappeared into the inky blackness at the door and the coach had driven away to the mews behind the house.

I waited a moment longer, then went to the front door and rapped upon it. I wished to arrive before the others, whoever they might be. A very proper butler pulled open the door. He asked no questions as he waited for me to act.

"I am expected," I said, somewhat doubtful this would win me *entre* into the house. In that I was wrong, for the butler drew the door wide and gestured me inside. The front hall was drenched in shadows. Only one tall branch of candles was lit and it stood at a distance from the door. I realized this was to prevent illumination from falling on any caller's face when the door was pulled to.

He took my hat and gloves and led me up the grand

staircase to the first floor by the light of single candle. I expected a gaming den to be arranged in a ballroom and was surprised when we went 'round the banister and continued up to the second floor, where the rooms generally were smaller and reserved for the residents of the home. I began to doubt that a gaming den was my eventual destination.

Finally, the butler rapped on a door; it was opened to reveal a very intimate gathering, indeed. Rather than a crowd of people playing at numerous tables about the room, there was one table by the fire. Drawn up to it was a small chaise upon which Lady Clara reposed, a glass in her hand. This room was almost entirely plunged in darkness as well, and the dancing of the flames was reflected in the deep red of her silk ball gown. No one else was in the room save the footman, whom she dismissed with a wave of her hand.

As the door closed behind me, I considered my options. The light was so scarce that I could not adequately plumb the depth of the room, nor did I know what, or who, it might contain. Choosing to ignore my misgivings, I spread my hands wide in surprise. "What of the others you invited here tonight?"

"They each felt that they had been separated from their money at my establishment far too often," she said with a pout. Then she brought the glass to her lips and eyed me over the rim. "You, however, look as if you could use a good game."

"There are limited games for two to play," I pointed out.

She shrugged a shoulder, smooth as marble. "I am persuaded you can afford to take the risk, my lord."

Money was one of the few resources I had not endured

a loss of during the course of the year. It was a pity as, to me, it was worth the least of all that I once had. "Let us be honest—we are not here to gamble; at least, not with money."

She heaved a deep sigh, one that afforded me a shocking view of her ample bosom. And then she proposed an offer I found difficult to refuse.

Chapter Seven

"Will you not sit down?" She patted the too-small space next to her on the divan.

Briefly I wondered if my reputation as a man who dallies with married women was responsible for her comportment. And yet, something told me she desired of me a boon that was not of the carnal realm. "Very well." I moved from the mantel to the divan at a pace that was neither too eager nor too languid. I had no wish to give Manwaring reason to call me out. "What are we to discuss?"

She smiled as if she had been given a great gift. It made her look younger than her years and impossibly naïve. "I actually do invite men to my sitting room to gamble. Should you wish to come again on an evening when I am receiving visitors, you are more than welcome. If the lamps by the front door are lit, do not approach. Any other night is one in which players are expected."

"Might I hazard a guess: Your husband does not know I am here?" Silently I wondered when she would reveal the subject under discussion.

"I'm afraid not; I claimed a sick headache. He will have assumed that I have retired."

"What does he think of your gaming hell?" I realized that I didn't know what Manwaring thought about much of anything.

"You surprise me, my lord. It was his notion from the start. It is his wish that I am entertained whilst he is consumed with his hobbies."

Since my conversation with Manwaring earlier that evening, I had developed a decided distaste for his hobbies. "Perhaps we had best get to the point as to why I am here." I was not anxious for my scar to become one of a pair, and thought it best to be quickly out of the house.

She heaved another sigh, though this one had little to do with enticement. "It is about the Gilbert boy, the one who died."

There was naught she might have said or done at that moment that would have caught my interest so fully. "Johnny? What do you wish to know?"

"Well, I had heard you were asking a great many questions—my servants speak with the Gilbert servants. You know how that is."

In fact, I did not. I hadn't the least idea what servants got up to when they weren't executing their duties. "The Gilberts have asked me to discover who has killed their young son, it is true. We have no reason to suspect any of the servants, specifically, but they cannot be ruled out."

"But I had thought the older Gilbert did it. Was he not carried off to gaol?"

"He is perfectly capable of walking," I said evenly, despite my vexation.

"Carried or walked, who can know? Of course, I did not see any take him away! But, it's true, isn't it, that there is something not quite right about him? Naturally, it must have been he who did it. A man like that can't be trusted."

"Why is that, Lady Clara?" Those who know me well would have trembled at my inflection.

"Well, he isn't right in the head. Such people are capable of anything." I made no reply, but she seemed to sense my mounting anger. "It's simply that I do not wish a killer to be loose in the square. If he is not imprisoned, then we are all at risk of becoming victims to a madman."

"A mad *man*?" I echoed through gritted teeth. "Could it not have been a crazed woman who killed William Gilbert?"

She blanched. "A woman? How could a woman murder a child?" she said, choking.

My head began to ache from the manner in which I clenched my jaw. "One with a lame arm and leg, perhaps?"

"Let us speak of something else," she said with an over-bright smile. "I shall be open for gaming tomorrow night. Do bring Lady Vawdrey's house guest. He looks as if he should be amusing."

By that I supposed she meant she thought him rich. "I imagine he shall be pleased."

"Yes, but do you think he shall come?" she asked with an insistent hand on my arm.

I began to wonder if she were financially embarrassed like the good señyor. "I daresay he is not much of a gambler, but he shall enjoy the company. Of that I have no doubt."

"Oh, well then, yes, bring him by all means. Manwaring shall be at home, as well. Sometimes he wanders in to chat with my guests."

I quelled the last of my anger so that I might pose questions of my own. "I wonder how you learned of Johnny's death."

"From my husband," she said with what I thought to be an over-wrought smile. "He had just returned from a ride in the park and saw with his own eyes the brother outside with the knife. He told me of it over rolls and hot chocolate," she said with a laugh more suited to a discussion of the latest Paris fashions.

"You are aware that William Gilbert and I are old friends, are you not?" My outrage at her lack of decorum nearly caused me to miss the fact that her version of events did not match her husband's.

"Oh! I *am* sorry! So, that is why it is you who is questioning the servants."

"Indeed, that and my status, as well as my connections to people of influence." I hoped my words did not make me seem a braggart. "If I might, I should like to question your servants as well. Perhaps one of them might have seen more than Manwaring did."

Her beautifully arched brows rose and her eyes grew wide. "What a splendid notion! They shall despise every moment of it, of course, but I find I cannot say you nay. When shall they expect you?"

"I am at your disposal, though I suppose they shall have quite enough to do in preparing refreshments for your gambling night tomorrow." The possibility that she did not serve refreshments was one not worthy of contemplation.

"It keeps them a good deal occupied, but I shall instruct my housekeeper to ensure that they each give you their utmost cooperation."

"Very well; I shall come tomorrow morning, shortly after ten. I trust the butler will allow me through the front entrance—I should dislike having to descend those evil-looking steps down to the kitchen door."

"But of course!"

"I am much obliged. Now, I believe I must be off," I said, standing. "Ten of the clock is so very early."

"Indeed," she said with a look of sympathy. We parted on good terms, and I hastily made my way home and up to bed before either Canning or Rey found their way to their respective doorsteps. I wished to be in excellent form for my questioning of the Manwaring servants.

The next morning was a rather vile, wet and, windy day, the sort one hopes not to see before winter. Contrary to expectations, when I presented myself at the front door of Manwaring House I was denied entrance. I found this puzzling in the extreme. I looked down the area steps; they did not appear to be so evil in the light of day. I pulled my caped greatcoat more tightly about me as I descended to the lower level and rapped on the kitchen door.

It was opened by a young boy with soot on his nose. His mouth fell open upon finding a swell standing at the bottom of the area steps.

"Is the housekeeper at home?" It was the most ridiculous string of words that had ever passed my lips.

He slammed the door in my face and, based on the sounds that issued forth from the other side of the door, scurried off. This commotion was followed by the sound of a hesitant tread coming towards me. When the door was again opened I was faced with a haggard woman, gray of hair and face, her slight waist girdled about with keys.

"Sir!" she cried in a voice riddled with astonishment. "What is it that you want?"

"I am Trevelin," I said with a thoroughly unwarranted bow. "I have been given leave to speak to the household. I have questions of a delicate nature."

She took her time in answering as she stared into the distance. I could not say whether her disinclination to look me in the face was due to our disparity in status or if it had everything to do with the scar at the corner of my mouth. Whatever the case, I reproached myself for dwelling on the maudlin.

"I live just to the other side of the square at Canning House." I knew I should one day have to refrain from relying on Canning's respectability, but this was not that day. "I should very much like to come in and have a cup of tea."

"Very well." She seemed nearly too weak to curtsy, but managed an unsteady descent that required my hand before she could rise. "I thank ye," she said as she motioned me to enter, whereupon she led me through the kitchen bustling with activity. "Molly, bring a tray to my sitting room for his lordship."

After the warm kitchen, her chamber felt as cold as Willy's cell at Newgate. We sat at a table across from each other on a set of uncomfortable hard-backed chairs, and said nothing until the tray arrived. The housekeeper stared into her lap whilst I looked about the meager room. A framed verse of scripture took up some space on a wall over a table upon which there was a prayer book and a candle stick. There was a miniature of a young man garbed in long out of fashion attire on the mantel, balanced on top of a pretty piece of lace. A small collection of clothing hung from hooks on the wall and there was a thin rug on the floor. That was all besides the bed, no wider than the one Willy currently occupied.

Molly arrived with the tea tray and set it on the table. The housekeeper poured it out and once we each had taken a few sips of the hot brew, she seemed warmer in spirit as well. "I am Mrs. Carrick." She risked a full glance into my face and quickly looked away again. "I hope the tea is satisfactory."

"Indeed, it is very good and most welcome on such a damp day. Mrs. Carrick, can you tell me why I was not admitted by the butler?"

She gazed into her cup. "That would be on account of the master. He does not like to admit gentlemen when there is no call for them to be here."

"But Lady Clara was expecting me."

"Espesh'ly then. I believe he don't trust her," Mrs. Carrick said with a sage nod.

It seemed I was speaking with a disgruntled servant. I continued to press her despite the mild repugnance I felt at my lack of delicacy. "Pardon me, but I wish to comprehend. He has no qualms with men arriving late at night, but won't tolerate callers during the day?"

She sat up straighter in her chair. "Aside from the parties, he only objects when he's to home. There's them who come at all hours when he's away," she said with a smirk.

I thought perhaps it was men of Huther's ilk who so offended Manwaring. "What of a man who used to be the tutor for the Gilberts?"

"Do ye mean Mr. Huther?" she cried, clearly enjoying

herself. "He was dismissed from Gilbert House after that poor lad was murdered, so Lady Clara has taken him on. Do ye wish to speak with 'im?" she asked in disbelief.

"In truth, I would, and in regard to that poor lad. Are you aware of other servants who might know anything useful?"

She heaved a sigh. "As to that, I couldn't say. I don't consort with the staff," she said, drawing herself up and looking me straight in the eye, "except to direct their duties. But as the mistress has given ye leave, ye can talk to them yerself. Ye may use me room here. I shall have one of the maids come in and do up the fire all nice and bright for ye."

"That would be most welcome." I had removed my gloves to take tea and they were now as cold as ice. I liked her well enough to delay rubbing my hands together for warmth whilst she yet remained in the room.

Presently, a girl who looked to be no older than sixteen entered with a shy bob of her head. She did not wait for my answering nod, but went straight to the hearth to make up the fire. Soon the logs were sufficiently riddled and the fire was flaming high.

"That shall do very nicely," I said in hopes of winning her over. "Might I ask your name?"

She turned and flashed me an uncertain look. "Sally."

"Sally, would you be good enough to answer some questions?"

She frowned, which was a pity as it made her too-thin lips all but disappear. Her poor teeth and skin were compensated for by a pair of exceptionally fine cornflower-blue eyes.

"Are you aware of the young gentleman who was deprived of his life a few days since?"

She nodded, but her expression gave nothing away.

"The man arrested for the crime is a friend of mine. I would like very much to discover the actual killer."

"What's that to do wi'me?" She wasn't defiant, merely curious.

"Only that this household is a near neighbor to the Gilberts. Servants do speak to one another." I took a sip of my tea. "With whom are you friendly?"

"I am walking out with Edmund, hims who works for Lady Vawdrey."

This was unexpected news. "I have met him," I said carefully. "He is a handsome fellow, is he not?"

"Yes, sir." She smiled, and her face took on a glow. Clearly, this was a subject with which she was comfortable. "We met when he came with his mistress to the workhouse. If he hadn't found me a position, I would still be there."

"How good of him. Tell me, how did Mr. Throckmorton arrange for you to be employed here?" In truth, I had no reason to believe the matter had a thing to do with Johnny's murder, nor did I have reason to think it did not.

"Alls he said was that the lady was needin' another housemaid. I was ever so happy to get out of the workhouse. People are disappearin' from there."

"What can you mean?"

She twisted her hands together in her apron. "I don't know 'zactly. Only, Betty Pitchfork was hired out of the workhouse to here before me, but when I got here she was gone. No one knows where she went to. And when I went to visit my friends at the workhouse on my first half day off, Lizzie Wright told me that Janie Cooper wasn't there no more. She hadn't gotten work or nothin'—she just vanished. And, Lizzie says that wasn't the first time, neither. And it's true, I know 'tis. That's why Edmund got me a job; so I could get away from there."

This was odd indeed, and not only because it cast Throckmorton in a heroic light. I decided I had possibly been wrong about him. "I am very sorry to hear that your friends have gone missing." I felt immediately chagrined the moment the words left my mouth; certainly peers of the realm failed to apologize to a servant for a thing. "Do you have reason to think these disappearances have anything to do with Johnny Gilbert's murder?"

"No, sir." She looked puzzled. "I don' see as to how."

"Are you acquainted with Mr. Huther? He was the tutor at Gilbert House but is now employed here, correct?"

She shrugged. "I s'pose. I've seen him a few times. He's bin comin' here to milady's gamblin' nights for a while, and often gamblin' days, too."

"Mrs. Carrick has just informed me that the butler has been told not to admit any men during daylight hours."

"I know aught about that. I've only seen him use the kitchen door like the other servants."

"Can you recall a time when he used the kitchen door whilst he was still employed at Gilbert House?" I wasn't entirely certain it was important, but if there were a connection between Gilbert House and this one, it was most likely through Huther.

"Yes, I think so." She looked uncertain.

"It's important that you remember. Take your time before you answer. Did you see him at this house at any time the day before Johnny Gilbert was killed?"

"I am not sure what day that was," she said fearfully.

"It was the day Mr. Throckmorton called at the Gilberts to ask for a recipe. Perhaps he stopped here to see you that day as well?"

"Oh, yes!" Her face cleared such that I knew that she had never considered Throckmorton to be involved in Johnny's death. "Mr. Huther was below stairs that day. It wasn't the next day, but the one after that he was here to dinner with the rest of the servants."

"Thank you, Sally! You have done well."

She left with a sunny smile, seemingly unconcerned as to the implications of my questions. She sent in the cook, but she knew nothing of import. I was unable to glean anything useful from any of the other servants except for verification as to the tutor having been in the house, including below stairs, the day before Johnny died. When I asked to speak with Mr. Huther, I was told that he was out of the house. Reluctantly, I departed the same way I had entered and literally ran into him on the area steps.

"Mr. Huther! What a surprise," I said as I rubbed the portion of my chin that had come into contact with his teeth.

He threw me a surly expression. "What are you doing here?" he demanded.

I was shocked. I hadn't expected to be treated such by a servant, least of all by the timid tutor. "I am here to learn what I can of Johnny Gilbert's death. What are *you* doing here? From what I understand, there are no children in need of instruction at Manwaring House."

He gave me a hard look. "If you want answers, you need look for them elsewhere. Try at the workhouse; the one that odd fellow is always haunting," he said with a jerk of his thumb across the square in the direction of Hampton House.

"Do you refer to the male housekeeper?" My dislike for Throckmorton was beginning to fade, but I was not yet ready to absolve him.

"People are disappearing. Whatever the trouble is, it began there."

I decided that I must visit the Bloomsbury workhouse as soon as possible. "Yes, these disappearances are indeed troubling. Would you agree that there is trouble here at Manwaring House as well?"

Huther shook his head. "Lady Clara has been very good to me."

"Good enough that you would conceal a murder?"

Huther's timidity might have fled, but it was evident that I had struck a chord of some sort. "Are you accusing Lady Clara of murder?" he demanded.

Had I been? It was a reasonable question, one to which I did not have the answer. "Of course not," I said, as I knew it was expected of me.

"Mark my words, it started at the workhouse!" Huther stepped around me and made his way down the steps to the kitchen door.

I remained unmoved and watched as he opened it, entered the house, and shut the door behind him. Something about this mundane action triggered in me a notion, one I could not, struggle as I did, put to words. And yet, I knew it pointed to a vital clue, one still in shadow and in want of illumination. With a sigh of defeat I returned to Canning House, ordered out the carriage, refreshed myself with the remains of breakfast from the sideboard in the morning room, and set out for the workhouse patronized by Lady Vawdrey and her man.

The distance to the Bloomsbury workhouse from Mayfair can be covered on foot in a reasonable amount of time. I chose, however, to take the carriage. I alighted outside the wrought- iron gate which was tended by a doorkeeper. It seemed that his assignment was to manage the comings and goings of those on both sides of the gate. Realization dawned as I watched people, much like Lady Vawdrey, arrive to perform charitable duties. Others were present to inquire after suitable domestic help, as had Lady Vawdrey on numerous occasions. Sally had been hired to Manwaring House from the workhouse with the help of Throckmorton. Others were permitted to leave only for the day to perform work that did not include lodgings. The power of the doorkeeper was impressive.

I had only begun to wonder what he might be able to tell me when Rey appeared at my side. I turned to him with what must have been patent surprise.

He shrugged. "Did you not request that I follow the housekeeper?"

"You mean to say that he is here now?" I asked in delight.

"*Si*, it is the day of the week that he and Lady Vawdrey journey here with food and medicines. But today she does not feel so well, so I thought to myself that he might go alone. Though I lingered at the front window so as to ascertain when the carriage would arrive, it never did. And then I saw him on the walkway with a basket over his arm; he seemed to be making his way on foot. As my hostess is confined to her chamber, I was able to rush after him with only the servants to wonder at my behavior most uncouth."

"My compliments! Has anything of note occurred?"

"Not as of yet, but perhaps when he departs we may observe him without Lady Vawdrey as witness to our suspicions of the man."

I nodded and drew my greatcoat up higher along my neck. The day was growing colder and there was no indication that the sun would emerge.

"What have you learned from your assignation with Lady Clara?" Rey asked. His tone was indifferent, but his anxiety showed in more subtle ways.

"Nothing of any use. She seemed concerned about whether Johnny's actual killer was properly incarcerated, and sought my opinion on the matter."

"This is all that she wanted?"

I had never felt so compelled to defend myself over so little. "I agree, it was peculiar of her to insist I attend her gaming hell, which was not in operation at the moment, only to ask me questions about the murder of a young boy. She did give me leave to question her servants this morning, but when I arrived I was not admitted. Upon rapping on the kitchen door, I was finally admitted entry, and able to speak with the servants. They informed me that when Manwaring is at home there is a standing order that no men are to be admitted."

"This is not so strange, is it? He is jealous of his wife."

"I suppose, but is it deserved? We were alone together,

but I never felt that what she wanted of me was something of which her husband should not approve."

"I see."

I thought perhaps he did not, but as we were being approached by the unfriendly-looking gentleman on the other side of the gate, I transferred to him my full attention.

"Loiterin' at the workhouse gate is not allowed!" he bellowed.

"You must be the doorkeeper," I said with all the respect I felt it wise to proffer such a large and belligerent fellow. "I am Trevelin. Perhaps you would be willing to answer a question or two about the disappearances here."

He narrowed his eyes at me. "Ye ain't one of those who writes for the newspapers, or one of them Bow Street Runners, are ye?"

"Not for a moment," I demurred, delighted to be conversing with the one person in London who seemed unaware of the scandal attached to my name. "I wish to discover the connection between those gone missing from the workhouse and a murder."

"Murder? At the workhouse? Ge' away with ye'!" He took a metal bar of the gate in each of his large, meaty hands and thrust his bulbous nose between them. "We have no use for such talk, d'ye hear?"

"Perhaps we should depart and return with the authorities most proper," Rey suggested.

"What a splendid notion, Señyor Rey. And when we do, we shall request an audience with the governor or matron of the workhouse." I suspected the doorkeeper knew exactly why I was there and did not wish for his part in it to be revealed. In that I was soon to be proven at least partially correct.

"No! No…there is no need to trouble them. Just ask me yer questions and I will answer them as best I can," he said with a grimace I thought some might consider a smile.

"Very well. It is said that a young woman by the name of Janie Cooper was present at the workhouse one day and was gone the next. What can you tell me about her?"

"Other than all of those moles upon her face, nothin'! I were told that she went to the Dark Room to pay for her crime of drinking Geneva."

"Has she not returned from this dark room?" I asked.

"'Tis her second offense so she won't get out for the better part of three mon's."

"Three months! That seems a great deal of time for a crime so paltry as taking a drink."

"Workhouse rules! We don't have any use for ruffians and their evil acts."

"And yet, here you are," I mused.

"I, a Catalanian, could not have said this any better, my lord." Rey's words were for me alone, but he stared up into the bloodshot eyes of the doorkeeper with the ferocity of a dog guarding his favorite bone. One moment longer and I feared he should growl.

I hastened to provide a distraction. "Might I speak to Lizzie Wright? I am given to understand she might be able to tell us something of use."

The doorkeeper had the grace to look abashed. "'Tis said it was she who informed the Matron as to what Janie had done. I confess, she might be dead, but if she wuz killed here at the workhouse, her body ain't been found. O'course she might have been done away with for the six-pence she was given as a reward for her loose tongue."

"It would seem that the workhouse is a dangerous place," I murmured to Rey. I returned my attention to the doorkeeper. "Can you tell me what has happened to Betty Pitchfork? She was hired out of the workhouse to be a maid at Manwaring House and has since disappeared from there."

"How am I to know what you swells do with your servants?" he demanded.

"It is not your betters under discussion," I informed him pleasantly enough.

"Isn't it? Those who go into service from here oft return to visi' those they left behind. That's at least two who went to Manwaring House who never did come back, not once!"

"Is that so?" Rey and I exchanged a glance. "What are your suspicions on the matter, then?"

"Don't have none, jus' know 'tis queer that they ain't come back."

"Are you certain they are the only two?"

"Well, Kat Davies is well and truly gone. Not that she is missed with that face of her'n."

"It does not become one to speak ill of the dead."
"W'at?"

I perceived that my admonition was akin to casting pearls before swine. "Let us return to the subject of those who have disappeared. Has Janie Cooper truly been banished to this dark room you speak of, or could she have gone the way of the others?"

"I dunno. I never go into that part o'the house."

"Do you suppose you might be able to discern the truth?"

"For a bit of blunt, I could find out anythin'."

I reached into my coat for my purse. "I shall return to hear what you have learned. So long as it is the truth, we shall deal well with one another." I placed a coin in his outstretched hand. "See that you do not spend it on gin."

The doorkeeper rumbled with laughter. Behind his shaking shoulder, I saw Throckmorton emerge from the house. I turned to Rey. "He is coming. Let us make haste."

"*Si*, my lord," Rey said, and the two of us repaired to the far side of the gate. I turned my back on it and adopted an air of nonchalance, one hand on my hip, whilst Rey, obscured by my height, kept watch from over my shoulder. (Or, if I am to be entirely truthful, under it.)

"He has come out of the gate and is returning back the way we have come," Rey reported.

I slowly turned to observe Throckmorton walking briskly in the direction of Mayfair. "Let us return to Hampton House in my carriage. There is a question I wish to pose to his mistress before he returns to her side."

"Oh, but she is most indisposed, my lord. She is not at home to callers."

I watched the retreating Throckmorton and nursed dark thoughts. "She will be at home for this."

Chapter Eight

As Rey's guest, I was admitted readily into the house. With a nod of dismissal for the butler, he ushered me up to the first-floor salon. We were most surprised, however, to find it already occupied by Lady Vawdrey, Mrs. Woodmansey, and the commendable Miss Woodmansey.

"Trevelin!" Lady Vawdrey barked. "Who allowed you to enter?"

"It was I who has done this," Rey quickly admitted. "I had thought you resting in your chamber and that we should have the room to ourselves."

"I am most pleased," I said with a smile for Miss Woodmansey. She favored me with a radiant smile in return. It seemed that she was one young lady who did not see a scar every time she gazed upon my face. 'Twas most refreshing.

"How do you allow such a person into your house?" Mrs. Woodmansey demanded.

"I confess, he is an acquired taste," Lady Vawdrey said with a dismissive wave of her shriveled hand.

"I cannot perceive why one should wish to acquire such," Mrs. Woodmansey said haughtily.

"Dear Señyor Rey," I drawled as I lifted my quizzing glass through which to observe Mrs. Woodmansey. "Note how she lifts all save one of her chins. Pray, how does she manage it?"

Rey gasped like an old woman, specifically, Lady Vawdrey. I never saw two such disparate creatures resemble one another so closely. Meanwhile, the singular Miss Woodmansey's face turned pink with the effort of repressing her laughter. *Oh, to have the pleasure of kissing such seditious lips*, I thought. The thunderous look on Mrs. Woodmansey's face, however, gave me pause.

Faster than I thought possible, Rey drew a chair to her side. He spoke to her in tones of such gentleness that order was soon restored to her features. I, however, paid no heed to his words; I was fully occupied in the sharing of a meaningful glance with the daughter. It seemed an age since a young woman had favored my face with the heat of her gaze for so long. As I unabashedly looked back the pink in her cheeks spread delightfully to her ears, and her eyes seemed to shine. Suddenly I realized I had no more than a moment to speak with her before her mother interfered.

I made no secret of the need for haste as I strode to where Miss Woodmansey sat upon the sofa, took her hand in mine, and kissed it. I knew that Lady Vawdrey watched, so I did not delay in releasing the tiny hand. Miss Woodmansey used it to brush the seat next to her and I lost no time in acting on her suggestion.

"Miss Woodmansey," I murmured once I had sat, "you have no idea how I have longed to speak with you."

"Do I not?" she asked in a voice that tantalized.

The breath caught in my throat. I thought perhaps she merely toyed with me, but proceeded as if she had not. "I should very much enjoy the pleasure of your company in a more discreet setting." Even should she be willing, I had no idea how I should accomplish such. This lack of knowledge did nothing to dissuade me.

She smiled. "And I should very much enjoy assisting you in your search for Johnny Gilbert's killer."

"Should you?" I was surprised at this admission. "It is no work for delicate young ladies."

"I had not realized," she murmured, her expression coy, "there was one in the room."

Utterly captivated, I gave her my best smile in appreciation for her cleverness as my mind madly churned. If she were to attend the gaming hell with Rey and myself, her mother need never know she had been in my presence. "Do you enjoy gambling, Miss Woodmansey?" I all but whispered.

She rolled her eyes. "I am my father's daughter, am I not? But I do not think it a horse race to which you refer."

"Indeed, I do not; an illegal gaming den. What think you of that?"

Her eyes glittered. "I think it sounds most thrilling."

My heart soared like a bird on the wing. "That is excellent," I said as calmly as the beating of my heart allowed. "Rey shall call on you at nine of the clock this very night."

"Nine? Is that not terribly early for such dangerous doings?" she asked excitedly.

"He can hardly knock upon the door any later; what would your mother think?"

"She attends a lecture this evening on the Formation of Religious and Moral Principles for Women and expects me to attend, as well. I have been dreading it lo these many days.

I shall claim a sick headache and slip out the front door at half past ten. Shall that do?"

Enchanted, I approved her plan. "We shall be there with the carriage and drive you 'round to Berkeley Square."

"Berkeley Square? We do not go to Hampton House again tonight?" she asked, astonished.

"No, but near to it. I shall explain all when there are none to overhear."

"Desdemona!" Mrs. Woodmansey called. "It is time we take our leave."

"Yes, of course, Mama."

Rey and I rose, whereupon the Woodmanseys rose also and took their leave of Lady Vawdrey. I fixed my gaze upon Miss Woodmansey until she disappeared behind the closed door. So lost was I in my thoughts of her that I did not at first hear Lady Vawdrey address me.

"Trevelin! How good of you to call on me when I am indisposed," she said, her tone sharp as a knife.

I turned and gave her a bow of contrition. "Señyor Rey informed me that you are feeling low, but I hoped you might see me on a matter of some urgency."

She appeared mollified. "Out with it, then! I am recovered, thought doubtless a relapse is imminent."

I had had my warning and knew that I must tread carefully. "Many thanks. What I have to say has to do with Throckmorton. The housekeeper at Gilbert House has reported that your man came to the kitchen last week to ask for the cook's recipe for jugged hare."

"So? What is remarkable in that?" She dropped her jaw in an over-abundance of surprise so that her already-long face took on fantastic proportions.

I was obliged to look away. "He claims to have gone at your request."

"Why should I need the recipe to that? Jugged hare!" she demanded. "What is there to know?"

"She claims you have a special fondness for her cook's particular recipe. Do you not?"

"No, I do not! My cook's recipe is perfectly adequate."

"If you say so, but I'm afraid it makes Throckmorton appear to be guilty of Johnny's murder."

"But, why?" Lady Vawdrey, who had been lounging on the divan, jerked upright. "You are touched in the head, Trevelin!"

"We must consider the facts. Throckmorton visited the Gilberts' kitchen the day prior to the murder, the same day the key to the kitchen door was taken. If he did not have a reason to be there—and it sounds as if jugged hare is not sufficient reason—then he must have been there for some other purpose."

"Oh, that!" she said with a sigh of relief. "He must have his eye on one of the girls in the kitchen."

I opened my mouth to correct her, but caught Rey's expression of alarm. "I am certain you are right." It was an utter pretense and I hated to say the words. "I ought to have arrived at that conclusion on my own."

"Yes, you ought to have! What is the trouble with that mind of yours, Trevelin? And to think it is upon you that my hopes rest," she said with a *tsk*.

I decided I had had enough of her insults. "We shall leave you to rest. I should be sorry were you to relapse," I insisted, and motioned to Rey to follow me from the room.

He gave Lady Vawdrey a bow and glared at me with his black eyes until I did the same. My bow was far sketchier, as I bolted for the door. I continued to move at a speed less than genteel until we gained the ground floor.

Rey led me into the study where a fire burned merrily in the grate. "I spend a great deal of time in here," he explained, "as I am not always of the most sociable disposition when Lady Vawdrey entertains callers."

"This is more than sufficient." I ensconced myself in a chair next to Rey's and the two of us contemplated the dancing of the flames whilst we collected our thoughts.

"Are you of the opinion that the jugged hare recipe has put Throckmorton in a bad light?" Rey asked.

"I confess I am of two minds on the matter. On the one hand, Lady Vawdrey denies that she ever requested the recipe for jugged hare from the Gilberts' cook and I thoroughly agree; how many ways might there be to prepare such mundane fare? On the other hand, perhaps the Gilberts' cook has landed upon something unique, in which case Lady Vawdrey would most certainly want the recipe. If so, her claims that she did not ask for it can mean very little."

"*Si*," Rey said with a fierce bob of his head, "she would wish it to seem that her jugged hare was always the best jugged hare in London."

"*Precisament!*"

"My lord," Rey asked in fervent tones. "Do you speak the Catalan?"

"Not at all. I know some Continental Spanish. It is short work to make the adjustment to Catalan for such a word. It is you, Señyor, who is admirable. How many languages do you speak?"

He had the grace to blush. "Eleven, my lord. I should like to add a twelfth when I am more at leisure."

I was duly impressed. "Do you offer lessons in all or only in your native tongue?"

"I teach all of the languages I know to those who have the aptitude to learn!"

"And Lady Vawdrey? She wished to learn Catalan?" Somehow I could not believe it was her foremost reason for having Señyor Rey in her home. I had no wish to enlighten him on the subject, however. I suspected if he knew how much pleasure she derived as an incomparable matchmaker, his pride would doubtless be wounded.

"But, of course. Have I not said so?" He spread his hands wide. "She is not a very apt pupil, however. I find that I must remain in England longer than I had anticipated."

His protestations served only to bring Miss Woodmansey immediately to mind. Perhaps she was proving more difficult to woo and win than he had presumed. "Perhaps, whilst you are among us, you might have time to tutor me in a language."

"I should enjoy that very much." He gave me a warm smile.

"So should I," I said with utter sincerity. However, the language I most felt the lack of was that of love. It seemed I knew little as to the wooing of women. Miss Woodmansey's face appeared before my eyes and I knew the time had come to inform Rey of my intentions—at least those having to do with the Manwarings. "Señyor Rey, I am to attend Lady Clara's gambling hell tonight. I should like you to come as well."

"Are you most certain it is a true card party this time?" he asked, half-doubtful, half-sly.

Though I thought his attempt at guile amusing, I ignored it. "I know nothing for certain, but she assures me there shall be others in attendance. At any rate, if there are not you shall be present to protect my virtue." I could see by the twinkle in his eye that he very much liked the idea of acting as my champion. The man truly had no notion of how ridiculous the notion appeared, he being so very short and I being taller than most men.

"I have a pistol in my chamber. I ought to bring it along, ought I not?"

"Ah! If that is a yes, then I accept. However, I should think firearms not needful. There is something else I must tell you, however. I have invited another to accompany us and I shall need you to assist me, or it shall not be possible."

Rey sat taller in his chair and shook his pitch-black curls. "I shall be most honored to assist. What is it that I must do?"

I required a moment to quell my laughter before I replied. "I have invited a woman," I all but choked, "one who has expressed an interest in helping us discover Johnny's killer."

"Ah, yes, Lady Vawdrey. She shall be a useful one to bring with us, is this not so?"

"Not Lady Vawdrey. This woman is younger. I shall need you to call for her so that she may join the two of us in the carriage. It shall be rather late and I do not wish to sully her reputation should any see her with me prior to our arrival at Manwaring House."

"But, it is to a gambling hell we are going, is it not? None will speak of having seen her there, for fear they shall betray themselves."

"One should hope." I drew a deep breath; the worst was to come. "The young lady whom we shall retrieve tonight at half past ten is Miss Woodmansey."

His face turned a dusky red. "No! She is a young lady most virtuous! She would never agree to go with two men, with no chaperone, and to such a place!"

"She has already, my friend. But do not fret—we shall treat her with the utmost respect and guard well her identity."

He looked at me as if I had run mad. "How are we to accomplish this? And how is she to help us if she is not to be discovered? She is to wear a mask? And not speak?" His face darkened more than I had thought possible. "I say again, no!"

I found that I could not adequately address his concerns. I had invited her so that I might bask in the glow of her presence, and she had agreed because she wished…what? To bask in the glow of Rey's? She claimed to wish to help solve the mystery of Johnny's death, and I felt the truth in that, at least. However, to my horror, I realized that I had taken no thought for her reputation. It seemed I was going from bad to worse when it came to the seeking of a young lady's hand in marriage.

"Señyor Rey, I find that you are wiser than I. Miss Woodmansey expressed a wish to assist us in our quest, but I did not give proper care to her reputation. I perceive her to be intrepid and determined. She quickly arrived at a plan that would make it possible for her to accompany us without her parents' knowledge, but I can see now that I have been quite wrong."

Rey stared at me for a moment as, slowly, the color receded from his face. "Miss Woodmansey wishes to help us to find the killer?" he asked haltingly. "She has thought of a way on her own?"

I nodded.

He vented a gusty sigh. "I find there is nothing I can deny Miss Woodmansey. If we take much care to hide her identity, to keep her safe, and her parents are not to learn of it, I shall agree."

It was a victory I found I could not enjoy. I was ashamed for several reasons, the least of which was my motivations. How could I tell him that I did it for purely selfish reasons—that I wanted to have a chance at love and being loved by her? It seems I had betrayed them both. But, what was done was done and all too soon I found myself waiting in the carriage as Rey rapped on the door to collect Miss Woodmansey.

I waited in the carriage in the dark of night, praying that the young lady I had invited to join me would have the courage to issue forth from her London townhouse beneath her parents' notice. There was no moon and I peered through the glass, straining my eyes. I did not see her until she was almost at the coach door, which I leapt to open for her. There was an air of excitement about her; naturally, she believed it to be Evelyn with whom she eloped. What she did not know, however, was that Evelyn had no such intentions. He would have ruined her; left her without virtue or husband. I intended to arrive before him and rescue her from such a fate. She did not realize my subterfuge until it was too late. As I read her a lengthy lecture, I frequently consulted my timepiece so as to ensure that Evelyn had given up on her. Finally, I deemed it safe and deposited her in front of her parents' house. To my dismay, she did not seem to appreciate my rescue of her virtue in the least.

My thoughts returned to the present, but the same aloneness that ate at my belly that night had merely packed its bags and made itself at home. Tonight there was a full moon, and I easily perceived Miss Woodmansey emerge from the house on Rey's arm. I nearly laughed aloud at the sight; they resembled nothing more than a pair of children draped in the garments of their elders. The emotions they seemed to emit, however, were perfectly real. Rey behaved as if she were already his, and she appeared quite happy to be at his side. Miserable, I wondered how I could possibly woo and win her from under the nose of one of my few friends.

They approached the coach in conversation both animated and hushed. It was clear they felt they were embarking on a grand adventure. I was reminded again of the young lady I had rescued from the clutches of my cousin. Gratitude filled me that no one knew of the night I had invited her into my carriage and driven off with her. I knew, only too well, that if details of that night were revealed I would not be painted the hero of the piece, no matter how deserved.

I felt the shift and sway of the coach as the driver descended, opened the door, and let down the steps. Miss Woodmansey entered with an air of excitement accompanied by a cloud of French perfume and a swish of skirts. She took up her seat across from me and the two of us shared a smile that I shall long remember. It was if the two of us existed in a world utterly separate from all others.

Then Rey entered, and it was as if a golden strand between us had been severed. He took his seat next to her and suddenly she was an ocean away. When he captured her hand and pulled it through his arm, I thought it a pointless act of chivalry. After all, there was no danger that she might trip and fall to the ground. She, however, favored him with precisely the same smile she had offered me. The gnawing sensation in my stomach stirred and demanded to be fed.

"I have never been to a gambling den," she stated, her voice eager. "Shall it be very dangerous?"

"Not at all," I said, just as Rey plunged in with his list of admonitions.

"Yes, indeed! But, you needn't fear, for I shall keep you safe. You must wear this mask," he said as he drew the soft black fabric from his coat pocket, "and you mustn't speak so as not to be recognized by your voice."

"Oh," she said, deflated.

"I imagine there shall be other women in attendance wearing masks, Miss Woodmansey," I soothed.

"We must refrain from calling her by name!" Rey demanded. "It is not too soon to begin. What shall we call her instead?"

"What about Miss Incognita?" I said, in the foolish hope my suggestion would render me daring and attractive.

Before she could reply, Rey had his own suggestion. "No, *La Mascarada!*"

"Perhaps Miss Masquerade would be better understood?" Miss Woodmansey asked.

"*Sí*! Of course. It is best this way," Rey said as if the proposal were his very own.

"Very well, the matter is settled," I said by way of including myself in their plans, but I do not believe that I was heard. Miss Woodmansey struggled with her mask and Rey helped her, his short, stubby fingers fumbling with the ties and taking much longer to produce results than was necessary. It allowed me a lingering view of Miss Woodmansey's back, which was quite lovely. All too soon Rey obscured it with the domino he arranged around her shoulders.

"This you must wear, as well. It shall make the mask seem less out of place."

Miss Woodmansey gave him another one of her lovely smiles. "Thank you. You have thought of everything. I know that I shall be quite safe in your hands, Señyor Rey."

As I lamented the willingness of young ladies to trust, my stomach churned. The fact that she was absolutely correct in finding him to be more trustworthy than I did little to console me.

The journey back to Berkeley Square was not a long one and nothing more was said until we arrived. The driver brought the coach to a halt as near to the door as possible, but his way was impeded by the plethora of transports in the drive. The sight filled me with relief, a feeling that was deepened when the door of our conveyance opened without the usual drenching of the interior with light from the house. If possible, the Manwaring residence appeared darker than it had the night prior. I thought perhaps Miss Woodmansey shrank back, but when Rey took her hand and led her out of the coach she seemed to rally.

I realized how short-sighted had been my plan; if it had been I who claimed her at the door I should have been by her side even still. As it was, I tarried behind like a dejected beau. Then I realized I was needed to say the proper words when the door to Manwaring House opened, and pushed past my friends in a manner that, to them, must have appeared arrogant.

I swallowed my dismay and knocked upon the door, which was immediately opened. "We are expected," I said as instructed and, just as before, we were welcomed into the house. Once again, the black interior was alleviated by the light of only one candelabra and we were led up the stairs in almost complete darkness. Rey and Miss Woodmansey followed behind me; I felt their apprehension like a wave of heat at my back. It served to accentuate my continued solitary state. Sharply, I reminded myself of the duty I owed Willy to forget myself and do what I must to ensure his release.

As before, we were led to the second-floor salon. My breath froze in my lungs as I wondered what might await us on the other side of the door. Perhaps Lady Clara was playing a deep game and I would be made to seem the fool. To my relief, when the door opened we were met with a blaze of light and noise. I narrowed my eyes against its brilliance and looked about. To the right was the too-small sofa that flanked the fireplace. To the left was the portion of the room that, the night prior, had been in shadow. It was full to bursting with tables, chairs, a roulette wheel, and more gamblers than I thought possible to be contained in such dimensions.

In the center of the room stood a table groaning with

refreshments; one side contained row upon row of bottled wines, a tower of crystal goblets, each one filled to the brim with champagne, and a fountain that sported orgeat. The other half was piled high with comestibles, both sweet and savory, designed to be consumed minus the inconvenience of wielding a fork or spoon.

The table was ringed with footmen, as well as female servants who wiped the floor and table free of the carelessness of the guests. Additional servants stood all about the room, waiting to fetch and carry whatever a guest desired. I recognized a great many of them, including Mrs. Carrick, who wore a curled white wig under her cap and bright red rogue upon her cheeks.

At the main table stood Lady Clara, her smile glittering, as she greeted the passersby. As we approached, her smile grew even brighter. "My lord, how good to see you here!" she said, exactly as if I had not been in the very room only twenty-four hours past. "And I see that you have brought your European friend. I am honored by your presence," she said as she turned her smile on Rey.

I sketched a bow. "May I introduce to you Señyor Rey of Barcelona. Señyor, this is Lady Clara, wife of Mr. Richard Manwaring."

"Thank you for your hospitality, Lady Clara," he said with a bow. "I have been most desirous to see an English gambling hell for myself."

Inwardly, I groaned. I ought to have warned Rey that one might do as he pleases at an illegal gambling hell, save call it such.

Lady Clara produced a well-practiced trill of laughter.

"You flatter me, Señyor, but this is but a card party. I do hope you enjoy yourself. Am I to know this young lady at your side?"

Rey stiffened. "This is Miss Masquerade. She is newly arrived in London."

I found myself amazed at his deceit. I hadn't dreamed he should stoop so low, even for Miss Woodmansey. At his words, she executed a curtsey just deep enough to imply that she might be of higher status than Lady Clara.

"Oh!" she cried. "It seems there is much about you we are not to know. How very theatrical! Now, I must see to my other guests, but do enjoy yourselves." She took herself off and I was left to wonder exactly what step we ought to take next.

Miss Woodmansey rustled to my side and spoke so quietly that I could not catch her words. She wore her hair in a less lofty style than the night we had met and the top of her head did not so much as reach my shoulder. I repressed the desire to scoop her up with one arm; two would not be required. Instead, I bent so that she might repeat her message into my ear.

"What shall I do? I should so like to be of service to poor Mister Gilbert who wastes away in gaol."

I felt immediately contrite. Willy's plight was my burden to bear alone. "You and Señyor Rey should choose a table and watch a game. It would be best to listen for the time being. Perhaps someone shall say something that should prove enlightening."

I thought she appeared somewhat crestfallen, and yet, she could not have been as disappointed as I. Sending the two of them off together was my punishment for forgetting Willy and putting my happiness before his liberty. I watched her walk away, her arm on Rey's, whilst the beast in my stomach dug into its meal.

Almost by rote I headed for the corner of the room, but was stopped short by the sound of a voice I thought I recognized. Hoping I had heard amiss, I cocked my head and listened; I heard it again. With caution, I made my way towards the sound but arrived at the end of the room without encountering its speaker. Just as I counted myself fortunate that I was mistaken, the hated voice sounded from over my right shoulder.

"Trev! It has been too long!"

My stomach sank into my shoes and I turned to face my cousin, Evelyn Rogers-Riemann. He had grown somewhat corpulent in the months since I had last seen him. His thick brown hair arranged in the windswept style had more territory to cover along his brow, and his eyes were pinched into mere slits. Even his fingers had grown fleshy. "Eve," I said stiffly. "I had not thought to see you here."

"But where else?" he drawled, looking around the room. "I dare not show my face amongst polite Society these days. Rutherford has seen to that."

A voice in some corner of my mind chimed: You are more courageous than he! However, I paid it no heed. "Rutherford has much to answer for," I said as pleasantly as my resentment allowed. "I see that Lady Clara's guests are far less particular as to with whom they associate."

Evelyn surveyed me with a jaundiced eye. "It is the same with any club whose members are bent on debauchery;

142

no one shall quibble about who is in attendance so long as all are discreet."

I shrugged. "Quite naturally I am in no position to tell any of your presence here tonight, not without revealing my own."

"Exactly my point," Evelyn said, with a sneer that owed nothing to any scar.

I was startled to recall that I had once considered him a friend. And then I was reminded that it was Evelyn who had saved my life when Rutherford took after me with a sword. My cousin might have done better to let me die and inherit my title, estate, lands, and monies, but he had chosen me over consequence in the world. In my gratitude, I had confused his actions with genuine affection. In fact, they were far less noble; he was but afraid.

"I shall bid you good night," I said curtly and began to walk away, but he put a hand to my arm to forestall me.

"Rutherford is not the only noble to present me with a list of his conditions. Am I to be so poorly rewarded for my deference to yours? I have stayed away from Society at his behest. I have refrained from calling on you at Canning House at yours. However, you go wherever you wish. Mark my words: there shall be a price to pay for your defiance."

I stared at Evelyn in astonishment. "How can he possibly harm me any further than he has already?"

"You might be surprised, Cousin. He might look for help. He might even find it." He looked at me, expectation glimmering beneath the heavy lids of his eyes.

"Ho! Do you think he would align himself with *you* merely to wreak more revenge on me?"

"You may depend upon it," Evelyn said, his voice cold as stone.

I stared down at his hand on my arm, then back at his belligerent face. "Unhand me or everyone shall know the truth about you."

Evelyn laughed and moved away. "You shall regret it, Trev. Revenge is too sweet to resist for long."

I wondered what he could possibly mean. Revenge? For what? In the past I had saved our friendship, his reputation, and even his life on more than one occasion. If he felt revenge a suitable response to my rejection, then I supposed he must take it. I stalked away with the heat of his gaze boring into my back, but he was immediately forgotten when I noticed Huther.

He was playing Hazard with a few others at a table near the center of the room. I approached slowly so as not to draw attention to myself, and watched as he noted the result of each throw of the dice. He must have been losing badly, for his dismay was evident; his entire frame shook so that the beaded perspiration on his forehead seemed to bounce along his brow. He was once again the timid tutor. When he turned from the game in disgust, I barred his way.

"Mr. Huther," I drawled. "How fortunate it is that we have met."

Chapter Nine

Huther scowled and attempted to step around me, something I would not allow.

"Clear the way," he demanded.

"Not until you answer my questions."

He gazed at me, stupefied. "I don't know anything!" he hissed. When he saw that I was unmoved, he relented. "Very well," he said, his gaze darting to and fro', "but not here; not where we can be seen."

Seeing the wisdom in his words, I took hold of his arm and drew him behind a potted palm in a darkened corner of the room. "When last we spoke, I neglected to question why you claimed to have received no letter of recommendation from the Gilberts when, indeed, you had."

"I don't know. I…" He drew a shaking hand across his brow, dislodging his sweat-damp hair. "I dared not tell you about this place," he mumbled. "Such is my obsession that I am no longer suited to be a tutor. I had no intention of seeking such a position. Lady Clara had a position for me, but that was not information I wished to disclose."

"And what of now; are you willing to tell me of the duties you perform in this household?"

He scowled. "I do what she asks of me, whatever that might be. I owe her a great deal of money. She feeds and houses me, and in return, I do her bidding."

"Would her bidding include the murder of a young boy?"

His face turned white. "No! I have already told you; I had nothing to do with Johnny's death."

"But you had already planned to leave the Gilberts' employ for the Manwarings' when he died, is that not so?"

"Why should I have? I had a position!"

"'Tis a good question. Shall we explore the answer?" I took out my quizzing glass and began to buff it against my coat sleeve.

Huther's agitation grew. "It happened as I told you. I had a position as tutor at the Gilberts. The mistress...was fond of me. Despite the neglect of my duties, I never expected to be dismissed. To my good fortune, I performed a task for Lady Clara in exchange for money owed. When I found myself without a position, she took me in. It is that simple."

I viewed him through the glass and was satisfied with what I saw. "I find that I believe you, Mr. Huther. Tell me, then, the nature of this task."

He looked profoundly unhappy. "It was merely the delivery of a letter." He crossed his arms and pressed his elbows against his hands to still their trembling. "That is all!"

I perceived that this was a lie. "From Lady Clara? To whom?"

He drew a breath and the air rattled in his throat. "Does it matter?" he asked as he looked about the room.

"If it did not, you should not hesitate to tell me," I pointed out.

He ceased his survey of the room and returned his gaze to me. "Very well, then; I shall tell you. Do not hold me accountable for the fate that may befall you as a result."

"You believe I am in danger?" I asked, rather breathlessly. I could not say if it were due to the elation I felt at the possibility of saving Willy's life or fear for my own.

"You are attempting to discover a killer, are you not?" His eyes bored into mine.

"Then you do not for one moment believe it was Willy who did away with his brother?"

His face blanched again; clearly it was a question he did not wish to answer.

"Then tell me; to whom did you carry Lady Clara's missive?"

"I should prefer not to answer that question."

"Very well," I said briskly. "I find I have another. When Señyor Rey and I questioned you at Gilbert House, you said that it was you who went to inform the butler of Johnny's death. However, the butler insists it is not so. Why should you lie about such a thing?"

Huther drew a deep breath. "I was afraid, so I hid myself. I was not proud of that. I chose, instead, to characterize myself as helpful."

"Afraid of what?"

His eyes grew large and his face broke out again in perspiration. "The one behind the knife."

The man was truly frightened. Doubtless, he knew, or at least suspected, the identity of the killer. I decided to force the truth from him by other means. "I believe you to be lying, Huther. I think it was likely you who killed Johnny. As a servant in the household, you had access to the kitchen. It was a simple matter to steal the key in order to make it seem as if it were someone else. You told Johnny to dress and meet you in the vestibule at a certain time during the night so as to go on some sort of adventure. And then you killed him."

"No! Why? Why should I?" he all but screeched under his breath.

I was favored with a flash of inspiration. "Because he saw something; something that would put you in a very difficult position if he were to tell anyone of it."

Huther's reaction was electrifying. "I didn't do it!" he hissed in a panic. "I swear that I did not!"

"But you know who did."

He looked for a moment that he would agree then began to vehemently shake his head.

"Then tell me, to whom did you take Lady Clara's message?"

He wished to tell me, I could see that it was so. His face began to change color with the effort of forcing his lips together. His eyes seemed to bulge from their sockets as his entire frame swayed back and forth.

I vented a languid sigh. "I believe I shall alert the constable."

"No!" he cried so loudly that people turned to look in our direction. He again surveyed the room before he fell against me and pushed me deeper into the shadows. "Throckmorton. It was Throckmorton," he hissed before he closed his eyes and collapsed in a heap at my feet.

Throckmorton. Somehow I was not surprised. Quietly, I leaned over and placed a finger beneath Huther's nose; he yet breathed. A better man than I might have alerted someone to his plight. Instead, I slipped my leather pumps from beneath his prone form and stepped out into the light of the game room. Huther had been looking for someone; someone of whom he was terrified. I thought perhaps he had found him.

I effected an air of nonchalance as I walked about, inspecting the faces around me from the corner of my eye. Evelyn was capable of inducing fear in a man such as Huther but, unlike myself, my cousin had been adhering to Rutherford's expectations. At any rate, why should Evelyn want Johnny Gilbert dead? Throckmorton was not present, nor had I expected him to be. Everyone else in the room was most likely who they appeared to be; mostly men with more money than they knew what to do with and who wanted a bit of sport.

I turned my attention to the few women who were present. My gaze was drawn first to Miss Woodmansey, who looked quite charming on Rey's arm. There was another lady in a mask and domino who seemed to have arrived under the protection of Lord Vane, one of Evelyn's cronies. Lastly, there was Lady Clara whose husband, Manwaring, had now joined her. They sauntered about the room, arm in arm, chatting with those of their guests who, I presumed, were losing the most money. Soon they would come upon Huther still collapsed on the floor.

Deciding that I had learned enough for one night, I strode directly to Rey and Miss Woodmansey and informed them of my desire to depart. They immediately complied, leaving me to wonder what I had done to deserve such loyalty. I was grateful to have them by my side when we left the room and were once again plunged into darkness.

We felt our way to the staircase, myself in the lead. If we were to meet with misadventure, I wished to protect my friends. We descended the stairs in a velvet-dark silence, save the swishing of Miss Woodmansey's skirts. As the carpet on the treads absorbed our hesitant footfalls, I was suddenly filled with dread; were anyone following us, we would be none the wiser. Huther had feared that the true killer was in the house; the very thought caused every hair I possessed to stand up on end. The flesh on my back crawled most particularly despite the fact that it was Rey and Miss Woodmansey who were directly behind me.

My concern was now for them. "Wait a moment," I whispered. I stepped aside, taking Miss Woodmansey's arm. As I drew her forth to go ahead, I knew Rey would follow. "I shall be just behind you," I murmured. The darkness deepened just before we reached the front hall. I strained my eyes in search of the glimmer of light that should have been cast by the lone candelabra by the front doors. It did not come. I arrived at the only conclusion of which I was capable: someone had put it out.

Desperately, I attempted to determine from which direction danger was most likely to strike when I heard it: the plodding tread of someone walking upon the marble floor in the vestibule. My muscles tensed, ready to spring at any moment, and my heart beat like a drum such that I felt certain all could hear its beat throbbing.

"What was that?" Rey asked, his voice tense and hushed.

"I believe it was a footfall from down below."

There came a short silence, followed by a rustling of the sort made when a lady in silk throws herself into the arms of the man at her side. I repressed the desire to analyze her motives and listened intently for a repetition of what I had before heard. It did not come. Either someone had walked away, or was lying in wait for us.

"What shall we do, my lord?" Rey whispered.

"Remain here whilst I investigate." The darkness was so complete that I was in danger of losing my balance. I placed my right hand on the banister and brushed the wall to my left with my fingers. Carefully, I crept down one step; past Miss Woodmansey who was doubtless still clutched in Rey's arms, then another, and another. Just as I thought that I had surely reached the bottom, something flew at my face. Crazed with fear, I clawed at the air as my heart pounded with impending apoplexy. Little by little, I realized the danger was merely a shadow created by the light of a single candle. It was held aloft by a dark figure one step below me.

"My lord?" It was a deep voice, and sinister; his breath noxious as it wafted, hot, into my face.

My heart leapt up into my throat. "Show yourself!" I demanded.

The figure below moved the candle to his face. I knew him: it was Short the butler to whom I had spoken in Mrs. Carrick's room earlier that morning.

Flooded with relief, my knees buckled. I went down far enough for the banister to catch me under the arm and bang painfully into my ribs. Rey rushed to my aid. Once I had found my footing, I turned to ascertain the status of Miss Woodmansey.

"I am quite all right," she said in a strained voice, her face still in shadow.

Rey returned to her side and we followed Short down the remainder of the stairs, his apologies ringing in our ears all the way down.

"My wish was only to cast light to guide your way," Short repeated as we gained the ground floor. "I should have been here sooner, but had not expected any to depart this early in the evening."

He seemed quite sincere, but he could not have looked more different. He appeared to be nothing but a freakish head with chin, cheeks, and nose grossly exaggerated by the light. His eyes were deep, dark cavities overhung with fiery brows, and his gray hair resembled a vaporous, ghostly caul about his head. He looked sufficiently fiendish to be the murderer for whom we had been searching.

"My lord?" Short asked when I made no reply.

I gave myself a mental shake and said the first thing that came to mind. "Throckmorton; is he in the house tonight?"

"I do not believe so, my lord. All the servants, save myself, are above stairs in the game room. He might have been here earlier to pay a call on Sally in the kitchen."

"I did not see Sally in the game room," I said. "Could they be somewhere together?"

"It is not her half day, besides which, she is always needed on card party nights. But, who am I to say? Despite my best efforts, this is a rather topsy-turvy household."

I exchanged a glance with Rey. It was an act of futility; his eyes were pools of ink that said nothing.

"Why is that?" I prayed he would not find my question too impertinent to answer.

He took a step closer, prompting Rey and Miss Woodmansey to do the same. Our faces circled the flickering candle as it cast ghostly shadows that leapt against the walls. "This house," he said quietly, slowly, even fervently, "is full of odd occurrences."

I frowned my displeasure. "Why did you not disclose this when we spoke earlier today?"

"I was afraid," he whined. "But, it is true. When everyone from the mistress to the boot boy is above stairs tending to the guests at these parties, the house...*screams*."

"Screams?" Rey echoed in bewilderment.

"Yes! Screams!" Short nodded wildly, like a man demented. "Or sometimes it moans, or groans. But often it is definitely a scream—a very high-pitched scream."

I thought him quite mad. "Has anyone else heard this screaming?" I asked.

The butler leaned back out of the circle. "No. Only me," he said, as if his statements were perfectly sane.

At these words, all the fear, foreboding, and anxiety I felt spilled from me like water over a fall. "Thank you, Short. We shall consider what you have said most carefully, shall we not Señyor Rey?"

"Indeed, we must." His rich voice, so at odds with his size, boomed in the grand hall. "But, I fear that Miss Masquerade is fatigued. I believe we should escort her home immediately."

The butler bowed, and opened the door. The three of us eagerly stepped out of the house into the benevolent night. Once the door had been shut, we stood for a moment reveling in the banality of the chill, October air, flooded with the light of a full moon. I took a deep breath and hurried down the black and white checkered front steps of Manwaring House, Miss Woodmansey and Rey just behind me.

"That is a house of evil," he pronounced.

"There certainly was something odd about it," Miss Woodmansey mused.

"It is unquestionably occupied by a cast of strange characters," I added. "Come, let us walk to Canning House and order out the carriage to escort Miss Woodmansey home."

"*Si*, it is time that she was safe in the arms of her *mare* and *pare*."

"Truly?" she asked. "It seems so early, though I suppose my mother shall soon arrive at the house."

We all agreed 'twas a pity and walked together in congenial silence, arm in arm, Miss Woodmansey in the center, for the length of a house or two. However, my mind worked to determine a way to prolong my association with her. "I have no wish to retire so early. Is there not a ball tonight?"

"There is!" Miss Woodmansey said with a triumphant smile. "Lord and Lady Monteer host a ball tonight for their daughter. She has just made her curtsies to the queen."

"Will your *mare* not be concerned for you when she is to arrive home and you are not present?" Rey asked.

Miss Woodmansey dipped her head in what appeared to be a fit of sheepishness. "I informed Mama that I would be attending the ball with you and Lady Vawdrey. If we do attend, I shan't have the need to invent answers to what shall prove to be numerous questions."

Señyor Rey made a sound indicative of his obvious delight. I, however, felt as if she had thrust a dagger through my heart. I reminded myself that it would have achieved nothing for her to have said she planned to attend the ball with me, but it did naught to assuage my feelings.

I forced my lips into a smile. "How clever of you!" I meant every word. "Is it too bold of me to request the first set upon our arrival?"

"Not at all. Shall I reserve the second set for you, Señyor Rey?"

"Yes! *Definitivament!*"

I wished to request the set after Rey's, as well, but restrained myself; I did not want her to grow weary of me. "I shall hurry ahead and bespeak the carriage. Hopefully Canning does not have use of it tonight." I did not wait for a response but unlinked my arm from Miss Woodmansey's and increased my pace to just under a run. It was undignified in the extreme but I would have no dances with her if the carriage had been called out already.

Moore answered the door and informed me that the Cannings had walked to dinner at the home of a friend in the square. My delight at this piece of luck soon waned as I waited for the others longer than I had expected. As I cooled my heels in the front hall, I tortured myself with imagined scenarios as to what was being said; what liberties were being taken. If I had been required to wait a moment more, I should have pulled open the door and rushed to join them, but soon enough we were reunited in the front hall.

More relaxed in my own domain, I took the opportunity to better appreciate Miss Woodmansey's appearance. I knew she was no beauty, but she had something other young ladies of her age did not possess: self-assurance. It drew one to her side, especially when she laughed. Her smile was nearly as bright as her golden hair, which seemed to glitter like gold in the light of the chandeliers that illuminated the vestibule. Her gown was as tasteful as always and the high-waisted style made the most of what little height she had. What I admired most about her, however, was her ability to perceive what lies beneath the obvious. This, to a scarred man with a sullied reputation, was beauty indeed.

We hadn't long to wait for the carriage, and soon we were off to the ball at the Monteers'. It was a grand townhouse that took up one entire side of Hanover Square. It naturally followed that the ballroom was enormous. If someone had informed me that all of Society was present, I should not have been the least surprised. Immediately, I bemoaned my plight; this was the sort of ball that required a new coat and I had already worn my royal blue superfine on numerous occasions. Never mind that it was only a month old, cost a small fortune, and fitted my trim figure like a glove: I suddenly felt a farmer.

It was in this deplorable state that I realized Rutherford was in attendance. My gaze was drawn to him almost instantly and not only because of the animosity between us. He was the sort who commanded notice regardless of surroundings. His penchant for unfashionable powdered wigs, the more ornate the better, made him a target of comment, scorn, and the wittiest of insults. (Certainly mine were known to be, though I never spoke them aloud.)

"Come, Miss Woodmansey, let us join in the dancing."

I took her arm and led her in the opposite direction of the duke. The last circumstance for which I wished was for Rutherford to renew his prohibition against me in her very presence. I strode away with her with such speed that she had no small amount of difficulty in matching my pace. As the dance was a Promenade, her predicament was furthered by the disparity in our heights. It also had a negative impact on our ability to converse. There was so much I wished to say to her, but I was forced to refrain. We danced the first set as promised, and then I was obliged to release her to Rey, my heart unburdened.

Determined to be on hand to claim another dance as soon as may be, I remained where I was with no thought but to keep her in my purview. Very shortly, however, Mr. Gilbert strode by with a young lady on his arm. I could not comprehend his presence or his association with this young lady when his wife grieved her sons at home. My suspicions were aroused: could it be true that Mrs. Gilbert took lovers and that Johnny was not Gilbert's son? Could that explain his lack of concern as well as his seeking the company of other women? Either way, it was bold of him to be seen with the same young lady as the night prior.

I knew, then, what my next step should be. However, I remained rooted to the spot until Rey returned with Miss Woodmansey. She was breathless but happy, her cheeks rosy; whether with exertion or love, I could not say.

"Miss Woodmansey, you must be parched." I held out my arm for her, which she took without hesitation. I had little time to enjoy my small victory as I led her directly to the refreshment room; it was where I had last seen Mr. Gilbert. I was only somewhat aware that Rey followed us.

"Are you still wishful of helping to solve the murder of Johnny Gilbert?" I asked.

"Yes, indeed," she replied with a nod.

"I saw his father enter this room," I said as I indicated the doorway to the supper room, "with a young lady on his arm. I cannot like it."

"I agree that it is not *de rigeur* for a man in his circumstances to attend a ball," she agreed. "However, I do not see that it makes him a murderer."

"He is not enough of the sorrowful father," Rey supplied from behind. "A man who cares so little for his son might not quibble at the killing of that son."

She turned to him. "But why? Why should he wish his son dead?"

"Revenge," I said without explaining for what that revenge might be. "A fit of anger gone too far; perhaps to make a statement."

"What statement might that be?" Miss Woodmansey mused. "It seems so very dire."

"It most certainly is, regardless of who killed him or why. However, that is he, there, by the table. He's the one with the dark-haired young lady on his arm; she is dressed in white spangles." She was indeed attached to him in an overly-familiar manner. Each time he spoke, she looked up at him and smiled in patent admiration. Neither did he take the trouble to hide his equal admiration of her; their mutual affection was an affront to Willy and his pain.

Miss Woodmansey seemed to sense my distress. "You and Señyor Rey shall discover what is amiss and make things right, I know you shall."

I repressed a self-pitying sigh. "I am honored by your confidence." Secretly, I was doubtful. "Let us draw closer and attempt to eavesdrop on their conversation."

Miss Woodmansey smiled in delight. "This is precisely the sort of behavior I have been warned against by my mother, nanny, and governess for all my life."

"We know that it is for the sake of Mr. Willy who pines away in gaol, is it not, Miss Woodmansey," Rey stated.

I jumped at bit at the sound of his voice; I had quite forgotten he was present. I recovered myself, and indicated that we should make our way along the length of the table as if we were in search of a certain liquid refreshment; the one at the elbow of Mr. Gilbert in particular. I said little and kept my back to him, as I had no wish to be recognized. The clever banter that sprang up between my two companions rent my heart, but it was perfect for my immediate purpose. It was not so loud that their words were discerned, but constant enough to attract notice. Those nearby would feel confident that nothing they had to say would be overheard by any in our party.

As they chatted, I backed slowly towards Mr. Gilbert and the young lady, selected a glass of orgeat, and pretended to sip.

"You have never looked more beautiful," Mr. Gilbert said.

It was all I could do to refrain from whirling about and striking him in the jaw.

"I am so pleased that you were able to leave your wife tonight. It means so much to me to have you by my side."

"She doesn't like it, of course, but she will accept it in time."

"Oh, my dear! Does this mean that I might count on your support for as long as I shall need it?"

"How can I do otherwise?" Mr. Gilbert responded with sickening affection.

I had never felt so selfish in all my life. Love had eluded me but I could not count my lot hard when I had yet to suffer as Mrs. Gilbert must from the actions of her husband. Having heard enough, I signaled to Rey and Miss Woodmansey that we should retreat. We walked in silence until we had regained the ballroom, where I revealed all that I had just heard.

"*Inconcebible*! That the husband of that poor woman could behave such—it defies all reason! A man such as this must be capable of anything!"

"I do not know," Miss Woodmansey interjected. "Many husbands betray their wives," she said, so matter-of-factly that it caused me to wonder about her father. "And yet, they do not murder their sons."

"You are correct, Miss Woodmansey," I conceded. "However, Señyor Rey and I have reason to believe that Johnny's death might have been the response to a long-building resentment." I did not add my suspicions that Johnny was not Mr. Gilbert's natural son, however. It was not for the delicate ears of an unmarried lady.

"What shall you do now, my lord?" Rey asked.

"The only thing that remains to me," I mused. "I must ask Willy."

∽

The next morning I found myself again on my way to Newgate Prison. Rey wished to join me, but I had no wish to humiliate Willy. It would be hard enough for him to respond to my queries in regard to his mother's faithfulness without a stranger in the room to hear his answers.

To my surprise, it was more difficult to see Willy in his desperate state than it had been the first time. I assumed that I knew what to expect, but the reality was too terrible. He scarcely registered my presence when I entered the chamber in which he lay, though his gaze briefly touched my face. His frown bore a sorrowful weariness as I approached him, and he did not rise from his prone position on his cot. To my dismay, it seemed that he wasn't eating; despite the quantity of gruel adhered to his shirt, his face had grown thin.

"Willy," I said as I drew up the chair to the edge of his bed and sat. "How long has it been since you have had anything to eat?"

He lifted his gaze to mine but said nothing.

"Have they been mistreating you?"

He shifted his shoulder in a meager shrug.

"Have your mama and papa been to see you?"

Tears started in his eyes, and I knew that they had not.

"There is much to do for the funeral. But they sent the extra clothing and blankets? And food? They sent good, hearty food, did they not?"

Slowly he turned his head to fix his gaze on a mound in a corner of the room.

I hurried over to inspect it. I found the promised blankets and clean clothing, but there was no food. I supposed the guards had stolen it.

"Willy, why hasn't anyone helped you to change?" I asked, vastly chagrined.

He lifted his sound hand and tapped a finger against his chest. "D'ape."

"The Ape? They refer to you as the The Ape?" I had never been so angry in my life. "Are you to say that they do not deem you worthy of the assistance you require? They won't even throw an extra blanket over you?"

His face contorted as he broke into a storm of weeping.

I rushed to his side, took him by the shoulders, and cradled him in my arms. He lay against my chest, his face in the crook of my neck, and sobbed until my neck cloth was wet through.

"All shall be well," I crooned. "I vow that it shall all be made right. Here…" I lowered his head to the pillow. "I shall help you myself." I went to the pile in the corner and first took up a clean blanket. As I returned to the cot, I wondered how I might accomplish what needed to be done without making him feel diminished. I placed the shirt and breeches at his feet and returned to my chair.

"Willy, you might think a swell such as I an utter greenhorn when it comes to dressing a man. However, I shall have you know that now I am at Cannings', I haven't had a valet of my own."

Willy looked up at me. His eyes were swollen, but there was no mistaking the mocking slant of his brow. He knew well enough that I was a hopeless case when it came to dressing myself.

"'Tis true!" I insisted. "As such, I have found it needful to do most everything on my own at one time or another. You shall be astonished to learn that I have even tied my own cravat once or twice!"

Willy opened his mouth as if to laugh, but fell into a fit of coughing instead.

"Willy, you are ill!" I strode to the door and thrust it open. "Get this man some water! And bring me a clean cloth whilst you are at it!" As long as I was to dress him, I intended to give him as much of a wash as I could manage.

While I waited, I went about the business of undressing my friend. First, I thrust away the dirty blanket he had been using and replaced it with a clean one. I pulled this up to his chin so that he would remain as warm as possible. Reaching under the blanket, I freed the buttons at the front of his breeches then gently rolled him onto his side so as to untie the gusset at the back. I then went to the foot of the cot and undid the buttons at his ankles, slipped the loops from around his bare feet, and dragged the garment from him. This task was made more difficult by virtue of his lame leg, which was permanently bent somewhat at the knee. The pain I still felt in my ribs from the collision with the banister at Manwaring House the night prior did little to help.

Next, I untied the top of his shirt and widened the opening. I drew the sleeve from his sound arm; freeing the lame one proved to be more of a task. Once they were both unencumbered, I pulled the shirt down past his shoulders. Replacing the blanket to preserve both warmth and dignity, I then returned to the foot of the bed and pulled the shirt from the bottom until I had dragged it off. I threw the two soiled garments into the corner farthest away.

The water still not arrived, I sat and held his hand whilst Willy drifted into sleep. When I had what was needed, I poured some water into a cup and used the rest to wash his face, very gently, until his eyes, nose, and the stubble on his chin were free of crusted food and tears. I then cleaned his body as best as I could. I had no wish for him to feel the cold or to wake him. As I felt his muscles begin to relax under my touch, tears came to my eyes. That he, even in his sleep, should feel the peace of being properly cared for, was humbling.

I came to my senses and looked about me; a dresser, a mirror, a chair, the bed I was lying in. I recognized nothing and feared everything. Then I realized Evelyn must have rented rooms somewhere, very likely under a name not his own. The pain that centered at the corner of my mouth was ever-present, but now seemed tolerable. Safe at last, I could not help but notice the pure cleanliness of the sheet pulled up to my chin, the orderliness of the room around me, the perfect softness of the pillow beneath my cheek. I closed my eyes and drifted into slumber.

With my hand on his arm I felt Willy shiver and knew he felt the cold. I retrieved the rest of the clean blankets and employed them to prop him up. Then I gathered the full length of the shirt in my hands and drew it over his head. I soon had it in place to his waist. Removing the blankets I lowered him so that he was again prone, and proceeded to work the shirt down past his haunches. Five days in prison had amounted to a shocking amount of weight loss, so this was not difficult. Once the shirt was pulled down to his knees, it was time to replace his breeches.

This proved to be the most challenging task yet. I had only a tender set of ribs about which to complain, a circumstance that required the assistance of Canning's valet at nearly every stage of dress that morning. Willy, however, was completely dependent on others to properly clothe him. I had been told that this task often fell to Willy's father and I marveled at the devotion required. I began to have a better understanding of the depth of Mr. Gilbert's love for his son and the sorrow he doubtless felt at the expected loss of Willy's life. I was not certain that it gave Mr. Gilbert a motive to kill the son who would take all that the brother might have had, but the notion was worthy of my consideration.

By the time I had managed to drag the breeches above Willy's knees, the pursuant tugging, pulling, dragging, and squeezing woke him. I thought that perhaps, now he was awake, he might do something to assist me, but he did not.

"I am vastly relieved you haven't a jacket!" I playfully derided. "That is one garment that requires two to properly don!"

It was clear to me that Willy wished to smile his amusement, but he fought the curving of his mouth.

Once he was fully clothed, I straightened out the blanket and added the others as well. Then I put the cup of water to his lips for him to drink. His lips were blue from the cold and his face white. To my dismay, he looked worse than before. The process had exhausted him more than it had even me; I perceived that I must pose my questions soon.

"Willy, you know that I am searching for the one who did this to Johnny—and to you. There is yet time. The trial date shall not be set until after you have appeared before the Grand Jury. Gratefully, I am very close to discovering who it is that should be here in your place. In the meantime, I need to ask you something…rather delicate."

Despite his fatigue, his gaze was stronger than before. It struck me how very much like my old friend he looked in that moment.

"There is no kind way to ask this: was Johnny your father's natural son?"

Willy frowned; a lop-sided grimace was the result. "Yesh!" He stared at me, his gaze hot and demanding, but there was nothing I could say, or explain, that wouldn't deepen his distress. When he saw that I would not relent, he rolled over and turned his back to me.

I sat in the chair, my chin propped up by an elbow to the knee, and pondered the morality of asking him such questions. Soon, to my profound regret, I heard the unmistakable sounds of weeping. I reached out to comfort him, but he was yet strong enough to pull himself from my grasp. When the cot began to shake with the violence of his sobbing, I put my face in my hands and did the only thing left to me to do: I joined him.

Chapter Ten

When I quit Newgate, I went directly to Gilbert House. My hatred for the person who had done this to Willy would not be forced aside. If it were Mr. Gilbert who had killed Johnny, I determined to expose him or die in the attempt. I instructed the coachman to pass by Canning House and press on to the Gilberts', the sooner to assuage my rage. Before the carriage came to a complete halt I threw open the door, tossed out the steps, flew down them and up the steps to Gilbert House to bang upon the door with my cane.

It opened to reveal an alarmed Bugg. I did not wait for him to admit me, but pushed past him far more savagely than he deserved. I took the stairs to the first floor two at a time whilst he cried out that this was a house in mourning and the master and mistress were not home to callers. I knew well enough where to find the sitting room, and I burst through the doors without aid of a footman. I was never happier to find Mr. and Mrs. Gilbert in one place; I would have answers from them and I would have them now. However, to my chagrin, the room was also occupied by Lady Vawdrey.

"My apologies," I gasped out. "I had not expected…"

Lady Vawdrey rose to her feet and raked me with a glare. "What? That anyone but you would come to call?"

"It is a house in mourning," I echoed the butler.

"I am one of Mrs. Gilbert's dearest friends! It is entirely proper that I should take a moment to walk across the square to see how she fares. It is not at all the same thing as paying a morning call." She treated me to another head-to-toe scrutiny. "What, pray tell, is your excuse?"

"I am merely in pursuit of a killer." My anger burned hotter than ever, but I was wise enough to swallow the home truths for the intractable Lady Vawdrey I longed to air.

She turned to the Gilberts. "He is correct, of course. He seems a good deal ruffled. Perhaps he has learned something of use. 'Tis about time!" she added as she swept past me and left the room.

My gaze fell upon Mrs. Gilbert, who sat with her handkerchief to her face. I forced myself to look away and collect myself. If her husband was the murderer, I had no wish to distress her any more than was needful. I decided to begin with the most pleasant news I could contrive.

"I have just been to see Willy. He is most grateful for all that you sent him."

"Is he?" Mrs. Gilbert asked, almost joyfully. "Is he getting enough to eat? Is he sleeping well?"

"Well enough." I had no wish to embitter them as to the state of their only surviving son.

"We are grateful to you, my lord."

I could not recall Mr. Gilbert ever before having addressed me as anything but 'Julian'. He had known me since I was a boy; it must have galled him to address me as his superior when I came to my title at the age of fifteen.

"I am grateful that I have yet the time to determine who deprived Johnny of his life. Whilst I was there, I was informed that Willy has yet to come before the Grand Jury."

Mr. Gilbert dropped his head in relief and his wife became more animated. "I am so grateful! Surely that is enough time to find who truly killed my boy!"

I realized that I could not delay any longer. "May I sit?" I asked, eyeing a chair adjacent to Mrs. Gilbert. I did not wait for a reply before I took a seat and leaned towards her. "Mrs. Gilbert, we have been acquainted for a long time. You have watched me grow from a boy to a man. Your son is a friend of long-standing, and I am determined to save his life. However, I find I am forced to ask questions that are most difficult. I must beg your pardon in advance."

"Very well," she said calmly. There was nothing in her manner to indicate she feared what I might ask.

"Thank you. Mr. Gilbert, I must ask that you refrain from answering for her or compelling her to answer according to your wishes. Might I depend on you for that?"

"Yes," he said shortly. His expression spoke of far more concern than that of his wife's.

"Thank you. Now, Mrs. Gilbert, I have been told that Mr. Huther was an incompetent tutor; that he left the house when he should have been giving lessons and left Johnny too often to his own devices. In truth, Johnny often left the house to follow his tutor, and perhaps found himself in some difficulty as a result. Were you aware of any of this?"

Tears welled in her eyes and a choking sound rose from her throat, but she nodded her agreement.

"Then, why was it you kept Mr. Huther on? Why did you not find a more suitable tutor or send Johnny off to school?"

She dabbed at her nose with her handkerchief. "I don't

know precisely. I suppose the best answer I can offer is that Johnny did not seem entirely suited to living away from home. He was a sensitive boy, not at all like William who loved to hunt and shoot and spend the day away from the house, even during school holidays. Johnny had no such ambitions or interests."

"Not for want of trying," Mr. Gilbert muttered under his breath.

I ignored him. "So, you engaged a tutor. But when he proved unsuitable, why did you not dismiss him?"

"I do not know," she whispered. "I suppose it was because Johnny seemed content at long last. I knew he wasn't spending as much time with his books as he should have been, but he was happy. He was somewhat young for his age; I felt that, in time, he would catch up."

"So, it had nothing to do with your attachment to Mr. Huther?"

She threw her head back in disbelief. "Mine? It was Johnny who was so attached. He did not endure changes well and, as I said, he seemed even happier once Mr. Huther began to be less demanding in the schoolroom."

I turned to Mr. Gilbert, who avidly watched his wife's face. He seemed to wonder if his wife told the truth every bit as much as did I.

"If Mr. Huther meant nothing to you beyond his positive affect on Johnny's disposition, has there been one who has meant more?"

Her brow furrowed with her frown. "I do not understand."

I decided I had best be more forthcoming. I had not

forgotten the effect my question had had on Willy, however. My throat constricted at the thought and I was forced to clear it before I could proceed. "Mrs. Gilbert, I cannot help but notice your decided preference for your younger son. I find it necessary to inquire as to why that should be so."

Mr. Gilbert's face turned scarlet. "Julian! You mustn't!"

"Mr. Gilbert, I crave your indulgence," I said with a dismissive wave of my hand. "Mrs. Gilbert, do answer the question. Did you prefer Johnny over Willy?"

She looked into my face without qualm. "Of course not. They are both my sons, and I loved each one of them as much as the other. I still do!"

"That is a lie!" her husband bellowed as he jumped to his feet. "You never loved Willy as you loved your beloved John!"

She looked up at him in astonishment, the hand holding the handkerchief suspended in the air. "What are you saying? He was as much your son as mine."

"Was he?" he asked explosively. It was clear that it was a question he had longed to ask.

Bewildered, she rose to her feet. "How can you ask me this? You are my husband. He is your son, as is William."

Her husband sucked in his breath as if he had refrained from taking a breath for a good deal of time. I thought perhaps he held back a sob as well.

I was obliged to rise, dismayed at the mayhem I had prompted. "Mrs. Gilbert, it pains me to have your honor so questioned. It is only on account of Johnny's death. I must leave no stone unturned. Please, let us sit. It is your husband's turn to be questioned now."

Slowly, she lowered herself into her chair; her expression offered no clue as to her emotional state. Mr. Gilbert demonstrated an unwillingness to reclaim his seat, but once his wife had obeyed, he did as well.

"Thank you. Now, Mr. Gilbert, in the recent past I have seen you in the company of a young woman on two occasions. It needn't be said that it is unsuitable behavior for a man mourning his son. That, combined with your behavior on other occasions when we have met, I have wondered if perhaps John was not your natural son. I perceive that you have wondered the same."

He nodded very slightly and stole a glance at his wife. "She has said that he *was* my son. I believe her."

"But you confess that you had previously believed that he was not."

Silent, he stared down at his knees whilst his wife looked at me, astonished.

"How dare you suggest that it is my husband who has done this to Johnny!" she said in a voice stronger than I had heard her use since Johnny's death. "He is an honorable man! I shall explain the young lady to you since he will not. My husband's brother died some years ago. It is his daughter, who is enjoying her coming out, whom he has been escorting. Under the circumstances, it is not at all seemly; I confess that I do not entirely like it. However, as her uncle, he has been the only father she has had for some time and he did not wish to deny her. Fortunately, a man is not required to adhere to the rules of mourning as rigorously as a woman," she added as she smoothed the folds of her black bombazine gown.

"I beg your pardon, Mr. Gilbert. And, Mrs. Gilbert, I must beg yours, also. I did not wish to believe that anyone in this house could possibly have hurt Johnny. And yet, if I am to find who did, I must ask a good deal of difficult questions. I pray that you can forgive me."

"Find who did this to *our* son, and all shall be forgiven," Mr. Gilbert said. His wife smiled and held out her hand. He folded it in both of his, brought it to his lips, and kissed it with infinite tenderness.

I felt decidedly *de trop* and looked quickly away whilst the beast that ate at my insides availed itself of another meal.

"My dear William!" she suddenly cried. "He must be freed! I do not know how I shall endure it if we are to lose him, too."

At her words, a wave of determination rose from the soles of my feet and up into my chest. I could not fail her. "I shall do everything in my power to do so. He has asked me to express his deepest sorrow for the loss of his brother, and the deepest love for the two of you." He had not said so, but it was the truth nonetheless. "He is a good man, and I am honored to call him my friend."

Both hung their heads and wiped away tears. I deemed it time for me to take my leave and, slowly, I rose to my feet.

Mr. Gilbert looked up. "My lord, a moment; due to the circumstances, Johnny's funeral was a private one. Please do not construe your lack of an invitation to be due to any other consideration."

Shocked that it had happened without my knowledge, I managed to mumble a remark. "Of course. I am desperately sorry." In deference to their grief I bowed far more deeply than necessary, and made my way to the door. As I quit the room I looked over my shoulder to see them with their hands entwined, their heads together and bent over the tears that fell as if from one set of eyes. I ought to have been happy for the Gilberts, satisfied that I had done away with the needless pain that had lain between them. I felt only desolate.

I held back tears of my own as I exited the house. I waved away the carriage and walked back to Canning House, one hand holding fast to the black band around my upper arm. It was a short journey and the day still young, but I found myself exhausted. Retiring directly to my room on the second floor, I removed my shoes and cravat which I tossed into a corner with as little ceremony as I had Willy's filthy clothes. As I could not remove my close-fitting coat on my own, I lay myself on the bed as I was and closed my eyes. I thought at first that I might lie there with my sorrow forever, but I soon fell into a welcome oblivion.

It was dark when I was awakened by a knock on my door. "It is open," I called, unsure of who might stand on the other side.

Canning entered and stood over the bed, his arms akimbo. "Trev, are you quite well?"

I struggled into a sitting position as the seams of my waistcoat bit into my sore ribs. "Indeed, yes. Why do you ask?"

"Only that it is unlike you to sleep at this time of day, not to mention that you are nearly fully clothed. I should be tempted to think you have only slept late save that you still wear your jacket."

I rubbed a hand over my face. "I ought to acquire a valet

of my own, but where shall you put him?" The Canning townhouse was tall and spacious but it did not have the commodious servants' quarters found in their enormous pile in the country.

"Pray, do not take this amiss, but you might have a dozen valets if you moved back into Silvester House."

"I shall take it under consideration," I said, though I rather doubted that I would.

Canning gave me a knowing smile. "We are going to Covent Garden for a play. Joan thought you might enjoy a diversion."

"I should like that, though I doubt it shall move me any closer to knowing who has killed Johnny Gilbert."

"You might be surprised. The change might do you some good. Heaven knows you could do with some of that."

"If you say so," I said with a smile.

"Excellent! Dinner is at eight and then we shall proceed." He opened the door and was about to leave when I stopped him with a question.

"Might I invite a guest?"

He looked surprised. "Of course. We should be delighted to have a friend of yours along. It is too late to inform Cook of guests, however. Perhaps you might invite him…or her…to meet us at the theater at the foot of the grand staircase in the entrance hall."

"Yes, I think that would be best," I replied, without satisfying his curiosity as to the identity of my intended guest.

"I shall send up a footman to deliver your invitation, shall I?"

"Yes, thank you." Before Canning had fully shut the door behind him, I rose and went to the escritoire to pen a note to Miss Woodmansey. To abide in her company without Rey present was an opportunity I could not refuse. As she was being invited to the Cannings' box, I felt it not in the least required to invite her overbearing mother. I wrote out my invitation with a glee that threatened my perfect penmanship, sanded the parchment, folded it, and wrote the direction on the outside. I blew on the ink to ensure it was dry before I slipped it under the door for the footman to take away.

I then turned to my wardrobe to select an ensemble that was certain to make the most of my few beauties. My black velvet breeches and long-tailed coat suited me very well. It was to be worn with a waistcoat in the same pale blue as my eyes and a sapphire stickpin. Resolved to look my best, I rang for the valet before Canning had the chance. As such, I was dressed and ready to leave my room long before eight o'clock. I repaired to the study to warm myself by the fire until the dinner gong rang. When I heard a rustling of skirts, I looked up to find Canning's wife, Joan, a lovely lady with brown eyes and hair and a soft Scottish burr.

"Ah, Julian, how good it is to see you!" she said as she came to my side.

I sprang to my feet and kissed her on the cheek. "It must be a sen'night since I've so much as laid eyes on you."

"Yes, George Charles has been sickly again and I have sat up with him most nights. I confess, I am worn to a thread and only hope that I shall be able to keep my eyes open for the duration of the play. You needn't fear; 'tis not the Scottish one," she said with a twinkle in her eye.

"I have no quarrel with *The Tragedy of Macbeth*. As for the little one, I am sorry to hear that he has been ill. He always seemed to be the halest of boys. I am persuaded he shall make a full and swift recovery."

"I do hope that you are correct," she said briskly as she adjusted her pearls via the mirror over the mantel. "He is such a dear, wee lad, but it seems never to fail that he comes down sick at the most inopportune moments: each and every time we arrive in London for the Season, it seems."

"Perhaps there is something in the air that does not agree with him."

She turned to me in wonder. "I have said the same thing, but George does not agree. Now he shall have to listen to me."

"'There is nothing wrong with your notions," I said gallantly. "He is merely being disagreeable."

"You are right, of course. He still frets that he was passed over for Prime Minister in favor of Perceval. I wonder if he shall ever recover."

I opened my mouth to offer my opinion on the matter, but her husband appeared in the doorway just as the gong rang.

"Shall we go in?" he asked, arm held out to his wife.

She went smilingly to his side and we proceeded to the dining room. As I took my seat I noticed that the table was, as always, beautifully laid and lit by copious candles. The Cannings rarely stinted on anything, especially not white wax candles. There was always a new one in my candlestick on the table by my bed each morning regardless of how little of it I had used the night prior.

"What play do we see tonight?" I asked.

"*All's Well That Ends Well*," Canning replied.

"That's the one that takes place in that strange country," Joan remarked. "Not Spain, not France, but…"

"Catalan," I said, despite my tongue having turned to lead.

"Is that not from whence that fellow hails? The one who stays with Lady Vawdrey?" Canning asked.

"Yes." I returned my fork to my plate and contemplated its contents. It seemed as if the fish was staring back at me.

"What is it, Julian?" Joan asked. "Is the cod not to your liking?"

I offered a wan smile, one that doubtless added to my sickly appearance. "It has proven to be a difficult day. I called on my friend William Gilbert, where he is held for the murder of his brother."

"Oh, yes!" Joan breathed. "I am so very sorry. I ought to have mentioned it sooner only, in my fatigued state, I had quite forgotten about it. George has said that you are doing all that you might to absolve the poor, wee soul."

"To put him to death would be but another murder." I picked up my glass and replaced it again without drinking. "I have stumbled upon only one clue that might be of use in his release. It seems that the only way to prove his innocence, however, is to find who has actually done it."

"Yes, the information in regard to his shirt is a compelling clue to his innocence," Canning mused. "However, until that fact is verified by the constable who arrested him, we have nothing."

The shirt! I thought how carelessly I had tossed it into

the corner of Willy's chamber and knew that I must retrieve it as soon as possible. Suddenly it was all I could think about. My delight at the prospect of spending the evening with Miss Woodmansey had vanished.

I spent the remainder of the meal as a spectator of a different play; one that centered around two people who are very much in love. Though I considered Canning to be as a father to me, he was only thirty-seven at the time, his wife even younger. Their marriage had enjoyed a sufficient number of years to deepen their affection for one another, but was still recent enough that it had not grown stale.

I attempted to imagine Miss Woodmansey and myself caught up in such delicious banter and could not; the man from Catalan was there at every turn. Bedeviled, I wondered what she might think of having been invited to a play that partially takes place in the country from which her beau hails. It was about as far from a declaration of love that one could muster.

Though I made certain to pick up my fork and bring it, laden with food, to my mouth at regular intervals, I ate very little. Despite that, I was not the least bit hungry as we boarded the carriage and started out for Covent Garden. I was fiercely glad that we were not to stop at Grosvenor Square to collect Miss Woodmansey. I required more time to put aside my melancholy.

It was not a long journey from Mayfair to Covent Garden. I might have walked it in less than a half hour. However, the roads were thick with carriages of every variety on their way to various entertainments. It was the Little Season, after all, and much of Society was in Town.

We did well enough along Bruton Place and on to Regent Street, but made very slow progress from there on. I began to fidget and be anxious that Miss Woodmansey should be forced to wait for us an unconscionable amount of time.

It was with decided relief that I emerged from the carriage into the crisp, night air. I followed the Cannings into the opera house, my stomach flopping about like a live fish in a kettle. I half-hoped for, half-dreaded the moment I should see her standing at the bottom of the grand staircase. It would prove to be the pinnacle of my evening, of that I was certain.

As we made our way through the crowd, I ran my fingers along the buttons of my waistcoat, tugged at the sleeves of my jacket, and checked the seams on my opera gloves. All seemed well save the scar at the corner of my mouth; there was little I could do about that save adopt a smile much too broad for a marquis to offer all and sundry.

However, when I finally clapped eyes on her I could not keep my lips from breaking into a wide grin. She stood facing away from our approach, her golden hair piled high upon her head, her gaze fastened to the doors leading to the lowest level of the theater itself. I delighted in watching as she plied her fan to ward off the heat of the enormous chandelier over her head. She put the other hand to her hair as if to ensure every silky strand was in place. My smile grew wider.

The Cannings drew away so that I was the first to approach her. "Miss Woodmansey," I said, prompting her to finally turn her head in my direction. "I am delighted that you accepted my invitation." I knew that I yet smiled like a loon, but I could not persuade my lips to do otherwise.

She stared up at me, as if seeing me for the first time and best pleased by what she saw. "My lord, I must thank you for the invitation." She held out her hand, which I took and kissed without actually brushing my lips against the white purity of her glove. "May I make you known to my good friends, Mr. and Mrs. George Canning?" I turned to him as he drew his wife forth to properly greet Miss Woodmansey.

"Mr. Canning," she breathed, "it is my great honor to meet you. And you, Mrs. Canning," she said with a deep curtsy for both.

I did not well endure the ensuing small talk. At long last, I was able to take Miss Woodmansey's arm in mine and proceed up the stairs to the Cannings' box. They took the seats at the front, leaving two slightly farther back for me and my guest. I drew her by the hand to sit in the chair next to Joan's and sat down on the last. As we settled into our seats, I felt a thrill invade my heart. She had come!

"The theater is very crowded tonight, is it not?" Miss Woodmansey pointed out.

I looked around and noted that every box, as well as the ground floor, was overflowing with humanity. "I suppose that is what accounts for the absolute hum in the air. I wonder if we shall be able to hear the actors above this bedlam?" I asked with a chuckle.

"I, for one, shall not mind in the least. I prefer to study the audience." She took a pearl-handled lorgnette from her reticule and balanced it across the bridge of her nose. "It would seem that the Duke of Rutherford is in attendance."

I felt my face flush and thanked the gods that Rey had not disclosed the name of the man who had supplied me with the scar. Very slowly I turned in the direction she indicated. I had no trouble in spotting the white-powdered wig of the duke. The fact that his wife sat beside him only made matters worse. I felt a flutter on my arm and was astonished to see that Miss Woodmansey had laid her hand upon it. She was gazing up at me with an expression so tender that the beast in my belly went utterly still.

I covered her hand with my own; to my astonishment she did not draw hers away. It had been a dreary six months since the duel and my ostracizing. And now it was as if the sun had broken through the clouds at last! Without disturbing the point of our union, I settled more deeply into my chair. For the remainder of the play, nothing proved capable of disturbing my equanimity: not the mention of Rey's country of Catalan, not the proximity of Rutherford, nor even that of his lady wife. The exception would be the moment the performance came to an end, and I was forced to rise and contemplate the beginning of the end of our time together.

"Miss Woodmansey," I said as I escorted her from the box, "I have not enjoyed an evening so much."

She smiled up at me, her expression coy. "I do not believe you heard a word of what was being said."

"How could I? The roar of the audience never ceased," I said with a deflective laugh. I had no wish to confess to wool-gathering, but I had underestimated her clear-sightedness.

"I had thought you to be enjoying quite the reverie."

There was no censure in her voice but I heard what I wished to hear. "Shakespeare is not my favorite." It was a lie.

"Then why have we come here tonight?" she asked, aghast.

Whether her dismay was for my lack of taste or my lack of discretion, I could not know. "I had thought that to be most evident." I looked down into her shining face and offered her a generous smile, one I knew looked as a smile was meant to.

She peeked up at me out of the corner of her eye and bit her lip, as if forcing back a smile of her own.

We had reached the grand staircase and I tightened my hand over hers to ensure her safety. The journey down these stairs was far different than that of the night prior, and I reveled in the light that revealed the truth to one and all: Miss Woodmansey was with me. Rey could have his moment with his arms around her in the dark of the Manwaring staircase; I had this very public moment. I had never felt happier.

Time passed far more quickly than a journey through crowds and a long wait in the damp, dark night for a carriage should have. At some point the Cannings had joined us and we spoke of this and that, but I could not say specifically what. I was conscious only of her tiny hand on my arm and mine atop it. When the moment came to assist her into the carriage and her hand finally slipped from my arm, the cold rushed in to banish any lingering warmth she had left behind.

I stood as if in a daze, watching her small face in the window of the coach as it pulled away and then for longer after. It took an arm on my shoulder from Canning to bring me out of my thoughts.

"She is a lovely young woman," he said.

"Indeed, she is; remarkable as well."

"Joan and I should like to know her better. Perhaps she would like to have dinner with us next week."

"Oh, yes, that would be lovely," Joan said over her shoulder just before she disappeared into the blackness of her own coach.

Canning and I followed, and settled ourselves against the velvet squabs. Watching the two of them together did not cause the pain it had at dinner. Rather, it was a pleasure to imagine how, one day, perhaps Miss Woodmansey and I might carry on just as they had.

When the carriage pulled up in front of Canning House, I wished to keep my thoughts to myself. I did not look forward to any awkward questions from Canning or his renewed insistence that it was time to return to Silvester House. "I believe I shall go for a walk," I informed them. "Thank you for the lovely evening."

"Of course," Joan said. She exchanged a look of repressed excitement with her husband, who merely shook his head. I knew that they each hoped the evening signaled the beginning of something quite wonderful nearly as much as did I. With an ambiguous smile, I took my leave and started down the walkway towards Manwaring House. To go the other way would mean to pass by Gilbert House, a circumstance I could not abide at the moment. The day had been a grim one, and I had no wish to disturb the beauty of its end.

A cold wind threatened to blow the hat from my head, and I turned up the collar of my many-caped greatcoat against the chill. Manwaring House was so deep in shadow as I passed I nearly missed it. I paused to admire the flickering of the light on the white and black checkered porch as the wind blew the clouds across the moon. The pleasant scent of wood smoke filled the air, and dry leaves from the plane trees skittered at my feet. Suddenly, a gust of wind dragged them all into a funnel of air and chased them down the walkway as if they could not wait to depart Manwaring House. It was then that I heard the scream.

Chapter Eleven

The sound chilled me to the bone, but I had myself half-convinced it was my imagination. Then I heard it again; it was fainter this time. I strained my ears, but I did not hear another. Moments passed with nothing to be heard but the scratching of the dry leaves along the pavement. When the rain began to patter against those still clinging to their branches, I retraced my steps and took refuge in Canning House.

When I rose the next morning, I thought the screams I had heard nothing but a dream. I remained long abed, took my breakfast of rolls and hot chocolate on a tray, and turned my face towards the weak rays of the sun that made their way across my counterpane. I was uncomfortably aware that I enjoyed a life full of simple pleasures made luxurious in contrast to what Willy endured. Fully aware that I must visit him again and offer him my most profound apologies, I still could not bring myself to stir from my bed.

Time and again I attempted to banish Willy from my mind in favor of a daydream of the life I planned to lead with Miss Woodmansey. Visits to the opera were only the beginning. There were picnics in the park, jaunts to Piccadilly Circus where I would buy her ribbons for her hair, fireworks of various kinds at Vauxhall Gardens, all chemical to be sure, and a grand wedding at St. George's in Hanover Square to which to look forward. We would look a sight standing in front of God and the altar, the top of her high-poke bonnet failing to brush as far as my shoulder, but the notion pleased me in the extreme.

Nevertheless, try as I might, Willy would not go. A new beast gnawed at my belly: Guilt. Not only need I apologize to my friend, but I needed to acquire that shirt. I felt no sense of urgency; the shirt was sure to lie where I had put it for eternity. However, the acquisition of the garment was only a portion of what must be done. I needed to discover the constable who took Willy away and make him swear that Willy's shirt had been clean when he was found on the drive of Gilbert House with that knife.

In the meantime, I realized that I must inspect the area steps of Manwaring House. Whatever it was I had heard the night prior, it had originated from there; of this I was suddenly certain. The notion had the power to compel me from bed and ring for the valet. My ribs were still bruised; more than that, to dress on my own seemed an affront to Willy. If a man as noble as he required assistance to dress, then a man full of foibles such as I certainly must. It mollified the guilt which I suspected had been keeping company with the loneliness all along. It only took better knowing the tragic details of Willy's life these past few years to fully rouse it.

When the valet had left, I stared at my reflection in the mirror. I raised one brow so that it was parallel to the angle of the scar in the corner of my mouth. Nothing had changed; I still looked full of disdain, arrogance, and bitterness. I relaxed my brow, and smiled so that the uninjured side of my mouth curved to the same height as the other. This was a face I did not much recognize; I had not been in the habit of laughing at myself in the looking glass. I owned that I looked far younger, innocent, and ingenuous, but it was not the proper demeanor of a marquis. I turned from the mirror, determined to put my scornful self to work in saving Willy.

I strode first across the square to call on Señyor Rey. I was led to the study on the ground floor, so like that of Canning's, and waited for my Catalanian friend to join me. However, when he walked into the room I could not look him in the eye.

"Señyor Rey!" I bellowed to the painting over the mantel. "I have come to invite you to accompany me on a quest to inspect the grounds of Manwaring House."

"But of course! I have just finished with Lady Vawdrey."

I supposed he referred to her lesson in the Catalan language. However, I could not find it within myself to mourn if Rey were in fact a lecher who preyed on those of Lady Vawdrey's stamp. Any man worth his salt would make it his duty to ensure that such a man did not walk off with a prize such as Miss Woodmansey. This thought gave me the courage to look into his eyes. What I saw was no villain, but my friend whom I had betrayed as surely as if I had run off with his intended.

I sighed. "Señyor Rey, there is something I must tell you."

"What is it, my lord?" he asked, his face glowing with affection.

"I invited Miss Woodmansey to attend the theater last night."

He became very still. I do not think he so much as breathed for half a minute.

"Did she accept this invitation?" he asked, his voice toneless.

"She did. We did not go alone. We were in company with the Cannings. It was all very proper."

"I see." He spun on his heel, went to the bookcase, and made a show of searching for a book.

"We saw *All's Well That Ends Well*, a portion of which takes place in Catalan." I could think of nothing else to report about the evening that might please him.

"The French portion of Catalan, yes," he said shortly, his back still turned to me.

"I hadn't realized there was a difference."

He turned again to face me, a book in his hand. "Only the language," he said with a flourish of his hand. "And the culture. And the territory." He shrugged and made what I could only call a moue.

This was a Rey I had not before met. As I did not much care for him, I cast about for a means to prompt the return of the old, familiar Rey. "After I returned home from the opera house, I took a walk."

"What does this mean to me?" he asked haughtily.

"I paused in front of Manwaring House. It was dark. And I believe that I heard a scream."

These were the words I needed. Rey's expression transformed from arrogant to one of alarm. "A scream? We must investigate immediately!"

"I thoroughly agree. This is why I have come. I suggest you don a coat; the air is nippy this morning."

Rey rang for a servant who arranged for his coat to be brought, along with his hat and cane, one so short as to be absurd. I refrained from saying so, however; I had already caused the man too much pain. Once we had fortified ourselves against the weather, we quit the house. I looked up to see that a bank of clouds obscured a weak sun. It was noon, but it looked as if it would be full dark within the half hour. I pushed my hat down tighter on my head. Rey and I walked along the square, the air between us uneasy, the sun coming and going with the vagaries of the wind. I questioned my wisdom in inviting him along after my revelation, but I had no wish to become alienated from him. For a man with so few friends, he was a gift not lightly refused. I decided it would be best to carry on as if nothing had happened in regard to Miss Woodmansey, but it was Rey who first broke the silence.

"It is strange what you have said about the scream, for something has been troubling me. The Manwarings' butler is an old man, this is certain. However, he is not *dement*. If he says he has heard screams in the house, what must I do but believe him?"

"I rather agree." I looked up at the sky through the branches of the plane trees that lined the pavement. The leaves quivered at the touch of my gaze, or perhaps it was the wind announcing the coming of winter. "After we have had a look around the house, we shall again question Short."

"*Perfecte*! We shall make him tell us all he knows."

I was tempted to admire Rey's benevolence for Willy,

but another motive for his enthusiasm occurred to me. Perhaps he believed that the sooner we found Johnny's killer, the sooner Miss Woodmansey would no longer seek out my company. I kept company with my thoughts (they were the most loyal of friends) until we reached the black and white tiled porch of the Manwaring townhouse. Turning at the area railing I began to clatter down the steps, and was instantly plunged into darkness. Startled, I turned to see the watery sun that shone just beyond Rey's head entirely swallowed up in another bank of black clouds. The steps were now mostly obscured, and the wind whipped up such that I was forced to hold onto my hat.

With far more grace Rey took steps to join me, and we felt our way, fingers to the wall, much as we had the night we had attended the gambling hell. Once I reached the bottom, I found I could go no farther. Rey fetched up against me and muttered a muffled "*oof!*"

"I beg pardon, Señyor Rey, but the toe of my shoe is caught on something. It is too dark for me to make out what."

He bent down and rose again too soon for me to have developed any confidence in his observations. "Your foot is caught in a cord of leather. It is," he choked, "wrapped around the neck of a girl."

My mind could make no sense of his words. "You are mistaken. Why would a girl sleep here? It is far too cold."

"My lord, this girl, she does not sleep. *Ella esta morta*," he murmured. "She is…dead."

I snatched back my entangled foot with such force that my shoulder slammed into the wall. "Dead? But how? Has she fallen?" Horrified, my heart began to pound into my chest and squeezed the air from my lungs. We stood, transfixed, unsure of what to do, until the wind blew the clouds from the sun and I could see what it was that Rey had seen already. 'Twas Sally. Throckmorton's Sally; a ribbon of red about her neck. Her mouth had been cut in both corners and the blood oozed out black as burnt custard. Against my will my knees bent until I crouched at her side, my shoulder wedged against the wall for support.

I stood before the pier glass in my cousin's rooms and studied the swath of bandages that obscured nearly half of my features. It was the first reflection of myself I had seen since the duel. The visible portion of my face looked as usual, save for the stubble that no one could be troubled to remove. Gingerly, I picked at the bindings that held the cloth tight against the corner of my mouth, and pulled. Blood, like blackened cake, clung to the bandage. I cleaned what was left of the dried blood to reveal a mass of swollen, red flesh. Through the center marched a curved line of hideous black crosses made of thread.

I steeled myself against the giddiness that threatened to collapse me atop the poor girl. "The cuts in the corners of her mouth; do you suppose it to be some kind of warning?" I realized that her death was no accident, and my stomach dropped.

"I do not know, my lord. A warning from whom?"

"The killer, of course. Perhaps this is a message to cease hunting for him."

Rey shook his head. "*No se.* But why does she wear a leather cord as well as a ribbon?"

I looked more closely. "The cord holds a key. There is

no ribbon—it's the mark from where her killer used the cord to finish her off. The cuts in her mouth must have been made sooner. That blood has already blackened. However, it's the garroting that killed her and not so long since."

Rey's eyes widened. "Do you suppose it was the screams of this poor creature that you heard last night?"

My stomach clenched at the thought. "What of the other screams? The ones to which Short referred? Had someone been torturing her for weeks? Months?" If so, I had failed the poor girl. My mouth went dry.

Rey turned his gaze up to the edifice that towered above us. "By someone in this house."

Swiftly, I removed my hat to catch what fell when I retched, but Rey took hold of it, dragged it to his chin, and voided the contents of his stomach before I had the opportunity. I did not wait for permission to do the same, and was grateful that it was a well-made, commodious example of its kind. I wiped my mouth with my handkerchief and looked around. There was no one. "We must alert the constable."

Rey took the hat from me. "Go. I cannot leave her," he said, his voice echoing against the walls of the small area.

For a moment, I considered banging on the front door and leaving the matter entirely up to Short. Then I thought better of it. "Rap on the kitchen door and ask for the boot boy. Do not tell anyone why." I reclaimed my once-beautiful beaver hat and went up the steps to empty it of its steaming contents. I heard Rey do as I asked and soon the boot boy emerged. I could see little of what he did at the bottom of those murky stairs, but I could hear his reaction well enough.

"Sally! Wot you doin' here?" he asked urgently. "You gonna be let go if you don' get back to work!"

There was a profound silence. "Sally?" he asked in a high, thin voice. "Wot's wrong w'you? Why won' you gi' up?" These poignant words were followed by a loud cry.

"Go fetch the constable," I called down to him.

He lost no time in darting up the steps. He flew past me, his white face streaked with tears and bootblack.

Once I was satisfied that he had gone in the right direction, I inspected my beaver hat. "Señyor Rey," I said as I pitched my beaver into the bushes. "Thank you for being here."

"It is nothing, my lord," he called up from his place at the bottom of the stairs.

"Ha! It is far more than that!" I knew I could put it off no longer; I went down the steps and crouched again over the bloodied body. "We must get that key before the constable arrives."

"But why, my lord?"

"There have been two deaths in the same square in a week. It cannot be a coincidence. Central to the first is the matter of a missing key."

"I see," Rey breathed. "Yes, but the cord must remain to demonstrate how it was that this poor girl died."

"I agree." Carefully I slipped the bloodied cord around her neck until the knot surfaced. I knew that Rey would have a difficult time in working it loose, so I had no alternative but to do it myself. Once I had the key I handed it to Rey, who took it with his handkerchief. I re-knotted the cord and slipped it back the way I had found it. I then rose to my feet, my fingers covered in blood.

Without waiting to be asked, Rey pocketed the key and handed me the handkerchief with which to clean off the blood as best I could.

"You are a good man, Señyor Rey." I gave him a curt nod, thrust my hands deep into my coat pockets, and returned to the top of the steps to await the constable. It began at once to rain.

"Many pardons for the ill usage of your hat, my lord," Señyor Rey called.

I stood, miserable, without words, the rain pelting my hatless head. The constable arrived in a timely fashion, or so I supposed. Having had no need to alert a constable in the past, I truly couldn't say. I do know that by the time he arrived I was chilled to the bone, and my neck ached where the rain had streamed down my hair and slipped beneath my greatcoat to wet the collar of my jacket.

The constable, whose youthful appearance denoted he was not likely to be any more experienced than I, glared at me as he approached. My hatless state most likely threw him off; 'twould be difficult to find an improperly-shod man in Mayfair. The closer he drew to my waterfall-tied neck cloth, Weston jacket, and waistcoat adorned with genuine silver buttons, the less surly was his expression.

He jabbed a thumb at the boot boy. "This one here claims to have seen a dead body." He sounded apologetic, as if he thought perhaps the boy was having a lark.

"Indeed, it is there at the bottom of the area steps." I followed his gaze down to see Rey staring back at me. "*He* is very much alive, despite being rather stiff at times." I gave Rey a brief smile before I recalled how twisted my terse smiles had become.

The constable did not look amused as he made his way down the steps in the driving rain. After a cursory inspection, he hurtled back up and heaved into the bushes in the same vicinity as my much-abused hat.

"Pray tell, is this your first corpse, Constable?"

He looked at me over his shoulder before he turned to heave again. He took a few deep breaths, wiped his mouth with the back of his hand, and turned to me. "Of course not! I was at the scene when the Gilbert boy was done to death by his own brother!"

"I believe you to be mistaken, Constable."

He drew himself erect and lifted his chin. "I ain't. This is me patch. Who else would have been fetched to Gilbert House? Tis the same square!" he insisted.

"Tell me, Constable," I said through gritted teeth. "What was William Gilbert wearing when you arrived?"

"Wot was he wearin'?" He stared at me as if I had run mad and then he grinned. "I remember, now! The simpleton was standing in the street wearing naught but a shirt!"

I adopted an air of studied indifference. "And what can you tell me about this shirt?" I asked as I examined my fingernails. They must have been found wanting, for I recall that I buffed them against my coat sleeve.

The constable shrugged. "It was just a shirt. It was long and very high quality, just as a swell's shirt ought to be."

"And in what condition did you find this shirt?"

He looked at me, perplexed. "Good, I suppose. What does this have to do with that girl by the kitchen door?" he asked with a jerk of his head in her direction.

"Perhaps nothing. Perhaps everything. I only wish to

know one thing and then you may be the one to pose the questions."

"All right, then," he said, crossing his arms tightly across his chest. "If that's the way it's goin' to be."

"Was the shirt clean or dirty? Think carefully now; a man's life is at stake."

The constable frowned. "I don' see as how it matters."

This admission was not in the least surprising. "As I have said, answer the question," I demanded, "and then I am at your disposal."

"I don' know. I truly couldn't say. It was not important."

"But it was!" I bellowed, play-acting having worn thin. "How does a man stab another without being spattered with blood?"

The constable staggered back in the face of my fury, his face white. "He did it. The eejit still had the knife in his hand! His parents ought to have kept that beast locked up in the attic. The world will be a better place when he's bin hanged."

My blood seemed to boil in my veins. Heady with the heat of it, I stepped menacingly towards the constable. Rey raced up the steps to forestall me, but I had the constable nearly in my hands before the Spaniard seized me by the wrists.

"No, my lord, you shall not do this thing!"

My fists were nearly level with his black curls; it would be the work of a moment to bring them crashing down upon his head.

When I did not relent, he tightened his grasp and gave my wrists a shake. "The man I know is of a character too chivalrous!"

It was if he had dashed cold water in my face. My arms went slack, the weight of their fall sufficient to break Rey's weakening hold. "I begin to see what Miss Woodmansey sees in you," I said as I turned away, rubbing my wrists. He was far more astute than I had realized. "See that the constable's questions are answered," I instructed over my shoulder. "I should be astonished should he arrive at any correct conclusions, but one must endeavor."

It still rained, so I made my way to the front door to stand under the roof whilst Rey answered the constable's questions. I could feel the gaze of the footman from where he stood by the long window alongside the door. I do not indulge in the smoking of cigars, but heartily wished for one regardless. It would have given me something to do other than ensure that I did not smudge the window with my wet coat, and seethe. That Willy should die because of the failures of such a gudgeon was intolerable!

As a man who had been assigned so much evil, I was determined not to be a back-biter. I willed myself to refrain from calling the constable every name for such a dull-wit as I could muster, and concentrated on a means to help Willy. When even Rey was forced to shout at the man through pure frustration, however, I knew that I had misjudged no one.

"Señyor Rey," I called as I hurried down the steps to the black and white tiled porch. "We have done our duty here. The constable knows where to find us should he have further questions." I reached into my pocket for a card and cursed when I could not find one. "Señyor Rey, you must give him yours."

"I shall, but to what purpose?" He drew one from his

vest pocket and handed it to the constable. "This is my name and occupation," he said, pointing to the card with his rather stubby finger. "This is my address. As you can see," he said as if speaking to a child, "it is in Barcelona. We are now in London, yes?"

The constable nodded.

"Very good. I stay at Hampton House in this same square." Rey turned and pointed down the street. "You may find me there; if you should require *his* assistance," he said, turning his finger towards me, "I shall take you to him."

I vented a breath I hadn't realized I had held captive. I was profoundly grateful that Rey had not revealed my name. I decided that if the sapskull of a constable wished to ask me further questions, he would have to find me first. I knew that asking any questions of him would be fruitless at best.

"Señyor, I believe a return to our friend at the gate is in order."

Rey looked at me blankly. It was clear that he did not remember to whom I referred. "Of course, my lord."

It seemed he trusted me absolutely. The man was a saint.

We went first to Canning House. After ordering out the carriage, I left Rey in the study to get warm whilst I went above stairs to towel my hair and fetch another hat. It was my best, the one I wore to the opera house with Miss Woodmansey, but it could not be helped.

I returned to the study to put my hands to the fire alongside Rey until the carriage was brought 'round.

"Who is this friend of ours at the gate?" he asked.

"The one with the nose at the workhouse."

"Ah, yes!" he replied. "You gave him money in exchange for information."

"Information I have not yet received," I pointed out. "I pray there is something he has to say that will exonerate Willy." I had to force my thoughts away from my sad friend's state or I would have been undone.

"Upon our return from the workhouse, we ought to stop at Gilbert House to ascertain whether Sally's key fits the kitchen door."

Rey nodded, and we said no more until the carriage arrived and we climbed aboard.

"Your friend, Mister William; shall we not soon call on him?" Rey settled deeply into the white velvet seat. He looked for all the world like a black seed in a sea of cream. "I fear that he is suffering too much from the loneliness."

I wanted to say that I had been to see Willy and that I would be happy to see him again. However, my lips refused to speak those words. "If you recall," I said rather too harshly, "our friend the doorkeeper was to discover whether Janie Cooper could be found in the dark room he spoke of with such loathing."

"Yes, and if she is there that says to us nothing. Is that not so?"

"Indeed. However, if she cannot be found within those walls, it means that another has disappeared from the workhouse, the very same from which Sally hails."

Rey cocked his head. "But I do not see how this information assists Mister William."

"It is only aids him if it aids us in finding the true killer."

As there was nothing more to say on the subject, I turned my head away. I did not wish to invite questions in regard to Miss Woodmansey and our evening together. I hoped I came across as mournful rather than recalcitrant. Either way, I knew Rey would honor my wishes. Not for the first time, I wondered what I had done to deserve such loyalty.

When we arrived at the workhouse, I approached the gate with eagerness. However, the doorkeeper was not at his post. I ran my cane along the metal bars; when it yielded no fruit I repeated my actions. Finally, an old woman came out of the house and made her laborious way to the gate.

She wrapped her wrinkled fingers around the metal bars and smiled brightly. "How may I help you?"

"Good afternoon," I said with a tip of my hat. "You must be the matron of this establishment."

"That is correct," she said kindly.

"Greetings. I wish to speak to the doorkeeper. He has information that I require."

Her face darkened. "The one with the nose?"

"Indeed! I should be grateful if you were to fetch him here."

"I am afraid I cannot." Her smiled slipped. "He is gone."

I was taken aback. "The big fellow?" When she nodded, I pressed her further. "Does he return or was he dismissed?"

She sighed. "Just gone," she replied shortly, her smile weakening further.

"Then what can you tell me about Janie Cooper?" I asked, dismayed. "Has she been found?"

She frowned. "She's gone, too," she said with a sigh. "Same as the others."

"Have you informed the constable?" I asked. I could find no fault in my assumption that he had to be more intelligent than the one who failed the residents of Berkeley Square.

"What good has that done me? 'Tis a puzzle to be sure, but no one cares what happens to these folks."

I was at a loss for words. A short time ago, I had not cared what happened to a one of them, either. "Well, then, can you tell me about Edmund Throckmorton?"

"Oh!" she cried in delight, her smile returning. "I was never so glad when one of my little ones found an important position out in the world. He arrived at the Foundling Hospital during my first year as matron there, years before I came to be here. Oh, he was a sight to see! Black curls, very much like those of your friend there," she said, pointing to Rey who had taken up his usual stance just to one side and slightly behind me. "And those eyes! They were as pretty as a flower! Still are! He comes to see me and bring things we have a hard time acquiring here."

"He came often to see Sally as well, is that not so?"

"Yes, Sally. She's a dear one! The two of them never looked at any other once they had seen each other. Like a fairytale it was!"

"I am so sorry," I said shortly. "Sally is dead."

Her eyes opened wide and filled immediately with tears. "No! It can't be! She just paid me a call last week!"

"Do you know who might have wished to kill her?" Rey asked.

"She was murdered?" She shrank back, aghast. "Are you certain it was no accident?"

"I'm afraid not. It is very plain."

She started to back away from the gate. "I don't know who would have done such a thing. All I can say is that it was *not* Edmund. He would never hurt her. He loved her. He told me that they were soon to marry, though not soon enough. The poor dear was anticipating their first child."

My heart sank like a stone. "I am very sorry to hear that. You remind me that I have a duty to inform her beau, if he has not heard already."

"I beg you to be kind to him." She drew close again and reached out her hand to grasp mine through the bars. "And give him my love." She released me without waiting for a reply, and returned to the house as quickly as her pains would allow.

I turned to Rey, who attempted to hide the fact that he wiped away a tear. "So it is left to us, is it not?"

He nodded, and I realized that he could not trust his voice to speak.

We climbed aboard the coach and returned to Hampton House in a heavy silence. When we disembarked, the sun shone exactly as if tragedy never happened in this world. The birds were singing and children were playing in the garden of the square, laughing as if they hadn't a care. It seemed ludicrous that anyone could be happy when there was so much sorrow in the world.

We entered the house, and went immediately to the first-floor salon in search of Lady Vawdrey. I decided it best to break the news to her. That way it would be she who informed Throckmorton of his sweetheart's demise. However, when we were ushered into the room, we saw that the two of them were, unfortunately, together.

Seated on the sofa across from his mistress, Throckmorton behaved as if he was her son. They appeared to be discussing a matter as frivolous as which of their invitations to accept for the week. As we entered the room, they both looked up in surprise. Instantly, he jumped to his feet to take up his customary place behind her chair.

"Lady Vawdrey," I said with a brief bow. "Señyor Rey and I have come bearing sad news. We believe it would be best if we spoke privately."

It was not Lady Vawdrey who replied. "There is no need," Throckmorton said in a voice hollow with grief. "I know what you have come to say. My Sally is dead."

Chapter Twelve

My mouth fell open in surprise. "Who has told you?"

"No one. I simply…know," he said, looking down at his hands. They trembled, as did his lips.

"Has the constable called on you?" If so, I wished to correct any of the misrepresentations he was certain to have delivered.

"A constable? Here?" Lady Vawdrey cried as she twisted her head to look at Throckmorton. "Who is this Sally?"

"I wished to tell you, my lady, but I feared you would disapprove." He took a deep breath and lifted his chin. "She is a housemaid for Lady Clara."

"A housemaid and *you*?" Lady Vawdrey accused. "How could you, Edmund? You are meant for better things!"

Throckmorton seemed to dissolve at her words. His hands dropped to his sides, his shoulders slumped, and his legs quivered such that they threatened to deposit him on the floor. "There was no one but her," he said, tears streaming down his face. "She was the most beautiful girl I have ever seen."

I knew he exaggerated, but it is often said that love is blind. "Mr. Throckmorton, can you tell us anything that might help us discover who did this to Sally? It is very likely that she and Johnny have been deprived of their lives by the same person."

"No!" Lady Vawdrey insisted, her lips warped with displeasure. "Whoever killed John Gilbert could have nothing to do with a housemaid. Where is the sense in that? I would suggest it was her lover who did it if Throckmorton weren't he."

"Which reminds me." I turned to Throckmorton. "The matron at the workhouse sends her love. She is very sorry to hear of Sally's death, as well." I did not mention the baby. I doubted Lady Vawdrey would be able to carry on under the weight of such news.

Throckmorton took no notice of my words. Instead, he collapsed into the chair next to his mistress. "I cannot credit it. How can she be gone?" The shock was settling upon him. I wondered how he could be so certain of what I was to say, and yet be so appalled when I had said it.

I looked to Lady Vawdrey. He was her man, after all. She, however, seemed put out in the extreme and had turned away from him.

It was Rey who came to the rescue. "Drink this," he said as he held a glass of something strong to Throckmorton's lips.

He obeyed, his throat and lips the only portions of his body that stirred.

Rey placed the glass on the table and joined me. "My lord, should we not question him about the key?" he murmured.

"Do you think he is capable of giving a coherent response?" I wondered.

"I shall ask him, yes? And then we shall see."

Rey returned to put the glass again to his lips. "Mr. Throckmorton, do you know anything about a key?"

He shook his head, but I saw how his body stiffened. Whether it was the drink that gave strength to his spine or fear, I did not know.

"I regret having to say such things to you," I apologized, "but Sally was found with a key on a cord around her neck. Do you know its purpose?"

He sat up straighter, licking the moisture from his lips. "It must be a house key. Why should she not have one?"

"Should she? Keys are meant to be in the possession of the housekeeper," I pointed out. "You of all people should know that."

"Of course. However, this key is not to any door at Manwaring House. It's merely an ornament."

"So you do know of it?"

"Well…yes. I gave it to her." He plucked the glass from Rey's fingers and drank.

"Then you know which lock it fits?"

"It's not about the lock it fits. Rather it's a symbol." He offered a wan smile. "We hoped to one day marry and set up our own establishment."

"With a housemaid?" Lady Vawdrey demanded. "When everything I have is yours?"

He turned to stare at his mistress. "You don't truly believe I would live here forever?"

"But why should you not? It shall be yours when I am gone. Who else should live here?"

Throckmorton sat as if stupefied. Perhaps the drink had been too much for him.

"From whence does it come?" I asked, in hopes of guiding the conversation back to the key.

He turned to look at me, dazed and uncomprehending. "From whence did what come?"

"The key, Mr. Throckmorton, "the one that Sally wore."

"I don't recall." He looked down at the glass in his hands. "I found it. How do you know of it?"

I had no wish to deflect the conversation with talk of our discovery of Sally at the bottom of the area steps. "I should prefer to talk about the key at the moment. I realize you have been dealt a dreadful blow, but it is important that you remember where you came by it."

"Well, I...I found it here in the square." His brow furrowed. "Oh, yes, I do recall! It was the morning that you saw me in wait of you at Gilbert House. You may recall that I bore a letter for you from my lady."

This was an interesting development, indeed. "Where at Gilbert House did you find it?"

"It was in the dirt where I was standing behind a tree." His gaze as he looked at me was unwavering.

"Did you not suppose it belonged to someone?"

"I didn't consider it for a moment. I had no thought for anyone save Sally and my dream for us."

"You do not wish," Rey asked, "to be a gentleman and live here until the end of your days?"

"Not without my Sally." He stared past me, the whites of his violet eyes reddened and his lids heavy.

"This is all utter nonsense!" Lady Vawdrey cried. "Edmund, you are meant for the life of a gentleman. Whoever your father was, he was doubtless a gentleman as well."

He snapped back to life. "I was born on the wrong side of the blanket!" He favored Lady Vawdrey with a look no servant ever bestowed on a master. "Is the word 'bastard' not the very definition of one who is not a gentleman?"

"But your blood, Edmund! Those eyes do not come from common stock!" Lady Vawdrey urged. "You are extraordinary!"

"In whose opinion? When you are gone, who shall be my champion? Who shall say I am worthy of this place? No one!"

"But..." Lady Vawdrey wailed.

I watched this scene of growing despondency with increasing impatience. I bent to whisper into Rey's ear. "Something is troubling me. I think we must see Sally again."

He looked at me in horror. "What? You wish to visit the *dipòsit de cadavers*?"

"If by that you mean the mortuary, then yes: the deadhouse."

"But why?" he said with a shudder.

"I fear that I missed a matter of importance." Something about her smile niggled at my brain, but I could not think what. "First, however, we should put her key to the kitchen door of Gilbert House."

"*No!*" Rey insisted. "First, we must dine."

I found I had no desire to argue. My appetite returned, and I could not account for its condition once I visited a house of the dead. We went again to my club where we dined on pig's feet and truffles alongside Timbale *Milanais*. It was delicious, but I had no wish to see it again.

I bespoke a bottle of brandy which I tucked into my coat pocket in the case some Dutch courage was required.

Our journey to the mortuary was one of incorrect information, false turns, routes up the river and back, and copious frustration, but we finally arrived at the squalid edifice in which Sally's body reposed. I was forced to part with the brandy in order to be allowed into the chamber where she lay, but it was well worth the sacrifice.

It was with some trepidation that we stepped across the threshold of the foul-smelling room. Pausing, our breathing shallow, we blinked rapidly in the fetid darkness as we attempted to make sense of our surroundings. The light of a single candle threw eerie shadows on the walls and ceiling, but little else could be discerned. In short, it was the sort of room in which one should expect a colony of bats to come swooping down upon one's head. Even so, I took a step forward and peered at the table that bore the candle. It kept company with a mound that looked as if it might be a body under a bedsheet.

Gagging at the odor, we made our way to the table and pulled down the sheet far enough to identify the mound as Sally. Rey quickly turned away, but I could not take my gaze from her. No one had taken the trouble to wash off the blood and in the light of the single flame it seemed black as night against her moon-white skin. Without additional illumination, there was little more to be seen. I turned around to find that Rey had already discovered more candles, which he lit with a spill touched to the existing flame. We arranged them around her head and shoulders and I bent to study her pitifully mutilated face. Looking at her brought to mind a question I had forgotten to ask: how did Throckmorton know she was dead?

"Señyor Rey, do you see those slices in her lips?" I ran a finger along the long horizontal wound in her bottom lip. "It's as if someone wished to open it up." I looked more closely and saw what it was that had troubled me. "See here? These teeth—those that aren't blackened with blood are far too white. I met Sally the day I questioned the servants of Manwaring House. I took note of the fact that her teeth were quite poor."

"It is very strange," Rey murmured as he peered into Sally's mouth. He ran a finger along the teeth and nodded. "Just as I thought: these teeth are carved from ivory...the whitest, purest ivory."

"Of course," I murmured. "I feel that I have seen these before." I could not recall where. "Many older people wear entire sets of false teeth, some of them made of those taken from cadavers. However, those are to replace the ones that have been lost to restore the appearance and aid in chewing. Why would a young girl such as Sally need false teeth?"

"Perhaps it was because her teeth were not beautiful? Perhaps Throckmorton wished her to have the best?"

"The cost of such teeth would be well out of the means of a servant!"

"True, but Lady Vawdrey perhaps pays him more than any servant. But, ah!" Rey said, lifting a finger. "There is the missing diamond necklace to consider. Could he have stolen it to pay for such a treasure?"

"Indeed, yes, Señyor Rey! I admire your sound intellect. In point of fact, I cannot think of who else might have stolen it and not have been discovered. And yet, Throckmorton found Sally beautiful. I do not believe he would have been troubled by her teeth, even if she were minus one or two."

Rey somberly wagged his head. "*Es un misteri.*"

"A mystery, indeed," I agreed. I pulled away the sheet to reveal the rest of her body which I examined in a manner Rey considered ruthless.

"You shall break the bones if you do not take care!"

"I believe she is past caring," I riposted. I ran my hands along all four of her limbs and removed the shoes from her feet in search of bruises. Then I rolled her over, undid the tapes of her gown, and held a candle to her back. "See here, Rey. There are bruises across her shoulders, as if she had been beaten."

"Could they have been made when she was thrown down the steps?"

It was an interesting notion. "'Tis true; she could have been thrown down them rather than carried out onto the landing through the kitchen door. However, these bruises appear to be older than the day she has been dead."

"How are we to know when she died?" Rey asked.

"If the screams I heard were hers, then we can assume she was alive less than twenty-four hours ago. But we know nothing of the sort." I rolled her onto her back and pointed to the line around her neck. "This was mostly red and raw when we found her; now it is darkening like the blood that had already blackened her mouth. Surely the mark from the garroting would have been just as black if it had happened as long ago as the bruises, which must have already begun to fade when she died."

"You can ascertain such facts simply from looking at her body?"

"Surely a man who learned to sword-fight from the masters ought to have suffered numerous injuries; enough to study the behaviors of blood and bruising," I suggested.

Rey drew himself up to his full dearth of height and lifted his chin. "I have never been wounded, my lord."

I was taken aback. "Never? Not once?" His fencing master must have been more than merciful.

"I am at my best when it comes to defense, my lord," he crowed.

It was a notion I could willingly entertain if his arms, which I had never seen bared, were as thick-set as his fingers. "Bravo then, sir! I am proud to call you friend."

"As am I," he replied with a bow. "Now, let us be away from here. I can no longer be troubled to breathe this foul air."

As I replaced the sheet, I was nearly overcome with a wave of sorrow. I pulled together the tattered edges of my sensibilities whilst Rey blew out all the candles save one. Again, we paused as we adjusted to the darkness, whereupon we found our way out the door, down the passage, and into the vestibule. The man who had granted us access was not immediately visible, so we let ourselves out with a sense of supreme relief of body and mind.

When we emerged, we found that the day had darkened into full night. Gratefully, we dragged the crystalline October air into our labored lungs and stumbled to the waiting coach. It had been my intention to test the key at Gilbert House, but I longed for the oblivion of sleep. Rey and I sat across from one another, but never looked the other in the eye for the entire journey. When we drew to a halt in front of Canning House, he quit the carriage without a word.

I knew very well the emotions that drove him. It was my intention to go immediately to my room without speaking to a single soul, but when I walked through the front door I was ushered into chaos. Servants were scurrying to and fro' and I could hear Joan's voice as she issued instructions all the way from the second floor. The door to Canning's study opened and the butler emerged, his face red and his expression one of extreme forbearance.

"What is it, Moore?" I asked, but he rushed past me as if I were as insubstantial as a ghost. I went to the door of Canning's study and rapped upon it.

"Enter!" Canning barked, such that I nearly slunk away. My hesitation prompted him to open the door himself. He went about it so angrily that the pursuant rush of air sent the lace of his cravat quivering. "What do you want?" he demanded.

"I beg your pardon. It is not important." And yet, I wished to know what had caused such a disturbance in this household that I so cherished.

"No, 'tis I who must beg your pardon, Trev," Canning said as he waved me inside. "Sit down and have a drink, and I shall tell you all about it."

"Yes, do," I insisted, though I did not sit. The amount of time I had spent in the carriage throughout the course of the day was enough to dampen my desire to fold my frame for even a moment. "What has happened? It is bedlam!"

"George Charles has a cough, and Joan is persuaded that

he shall not recover in the London air," he said somewhat mockingly. "The plan is to depart for home early tomorrow morning."

"All the way back to Kilkenny?" I asked in astonishment. When his face darkened, I refrained from informing him of the role I played in Joan's desire to quit London. "I am sorry that he is ill, and hope that he shall soon recover."

"Hmmm," he grumbled. "Thank you. In the meantime I am closing up the house, and shall be staying at the Clarendon."

"You are to remain in London?" I asked in some surprise.

"I yet have business and duties to which I must attend. Though I believe it better for you to take up residence in your own house, you are welcome to stay on here." He gave me an assessing look and sighed. "You shall have to take your meals out. Joan insists on having Cook with her. She claims that George Charles needs her especial concoctions."

I began to perceive the true source of George's irritation. "Ah, I see. We shall all be sorry to see the back of Cook and her delicious dishes." I felt far more distress at the loss of the Cannings, however. "I am for bed. I bid you all a fond farewell."

"Trev, wait," George said as he tried to smile. "Have you learned anything new that shall exonerate William Gilbert?"

I shook my head in dismay. "Not that is of any use. However, I am determined that I shall. I feel that I am very close to learning the truth. When I have, I shall come to you at your hotel."

"See that you do." He turned away as if I had already gone, and I knew that I was dismissed.

I made my way up the stairs, threading my way between a maid who, in her hurry, dared to use the front stairs and a footman who did the same. I knew that it would be pointless to expect the valet to attend me amongst so much chaos, so when I came upon the boot boy in the passage I instructed him to follow me to my room. After he had helped me out of my jacket, I gave him a few coins in exchange for remaining behind until I could arrange for another valet. I then told him to go to the kitchen and bring me up a plate of bread and cheese. The moment he shut the door behind him I shuffled the shoes from my feet, tossed myself onto the bed, and fell instantly asleep.

I awoke the next morning to an eerie silence. Though I did not normally take much notice of the hum created by a household of servants as they lighted the fires, clattered up and down the back stairs, polished the railings of the front staircase, and hauled the cans of bathwater along the passage, I found that I regretted the loss of it. Neither did I hear the chatter of children, the patter of their feet as they ran along the passage outside my chamber door, or the bouncing of George Charles' ever-present rubber ball.

In dismay I sat up, and was instantly sorry. The air was frigid, and there were none left in the house to light the fire. The candle in its stick had not been replaced, and as I had not bothered to blow it out before I fell into slumber it was burned down to the wick. The water in the washstand had not been renewed, either. I dragged my dressing gown from the chair by my bed and wrapped myself in it before I put my feet to the floor. Happily, my slippers were where I had left them and I padded over to the hearth to see about lighting the fire.

Once I had got the flames going, I stepped into the passage to call the boot boy, and trod upon last night's plate of bread and cheese. I picked it up and went down three flights of stairs to the kitchen to rummage about in the pantry. I managed to find a clean plate, upon which I placed fresh slices of bread and cheese which I then carried back to my room. I ate my meager meal in front of the fire and quenched my thirst with the wash water from the day previous. It was time to find the boot boy.

I found him in the scullery polishing my shoes. "Boy, how does one acquire fresh water in this establishment?" In my experience, water had always simply appeared.

He left off working on my shoes, fetched a wooden pole with a can of water at each end, and slung it over his shoulders. I followed him up the back stairs as I dodged the water that splashed out of the cans at nearly every step. Once we obtained my room, I was surprised to see that the cans were not completely empty of their contents. He took up the bowl and tossed the wash water out of the window followed by what remained in the pitcher, which he refilled with water from the can. He then filled the decanter on the night table and planted himself in the middle of the room in wait of further instruction.

"Er, uh," I hesitated as I cast about for something to say, "be back here with my shoes in half an hour."

He nodded and slipped out of the room. He was certainly respectful, but I found that I longed for the sound of another human voice. I went first to the decanter, in order to banish the taste of the wash water I had drunk earlier. Then I washed, shaved, and dressed to the extent I could without the boot boy's help. I lingered a bit over the tying of my neck cloth. I supposed that the boot boy couldn't have done worse; perhaps better if he stood on a chair to undertake the job. As I struggled with the stiff linen, my mind continued to veer towards the scene at the mortuary. A cherished life snuffed out by someone's utter lack of charity. 'Twas intolerable, and I refused to allow my mind to dwell on Sally's sad fate for a moment.

Worse was the thought of Willy's fate if I failed to rescue him. The red line around Sally's throat was but a shadow of the bruised and bloodied skin that would ring Willy's neck should he hang. With a curse, I slammed my hair brush against the wall; it was useless anyhow. It could not restore the beauty to my face. It was a small thing compared to Willy's and Sally's woes, but somehow it was all of a piece. Each was an injustice that scarred in a visible and permanent way.

It was then that the boot boy appeared, and I pressed him into service as my valet. It would not surprise anyone to learn that the donning of my jacket took some time. Finally, he climbed onto the bed in order to overcome the disparity in our heights so that he might coax the jacket across my shoulders. We both heaved a sigh of relief when it was done. I donned the shoes he had brought with him, admirably polished, and made my way out of the room. The boot boy followed me down the front staircase and paused at the door as if in want of something.

"Well?" I asked him. Perhaps now he would speak.

Instead, he merely shrugged his shoulders. I drew another coin from my pocket. "You are to set up a cot here in the front hall. Thereby you may let me into the house at whatever hour I arrive home."

Solemnly, he took the coin and ran off in the direction, I presume, of the household cots...or his own cot, or someone else's. I had not a clue, nor did I much care. I took myself out through the front door and headed directly for Gilbert House. I had the key from Sally's leather cord in my pocket, and I intended to use it. I paused when I arrived at the façade of the house. Not for the first time, I marveled at how short a trip it was from Cannings, and yet it had nearly always seemed too far to visit Willy once he was no longer whole. I descended the area steps that, despite the low sky, did not have the vile appearance of those at Manwaring House, and made my way to the kitchen door on the landing at the bottom.

As quietly as I was able, I tried the latch to see if it was locked. It was early enough still that I supposed no one had yet had occasion to lift it. But what did I know? The servants of this or any household might have reason to depart at any hour of the morning. However, I was in luck: the door was held fast. I then inserted the key to the lock and was part amazed, part smug when it fit perfectly. I turned the key as quietly as I could manage, though I could do nothing about the sounds made by the shifting of the tumblers. Once the key was fully turned I pushed at the door, and it fell away from my hand. There was no doubt; I had in my possession the key that had opened the door the night Johnny Gilbert was killed.

I slid the key from the lock and went to the steps, my heart heavy. I felt that I ought to have been delighted at my discovery, but my success with the key only made Johnny's murder that much more of a reality. All my grief for Sally, Willy, even myself, was partially misplaced; Johnny's fate deserved a deeper portion of my empathy. All that was left for me to do for him was to find his actual killer. As I put my foot to the first step my legs felt like water, as if each would instantly dissolve at the slightest pressure. Somehow, as I shifted my weight back and forth, step after step, they carried me onwards and upwards.

Chapter Thirteen

I have little memory of what happened during the course of that day. I know that I endured a stupor of despair, but where or how I came to my senses or occupied myself for the duration I do not recall. At some point I found myself in Canning's study at the mantel, taking up one item after another and turning it about in my hand before replacing it, imperfectly, in its rightful place.

One of these was an invitation to a ball at the home of Mr. and Mrs. Leavitt. I thought it seemed familiar, as if I had heard the name at some point in the not too distant past. I waved it back and forth, the frigid air wafting into my face, until I recalled: the ball was at the home of the debutante Lady Vawdrey had wished me to woo the year prior. I had instantly dismissed Miss Jane Leavitt for the fault of not having been born to a man with a title. Since then, events had unfolded such that the memory appalled me. And yet, a year on the Marriage Mart had not made her a wife. I decided on the spot that I would attend. If it did not prove fruitful in my attempts to solve Johnny's murder, at least I should have the opportunity to see she whom I had so callously rejected.

I sprinted up the stairs, the previous weakness of my legs thoroughly gone, and hollered for the boot boy as I went. He made it up to the second-floor landing nearly as quickly as I, and together we created an ensemble that depicted me as the elegant, intelligent, and confident peer of the realm I had once been.

I stood at the mirror in my chamber at Silvester House as I dressed for what promised to be a superlative adventure. "Come away from there, Trev," Evelyn insisted. "When did you become such a dandy?"

"It could not have been prior to my close association with you," I murmured, coaxing an errant curl into its proper place. "'Tis in your shadow I walk," I quipped. "Would I be off to a duel otherwise?" I lifted my brow and gave him a speaking look.

Evelyn laughed. "What have I done to deserve you, Cuz?"

"Twas merely an accident of birth." I placed my high-crowned hat carefully on my head, slung my cape over my shoulders, took up my gloves and cane, and gave him a sardonic smile, the one that made me look a perfect Adonis.

As it turned out the boot boy was a dab hand at the tying of neck cloths, and I was more than satisfied with my appearance. I checked my final appearance in the pier glass whilst taking care to turn the scar away from my gaze. There he was: the man I had known, once upon a time.

"You've done well, boy." I assisted him to hop off from the chair he was forced to press into use. "I am readily certain that I shall be home late. Keep the fire in my room going, as well as the candelabra by the front door to light my way upstairs, ensure that I have a fresh candle in my stick, and be in your cot to open the door when I rap upon it."

The boy gave me his usual shrug, and with a flick of my

many-caped greatcoat I went out the door and down the stairs. I had been afforded a solitary coachman who had hitched up a pair of inferior horses to the curricle I kept at Canning House. It would be a drafty trip but it was not far, and I did not much care what happened to me as long as I could find the means to save Willy.

I arrived at the Leavitt home with cold feet (I resolved to next time ask the boot boy to heat some bricks for my journey) and a hot temper. The house, however, was as warm as toast. As I made my way to the ballroom, my various parts were soon restored to the correct temperature.

For the first time in months, I did not inspect the room for a suitable corner in which to ensconce myself. Rather, I looked about for Miss Leavitt. My motivations were twofold. One, I might possibly put myself in deeper favor with Lady Vawdrey by dancing with the girl. Two, a girl at her own ball was a veritable font of information.

It did not take long to locate her; diamonds glittered in her rich red hair and her gown was a confection of silver spangles over white silk. She was tall and slender, and moved with a grace that I greatly admired. As I watched, she turned to meet my gaze. Slowly, her mouth spread into a canny smile as if she knew precisely who I was and liked me in spite of it.

It came to me quite suddenly that I had never seen eyes so green or a more adorable sprinkling of freckles across so perfect a nose. Lady Clara's blunt-ended nose was elegant, but it lacked the perfection of Miss Leavitt's. I went immediately to her side and bespoke a dance. To my astonishment, she did not say me nay.

"My lord, the set just prior to supper has not been spoken for if you are of a mind to request it." She smiled again, and I felt giddy as if the entire room had shifted along with my expectations.

"I should be honored," I said with a deep bow. Indeed, I would be guaranteed the chance to lead her in to supper on my arm with such a placement. I rose from my bow to find her still standing as before, smiling, and not fled away. I was far too pleased to wonder at her lack of temerity or the location of her chaperone.

It was then that her father approached, his countenance thunderous. I did not remain to learn what had put him in such ill humor. I sketched a brief bow and took myself off to while away the time until I might dance with her. However, my gaze fell immediately upon Miss Woodmansey. She stood with her mother, Lady Vawdrey, and Señor Rey. They smiled and seemed to enjoy the company of one another. I thought Lady Vawdrey looked especially delighted. I feared it was because she had successfully matched another couple. If so, it must have been balm to her wounds; Throckmorton's failure to fall in with her plans could not but rankle. And yet, there was yet time for him to come up to scratch.

I stepped behind a potted palm to gaze upon Miss Woodmansey undetected. She ought to have appeared less attractive to me after the glory of Miss Leavitt, but she did not. I drank in the kindness of her smile, the compassion in her gaze, and the wit that flashed across her face. She seemed to exhibit these emotions most broadly when she looked upon Señor Rey. Though I doubted not that he fully deserved her admiration, I begrudged him it. I could not so much as contemplate losing her to Rey.

I nursed the longing in the pit of my stomach and made sheep's eyes at her until I felt a presence at my elbow. It was Lady Clara.

"Lord Trevelin! You and Miss Woodmansey?" she asked with a twitter. "She is not in the least suitable for you."

I felt myself frown. "I fail to see how it is any business of yours, Lady Clara."

"Matchmaking is every woman's business," she said with a coy smile. "Not that I claim to have the talent for it," she added. "No, I much prefer to make money at the hands of hapless gentlemen."

I liked her candor, and turned to engage her in further conversation. I admired her as well, especially her beautiful, perfectly formed teeth. "Lady Clara, your smile is exquisite."

She did not appear pleased by my compliment. "Thank you," she said, rather dully. "Robert likes me to look my best. He seems to be nearly satisfied."

I could make no sense of such a comment. "You are a beautiful woman," I said, my words thoroughly genuine. "It is my opinion that your current status should be good enough for even the most discerning of men."

This time she blushed in response to my compliment. "Oh, well, Robert…He doesn't like my nose." She put a hand on my arm and, laughingly, looked into my eyes. "He tells me he is going to take a knife to it one of these days."

I was more bewildered than I had been previously. "For what possible purpose?"

"Who can say? He fancies he can whittle it into a shape he prefers. Is it not ridiculous?" Her smile was wistful now. "He hasn't any idea how much the thought terrifies me."

"'Twould terrify anyone," I insisted. "But I am persuaded that your husband merely jests."

"Yes, of course," she agreed as she linked her arm with mine.

I was taken aback by her fond response. If she had any wish to seduce me, she had had a far more favorable opportunity to do so the week prior. "I believe you are in need of a friend," I suggested.

"Yes! I expect that you are correct." She smiled up at me with such perfect amity that I assumed her to be somewhat disguised. "I have been longing to tell someone what I have done, but I must be most discreet."

My spirits rose with her ingenuousness. I pulled her arm tighter against my side and drew her to a more private corner of the room. (The usefulness of corners was a subject upon which I had become adept.) "And what is it that you have done, Lady Clara?"

"I have had way too much wine." She made a moue, and ran a finger along my jaw just below the scar.

She had said nothing that was of the least use, and yet she had my utmost attention. "I do believe you are three sheets to the wind," I retorted. It was a remark designed to withstand the sensations roused by the touch of anyone's finger to my face in many months, save mine.

"That is most likely true!" she said gaily. "But it does not invalidate the fact that my husband is very angry with me," she mused as her finger skimmed along my bottom lip.

I caught her hand before she reached the flawed corner of my mouth.

"It's rather absurd; you look either to be always

smiling," she said, then dragged our hands over to the unblemished side of my mouth, "or perpetually sneering," she added as she dropped her hand to her side.

My hand fell with hers and glanced off her shoulder. She jumped as if someone had bellowed in her ear.

"I do beg your pardon," I said, aghast.

"It is nothing. Only, my husband is very angry with me." She looked as if she were about to weep. "I am losing money at my game nights, yet I fail to comprehend why it is of any consequence. My dowry was more than sufficient. Besides, the gaming hell was his idea from the start. What did he expect; that I should win every night? 'Tis not possible."

"Do the losses make him angry enough to harm you?" I asked out of genuine concern.

She shrugged. "There is no law against it. I am his wife, to do with as he pleases."

I did not agree, but it would solve nothing to say so. "Surely he can see that you are one woman against Dame Fortune. How does he expect you to prevent losses?"

She rolled her eyes. "I cannot say. But there are moments," she said more quietly, "when I am very much afraid."

I recalled the screams I had heard coming from Manwaring House and wondered if it had been she who had uttered them. And then I knew that I had been a fool. "Lady Clara, has your husband harmed anyone else? Any of the servants?" I asked leadingly.

Her eyes filled with tears but she did not look away. "There is no law against that, either."

"There is one against murder."

Her lips began to tremble as the tears slipped from her eyes and down her cheeks. "What am I to do?"

"I shall see to it that you are safe. But you must tell me what you know. You are aware that Sally is dead, are you not?"

She bit her lip and looked away. "Is she?"

"She was beaten, mutilated, and finally strangled."

"That is dreadful, but…"

"But what?" In my eagerness, I dared to take her hand and squeeze it.

I was shocked when she stepped into my arms and laid her cheek against the silver threads of my striped waistcoat. "She should not have become with child."

I could feel her trembling against my ribs and knew that she was far more frightened than she had admitted. "I do not understand. Why should anyone kill her for such?"

She pushed away and looked up at me, blinking back tears. "One would think that ridiculous, is that not so? Especially as it was my husband's child."

I searched her face for any indication of jealousy. "Lady Clara, did you kill Sally?"

"How can you ask that of me? Why do you not suspect Throckmorton? He had as much cause." She stared at me, enraged, then the light in her eyes dimmed and she calmed. "I have done something dreadful, but not that," she said wearily. "I needed money. Robert was so angry that I was losing nearly every night. I knew Lady Vawdrey would keep that necklace tucked away until the Little Season began. So, I had Throckmorton steal it for me."

"How did you dare to ask him?" I asked in

astonishment. "He looks to Lady Vawdrey as a mother. Why should he do anything to risk his position there?"

"It was on account of Sally," she said sadly. "He knew she expected a baby; he thought it his. He had some romantic notion of setting themselves up as gentry. As if a bastard and a housemaid could ever be that! At any rate, I threatened to send her back to the workhouse if he did not do as I asked."

"I should think she would prefer it to Manwaring House if what you say is true." I did not believe it, but I wished her to be the first to mention the manner in which people had been disappearing from the wretched place.

"Should *you* wish to live at the workhouse?" Her voice trembled.

It was not the reply for which I had hoped. Yet the fear in her voice was palpable.

"There is more. I promised Throckmorton money once I had sold the necklace."

"But you lied," I prodded. "You needed the money to appease your husband."

"I would have given the man what was left after I paid my debts, and gladly! But, I took it to a very discreet jeweler to have it valued, and…"

"Lady Clara, do not be afraid. Tell me." I again pressed her hand.

"Very well!" she said with a devil-may-care toss of her head. "The necklace; it was paste."

"Paste?" I could not account for such a thing. "Is Lady Vawdrey aware?"

"I could hardly say," she said with an arch of her shapely brow. "I sold it anyway for the pittance it was worth."

"And when you could not produce enough money to cover the money you lost your husband beat you, is not that correct?"

I nearly shuddered at the manner in which she smiled; sickly and sweet on the same pair of lips. "My teeth—they flew out of my mouth like sparrows fleeing from an owl on the hunt."

I heard a gasp; it was a moment before I realized it was I who made it. "And this is why you wear this set of false teeth!"

She pulled her lips tightly over the faux beauties and nodded. "Lord Trevelin, I implore you, do not forsake me! If you do, I shall go to prison."

I looked into her deep brown eyes, wet and imploring. "It is your husband's responsibility to make it right. What is yours is his, including that necklace. He might have had good reason to be angry at what you had done, but once he learned of it he should have taken the matter up with Lady Vawdrey."

"Perhaps he has already?" she asked hopefully.

I shook my head. "She has elicited my help in discovering what has happened to it."

Urgently, she placed both hands on my arm. "If you tell her the truth, my husband shall beat me again. Perhaps I shall not survive it. Please, my lord," she begged. "I cannot bear it!"

I considered her words. "You have endured much. If he were not such a brute, you would not have had any reason to steal the necklace. In truth, I have more important matters which require my attention; the identity of Johnny Gilbert's killer, for one."

She seemed to flinch, but her voice was as strong as ever. "Thank you! You cannot know how much it means. I have no wish to end up like Sally."

I opened my mouth to question her further on the matter of the housemaid's death, but something held me back. When I looked up, Lady Clara's husband approached.

I took several hasty steps backwards and offered my most effulgent smile. "Manwaring! I had not thought you in attendance tonight." Better for him to think I dallied with his wife than suspected him of abuse, or worse. His expression, however, gave away nothing as to what his suspicions might have been.

"Trev!" he cried as if we were old chums. "How good of you to call on us the other night. My wife and I should be delighted to entertain you again any evening when we are at home."

I found his perfectly appointed face more loathsome than usual, but hid my feelings for the sake of his wife. "Not as delighted as I should," I said with a wink for Lady Clara. I took her hand and kissed it before stalking away, and prayed that he would be deceived by my ruse.

It wasn't until I was tooling my curricle back to Canning House that I put the pieces together. Once Throckmorton had stolen the necklace, he could not risk hiding it anywhere in the house. If it was discovered missing, a search would be made. He would have had to take it to Manwaring House almost immediately.

By that time, Johnny had been following Throckmorton about for weeks; perhaps months. He must have seen something that implicated Lady Clara, who could not risk her husband discovering what she had done. I had not wished to believe a woman could kill a child, but it was certainly within her physical power to have done so. I decided that Huther had doubtless been involved. It explained his abject terror.

I found I could not be angry with Lady Clara for depriving Johnny of his life. Neither could I place her in the role of monster I had imagined his murderer to be. The amorphous mass responsible for Willy's plight had inhabited the darkest corners of my mind. When Lady Clara stepped from those shadows Johnny's killer became a person, one with troubles of her own. Indeed, I felt such pity for her that I was determined to protect her if I could without risking Willy's freedom.

It was a conundrum, one that kept me awake most of the night. Once I deemed it a suitable hour, I went straight to the Clarendon and enquired of the porter for the direction of Canning's rooms. As I climbed the stairs, I was treated to the most delicious aromas. I realized why Canning had chosen to stay there; the French chef, one-time servant to Louis the XVIII, was much sought after. Despite such good fortune, Canning appeared unhappy when he discovered me standing at his door.

"What is it? Wait, you had better come in," he instructed as he held the door wide. He was still in his nightshirt, dressing gown, and slippers, and a stocking cap covered his bald pate.

"Do forgive me, sir. I would not have called if it were not terribly important."

"Has the house been infested with bees? Or perhaps it

has burned down. Might I remind you that you are in possession of your own dwelling?"

I was accustomed to Canning's acid tongue and refused to take offense. "I have come about William Gilbert. I have very strong evidence as to Johnny's killer and I am at *aux anges* to see Willy released."

"This is splendid news!" Canning tightened the sash around his middle and indicated that I should be seated. "Tell me what you have discovered."

"I shall tell you all save the identity of the true killer." I settled into my seat and waited for Canning's reaction.

He looked more taken aback than I had anticipated. "Trevelin, whoever has done this must be brought to justice! Without proof of someone else's guilt, how am I to exonerate Willy?"

"All that is needed is your good word," I insisted. "If you trust me, which I believe you do, you shall act on what I have discovered. Am I wrong to assume you would?"

He stroked his chin. "I can make no promise until you have told me all you feel free to say."

"Very well. It is a sordid tale about a beautiful woman who has suffered much at the hands of her wicked husband."

"What does this have to do with young Gilbert?" Canning demanded.

I told him what I knew, minus the names of the persons involved. I refrained from describing the necklace or even commenting on how extraordinary it was so he would not think of Lady Vawdrey, nor his suspicions fall on Lady Clara. I also left out the information about the gaming hell— I only said that the wife in question had gambling debts; it was common enough.

"I see," Canning mused. "But you have no proof of what she has done?"

"She all but admitted it. I am as sure as I can be that it was she who wielded the knife. More than that, I am certain that William Gilbert did not. All I am asking is that you get Willy out of that place." I leaned forward in my chair. "If you saw him there, my sense of urgency would be yours!"

He grunted such that I knew he felt my sorrow and desperation.

A quarter of an hour later I had read the letter Canning had written to the Grand Jury, requesting William Gilbert's release. I was uncertain as to how long it would take before anything was done, but for now I could go to Willy and give him the happy news.

Unlike the first time I visited him at Newgate, I cared not in the least that I had only the open carriage in which to travel. The whole of it seemed rather ridiculous; if Willy could live with being falsely incarcerated in such a place, I could certainly live with being seen on the premises. My heart was lighter than air as I expertly tooled my curricle through the dense array of carts and carriages. I had not even thought to douse my handkerchief with scent; all I could think of was Willy's joy when he learned that he should go free.

In a shorter amount of time than I thought possible, I was standing in front of a guard.

"I have come to see William Gilbert," I said as loftily, as if I named the Prime Minister of England.

The guard gave a curt nod, opened his ledger, and ran his filthy finger down a column of names. "William Gilbert, did ye say?"

"Yes, I wish to see him."

"I see 'im 'ere," he said doubtfully, looking up at me with a question in his eyes. "It says he's deceased."

The words he spoke did not hold their usual meaning. "Deceased? No, he has not yet appeared before the Grand Jury. How could he have been executed?" I scoffed. "There must be some mistake."

"True enough; t'ats 'appened afore. But, 'ere, 'e's jus' died early this mornin'."

I looked at him blankly, incapable of comprehending his words.

"How's about I take ye to the body?" he asked. I could not say if he were being helpful or cruel.

"Yes, that would be a very good idea." I looked forward to the moment when I would prove him wrong.

He waved a hand, indicating that I should follow. As we traveled the route to Willy's cell, I had my first misgivings. I fully expected to be led to the chamber of a different man, one who had been hung, or out to the yard where the gallows stood, or the dung heap, even. When the guard opened the door to Willy's cell without aid of a key, I felt truly alarmed. He left the door ajar and, with a touch of his fingers to his forehead, went away.

I lingered in the passage, listening to the pounding of my heart for an inordinate amount of time. Finally, I could bear it no longer; I had to know. I swallowed, lifted my chin, and willed myself to step into the shadows of the chamber. There, on the cot, wearing the same clothes in which I had dressed him, was Willy.

Chapter Fourteen

His face was pale, but the stubble on his cheeks shone like gold in the light that filtered through the bars of the solitary window. His eyes were closed, and the corners of his mouth turned down so far that he nearly looked a stranger. A bandana tied around his face and knotted at the top of his head prevented his jaw from falling open. He had not been hung, of that I was certain. There was no rope burn on his neck and his eyes did not protrude from their lids.

I pulled down the blanket that had been tucked under his chin and saw that his shirt was covered with blood. It was so startling a sight that it took me a moment to realize the truth: Willy had died of pneumonia. There was one thing I could not deny: that he looked utterly peaceful. I pulled up a chair and sat beside him just as I had the last time I called upon him. "Willy," I said, the tears beginning to fall, "I had thought to free you. I have spent every moment in search of Johnny's killer." The thought flashed through my mind that I had not. There was my pursuit of Miss Woodmansey for which to account.

It no longer mattered. Nothing did. Except for this: How was I to tell his mother and father of my failure? I remembered then the shirt that I had been so eager to procure. It was still where I had flung it the last time I visited my friend. *Much good it would do anyone now,* I thought.

I took Willy's lame hand in both of mine and put my forehead to the poor pile of flesh and bones. "My friend, I have failed you," I cried, with no thought as to any who might hear my words. "I most humbly beg your pardon." And then I wept in earnest.

I do not know how long I anointed Willy's hand with my tears. When I finally stumbled from the prison, I knew I must call upon his parents at once. Instead I went directly to White's, where I drank until I forgot my name, or even that I had one. I lost consciousness in my chair and was wakened an unknown number of hours later by a footman who held out a silver tray bearing a letter. There was a name scrawled on it—mine, presumably—but I did not recognize the hand.

I rolled back my head until I looked up into the footman's face, whereupon I presented him with a ferocious frown. When he did not flee in terror, I reluctantly slid the piece of parchment from the tray and dropped it into my lap. "Water!" I called to whoever was near. When I had drunk a full glass, I decided it best to fill the chamber pot behind the screen in the corner before I did aught else. Once I felt something resembling a man, I opened the piece of parchment.

It consisted of nine short lines that somehow did not form a proper paragraph. Each sentence seemed to refer to a meaning all its own rather than contribute to the whole. The fact that there was no signature only added to my bewilderment. It seemed merely the ramblings of a madman, but I was able to perceive that I was to meet him, whoever he was and whatever his state of sanity, *inside* Canning House before the sun set that night. Otherwise, I would never know the truth; of what I could not say.

Furthermore, someone was to die.

I crumpled the parchment into a wad and barked for my curricle to be brought round. I stomped up and down the pavement outside White's until it appeared, whereupon I quickly alighted and raced to Canning House. When I arrived, the front door was slightly ajar. To my chagrin, there was no sign of the boot boy. As unaccountable as it seemed, the author of the missive had done as he said: he was in the house.

There was little point in being cautious; my arrival had been announced by the approach of the curricle. Nevertheless, I pushed open the door as stealthily as I was able. Instantly, I heard the pounding of feet against the marble floor, its tread too heavy to be the boot boy's. From the deep shadows that obscured the lowest steps of the staircase emerged the silhouette of a man as he ran upwards.

I went after him, but somehow he was always too far ahead of me to be identified. By the time I had dashed up the flights to the second floor, I was winded; certain I would never catch him. These words rang in my mind: someone was to die. I feared for the boot boy. I feared for myself. I had to catch this madman before anything dreadful happened.

I could hear said madman crashing along the passage above me, but he had run out of stairs. As I arrived at the top of the house, I could see that a door was open to a chamber at the front of the dwelling. Quietly, I crossed the threshold and stepped into what appeared to be a room for storage. Signs of the Cannings' hasty departure were everywhere:

bits of silver tissue were strewn amongst the few hat boxes that remained, the trunks had all gone, and there were streaks in the dust from where they had been dragged along the floor. Dusk was falling, and very little light made its way through the small window. Squinting, I studied the shadows. In the corner under the window, heaped upon the floor against a chair, was a man. He held a small pistol to his head.

Once he realized that I saw him, he straightened his spine so that the last rays of light shone in his eyes. They were lavender, and stricken with terror.

"Throckmorton, do not do it. She would not wish your death."

"You speak of Sally to me?" His voice shook with emotion: grief, anger, and so much fear.

"Not if you do not wish it. Only, do not hurt yourself."

He dropped his head back against the chair and moaned. "You understand nothing."

I paused to consider. "I know that you loved her. I know that she meant something more for you; something more than being the housekeeper at Hampton House."

He gave a harsh bark of laughter. "Yes, something far more: Sally's husband to begin with, the father of her children, and she, the mother of mine. And the baby! The baby is gone with her…" The sobs wracked his body, and he eased his grip on the gun.

I dived for it, but even in his sorrow he was faster than I.

He threw the gun again to his temple. "She was mine. Mine! And now there is nothing to hope for; nothing to live for but pain and misery."

I could not disagree but did not wish him to do away

with himself, and not only for his own sake: I required answers to my questions. "I know something of pain and misery. Put the pistol aside and we shall discuss it, you and I, like men."

"No! I dare not. I did not hear the door to the house shut behind you." He sounded quite deranged. "I won't be taken like the others!"

"The others? Do you refer to those who have disappeared from the workhouse?"

Ignoring me, he sat up and peered out the window without lowering the gun even a fraction. The window framed a view of the houses directly across the square, including Lady Vawdrey's. Seemingly satisfied, he reclined again on the floor, against the chair, and made a shocking disclosure. "It was I who killed Johnny Gilbert." He began again to weep, the tears streaming down his face. He wiped at them with a dust-covered hand. It left streaks of dirt from his chiseled cheekbone down to his perfectly-cleft chin. "She gave me no choice."

"Lady Clara?" I was surprised at how calm my voice sounded.

He nodded. "How did you know?"

"I have suspected, only." I eyed the pistol. It was a very small ladies' muff gun of the sort a woman such as Lady Clara might carry. Despite its diminutive size, I could see that his arm was growing weak. "Please put it down and tell me more."

He behaved as if he did not hear me. "Before that, she made me steal the necklace."

"I see." Better than he realized.

"It was on account of Sally; can you not understand that?" He begged me as if he argued with anyone but his own conscience. "People were disappearing from the workhouse. No one knew why. The police were of no help. I was terrified for her." He drew a deep breath and seemed to calm a little. "The first time I saw her, I knew that I loved her. Her eyes, they were so beautiful. When she looked at me, it was if she was seeing straight through to my soul!" His expression of adoration suddenly shifted to anger. "I was tired of being no one. Tired of being unloved. She changed all of that. And then she told me about the baby…what else could I do?"

"Indeed. I know well what it is to be lonely." I suppressed the urge to tell him just how well. "Have you taken Lady Vawdrey into account? Does she not love you? Have you considered how lonely you should make her if you were to shoot?"

He stared at me as if I were the one unhinged. "I stole her diamond necklace! I killed," he moaned, "the son of her friend. How can she forgive me?" The tears coursed down his nose and cheeks, unrestrained. "She shall wish to never see me again, nor shall she. I shall hang if I don't first put a period to my existence." He wiped a dirty hand across his face. It shook. "How can I face her? How can I bear to see her sorrow as she comes to comprehend the mistake she made in taking me into her home and making me a gentleman?" He said the last word with a sneer. "I am common, nothing more than that! Nor should I have ever become more, despite her assurances that I should one day be accepted into Society. If it were not for her," he said in tones of condemnation, "I would not have wished for a better life. I would not have been tempted by the money Lady Clara promised."

"She promised you money?" I knew the answer well enough, but I hoped my question might prolong his eloquence.

"'Twas for me and Sally, so that we might live like swells in our own home, not at the beck and call of anyone, but it never came." In his fatigue he began to slur some of his words, and his original speech patterns bled through his well-learned, proper English.

"You have done wrong, Edmund, but you can atone for it, here and now. You must tell me exactly how it all happened, so that I may advise you how best to make amends." I cast about for a way to separate him from the pistol. "Are you hungry? Let us go down to the kitchen and find you something to eat."

"Never! It was in a kitchen that I stole a key so as to take the life of a young boy, a lad who did no wrong. He did not deserve it. But, sad as that is, it was not the first time I had taken what was not mine. That was when I took the necklace so that my love could *live*. Once I had done that, I was in Lady Clara's power. If I had refused to do her bidding she would have sent me to the gallows, and Sally back to the workhouse to await what fate I cannot know."

I thought perhaps he could; that he did. It was the very thing I wished to discover. "I understand. So, after you took the key, what did you do?"

He sighed, shifting his leg so that his foot fell to the side and the hand with the pistol somewhat relaxed. "I knew Johnny," he said dully. "He used to follow me around, for lack of anything better to do, I suppose. His tutor left the house at all hours to gamble at Manwaring House. At first Johnny simply followed him around, but he soon tired of that. That was when he began to follow me. When I went to the workhouse to make deliveries for Lady Vawdrey, Johnny followed along behind." An ugly sound started deep in his throat and rose into a sob. "The poor child!" he cried. "He saw too much!"

I did not weep with him. I had already shed my allotment of tears at Willy's bedside. Instead, I eyed the pistol as it bobbed against his heaving brow. I could not be sure how much time I had left to pose my questions. "How could he have seen you steal the necklace?"

Throckmorton froze and his eyes snapped open. He stared at me, but did not seem to see me. "Naturally, he did not! No, it was my journey to the house to deliver it that he witnessed. It was Huther, who owed Lady Clara *much* money, who took it from me. I slipped it to him right there on the walkway as I passed by the area steps. He waited at the bottom and I simply slid it from my pocket and dropped it over the railing as I went by. It was too easy." His face crumpled into a silent sob and his body shook.

"How long after this did she ask you to kill Johnny?" The words stuck in my throat. Until this moment, Johnny's murder was but a notion. I had not seen the lifeless body, had not seen him alive for some time before his death. My main concern had been to liberate Willy. Now, as I listened to Throckmorton speak of the events that led to Johnny's death, it became an intolerable reality.

"It's been months since I took the necklace. I have lived

in fear that she would ask to wear it, and then where would I be?"

The timing tallied with what Lady Vawdrey had said about how long it had been since she had worn the necklace, as well as Lady Clara's confession of how she threatened Throckmorton into stealing it.

He moaned. "How could I betray her so? She was the closest thing to a mother that I have ever known. She loved me as a son!"

"Loves you still," I urged. "Do put down the gun and we can go across the square. You can explain it all to her there before..."

He frowned and stared at me in disbelief. "You would do that? You would allow me to go to her before handing me over to the authorities?"

I nodded. "I do not think you an evil man, Edmund; merely a desperate one."

Just then there was a sound from across the square; perhaps a horse threw a shoe or a door had slammed. Throckmorton moved again to peer out the window. This time he did not seem as satisfied, and was suddenly more afraid than he had been before.

"What is it? What do you fear?"

"There isn't time," he breathed. I could see how his heart pounded through his coat.

"What can you possibly fear more than death by your own hand?" I asked in disbelief.

"It is all in there."

I followed his gaze to the crumpled parchment that I still held tight in my hand. It was then that I heard the shot, the one that put an end to Edmund Throckmorton. I stood for a moment in stunned disbelief.

I returned home from my first ball after the duel, and went immediately to view my reflection in the glass. In truth, it was no different than it had been prior to departing, but instead of seeing a comely man with an unseemly gash in the corner of his mouth, I saw what did everyone else—a villain. It was the end of the life I had known.

"NO!" I cried as I fell to my knees, and gathered him into my arms. I gazed upon his ruined face and wept impossible tears.

The boot boy saw to everything. He crept out of his hiding place in the chamber across the passage, wrested the body from my grasp, and covered it with a sheet. Then he sent the coachman in the curricle to fetch Canning. My little boot boy waited below stairs until Canning arrived, whereupon this taciturn lad trailed the man up the front staircase, regaling him all the while with the tale of what had happened. When Canning entered the room where I remained, seated on the floor, Throckmorton's blood on my hands, he took one look at me and put me to bed.

I remained in seclusion for a sen'night, the boot boy my almost constant companion. Canning returned to his rooms at the hotel once he had arranged for someone to cook for me, in hopes it would prevent my death by starvation. (He later described the discovery of a corpse in his house as a singular event, one that he dearly hoped should remain so.) The fact that I ate little was of no consequence. I mostly lay in bed and fancied myself on the cot where I had last seen Willy, his head bent over my weakening body, shedding tears of bitter regret. It was no solace.

Eventually I came to myself and looked about. The boot boy was asleep in a chair by my bed. The candle on the night table cast a soft yellow glow against the wall. The rest of the room remained in deep shadow. My gaze drifted until it came to rest on a wad of parchment on the table. It seemed to glow in the light, save where it was stained with Throckmorton's blood. I recalled that he had said the letter contained the answers I sought. I lay still whilst I considered whether anything mattered now that Willy was dead.

Finally, I remembered what was owed Johnny. I took up the wad and tugged it back into its proper shape. Nothing had changed; it yet bore the nine sentences that did not seem to match up. They told of the fact that Throckmorton wished me to meet him inside of Canning House, that someone was to die (not an improbable prediction, as it turned out), that I must come prior to nightfall, that I would learn the answers I sought. But there were other messages therein that added nothing to the relevant.

With a sigh, I placed the parchment on the table and left my bed to draw back the curtains. There was a hint of light to the east; morning, then. As I had had enough sleep to last a month, I decided I had best be up for the day. The boot boy stirred and I shook him by the shoulder. He opened one eye, very slightly, and when he saw that I seemed willing to live he jumped out of his chair and looked at me, eagerly awaiting my instructions.

"You are a useful lad, are you not?"

He merely looked at me and waited.

"I know that you speak; I have heard you."

Still: nothing.

"Very well," I said in defeat. "Go fetch me clean water and something to eat."

He was off in a flash and soon I was seated in front of the fire, eating bread and cheese just as I had my first morning alone in the house; the day prior to Willy and Throckmorton's deaths. That they should die the same day seemed monstrously unfair. And yet, I knew that Willy's fate had been sealed. Had Throckmorton chosen to tell me the truth days earlier, the pneumonia would still have put an end to my friend.

And then I thought better of it: if Throckmorton had confessed when I had first called upon his mistress to discuss Johnny's death, Willy might not have contracted the illness that killed him. I rose to my feet with my plate in my hands and threw it against the wall. It flew into a dozen pieces and landed on the floor, where it remained until my little boot boy, hearing the clamor, rushed into the room and cleared it away.

It was with a sense of profound relief that I walked out of the house a short time later. I had had no means of recognizing the pall that had fallen on it until I was no longer under its roof. The frigid air chilled my nose and ears as I stood in the center of the square, gazing at Hampton House. It was my first call of the day. The butler ushered me up to the first-floor salon, and opened the door to reveal Señyor Rey giving Lady Vawdrey her lesson in Catalan.

"My lord!" Rey cried as his face suffused with joy. He

jumped from his seat and rushed to my side. "How good it is to see you!" He wrapped his arms around me and buried his nose in the folds of my waistcoat. "It is high time that you joined the land of the living!"

"So that's where I am," I said faintly as I looked about. I felt that I somehow still dwelt in a world of dreams.

"Come and sit, Trevelin, and tell us how you are getting on," Lady Vawdrey crooned.

I had not expected her sympathies in the least. That she should be at home to me so soon after her Edmund had died in my arms was astonishing. I sketched a bow and seated myself on the sofa opposite her. "I wish to express my deepest sorrow at the loss of your man, Throckmorton."

Her expression hardened. "Thank you, Trevelin. He was, after all, but a servant."

I looked to Rey who shrugged, his expression wary.

I offered her a faint smile, forgetting entirely how much like a sneer it would appear. "He was quite agitated at the end. He loved you as a mother. He felt that he had disappointed you."

Lady Vawdrey's face fell and she turned away as if to gain command of herself. "Is that what he told you before you failed to pry the gun from his hand?"

I frowned, and looked again to Rey. His expression was full of sorrow, as if he understood her sentiments all too well.

"I assure you," I said, leaning forward in my earnestness, "it was my greatest desire to prevent his...doing as he did. I had only just paid my final respects to Willy Gilbert earlier in the day and I could not bear to see another death; neither for my sake nor for his. Nor yours," I said in perfect sincerity.

She bit her lip and nodded. "Thank you for that. I should not have presumed to know your intentions. I am grateful that you have come to explain." She lifted her gaze to look me in the eye. "Finally."

I drew a deep breath. "I most humbly beg your pardon. I ought to have come sooner. I have not been well."

"But, of course you have not been of the sound mind and healthy body," Rey said in hearty tones. "I am pleased that you have recovered!"

I gave him a nod. "Thank you. I hope that you have been keeping well in my absence."

He smiled, and inclined his head in return. At least he was still my friend, even after my betrayal with Miss Woodmansey. It was the first time I had afforded her a thought since that terrible day. I refused to question as to why it was so, and turned again to Lady Vawdrey. "You charged me with the task of learning what has happened to your diamond necklace. I have come, in part, to share what I have discovered as to its fate."

She looked at me in astonishment. "Fate? That does not sound as if you have found it."

"Not precisely, though I have learnt what happened to it." I drew another deep breath. "Throckmorton stole it. He took it to fund his new home with Sally." I refrained from mentioning Lady Clara's role in the matter.

"What a parcel of lies!" Lady Vawdrey snapped. "He would never betray me thus! I suppose you shall claim that Edmund himself has told you this."

"He has. He also told me that the necklace was but paste. Were you aware of this?"

She pursed her lips and narrowed her eyes at me. "What if I were?"

"Then this proves that I speak the truth; I could not have known the necklace was paste if not from him."

She looked down at her hands. "It didn't matter to me in the least! I have lived enough years to learn that beauty is that beauty does. Heaven knows it sparkled just the same."

I rose and went to stand at her side. "Again, I am very sorry for your loss. As to the necklace, it was sold. I imagine it could be tracked down and restored to you. Do you wish me to make an attempt?"

She looked up at me with an expression of hatred. "You? Why should I ask you to do anything whatsoever? You have failed at all with which I have tasked you: courting Miss Leavitt, retrieving my necklace. You could not even save your friend."

I could hear Rey's gasp, crisp and loud as a slap. I was too stunned to be angry, not at first. I did, however, stalk to the door of the room without so much as a word. Rey followed me out into the passage, down the stairs, and into the study on the ground floor.

He carefully closed the doors behind us. "My lord, I beg your pardon for her sake. She is not herself."

"If you believe that, it is only on account of the brevity of your acquaintance," I said testily as I dropped into a chair. "She is more herself than ever. What I cannot understand is how she expected me to do other than what I have done. I did not put the gun in Throckmorton's hand; I did not steal the necklace."

"*Si*, my lord; indeed, it is her dear Edmund with whom

she is angry." He moved to stand in front of the fire. "He has hurt her, very badly. However, he lies in state in the family vault, whilst you are alive. She resents it oh so very much!"

I barely heard the last of his remark. "In the family vault? A self-murderer?"

"The coffin has not been interred. It merely sits until she can be persuaded to part with it. She will not allow any to take it away. I find I cannot find fault in her for that," he said sadly.

"Does she know that he is a killer? Johnny's, to be specific." I realized that I had no idea what anyone had been told of Throckmorton's confession.

"Your friend Mr. Canning very kindly paid a call and explained the circumstances. He said that he had not yet spoken with you about it, but that a young boy in the house told him what he had overheard."

"I cannot account for what that one has said. To me he has yet to speak a word!" I wondered if the lure of gold was the boot boy's only motivation in serving me. Perhaps he feared me, or at the very least, did not like me. Few did in those days. I shifted uncomfortably in my chair as I considered my next words. "And what of you, Señyor Rey? Do you resent me?"

He looked his surprise. "For what, my friend?"

I considered my reply with care but, in cowardly fashion, selected the one that promised the least risk of a falling-out. "That I did not include you in the discovery of Johnny's killer."

He nodded gravely. "I should have liked to be there, if only to comfort to you. I have walked across the square to call on you twice a day since it happened, but no one ever came to the door."

I grunted my appreciation. "The servants have all gone away, save one, and we were neither of us in a position to play footman."

"I merely wished you to know that I should have offered you my assistance as well as my loyalty, had I been allowed."

His words smote me in the breast. I wished to express my gratitude, but words did not come.

He gave me a gentle smile. "I am so very sorry that Mister William has been taken from this world."

He was the only one to have said such words to me. I forced away the tears that threatened with a change of subject. "I pray you have had more to do than comfort Lady Vawdrey for the past week."

At my words, Rey looked down at the floor. "I fear that I have not been a very good friend. I have been to balls and other entertainments whilst you were abed, and often in the company of," he said as he looked up, his eyes bright, the expression therein challenging, "Miss Woodmansey."

Chapter Fifteen

It was a depth of betrayal I had not yet known. It was not a matter of his having chosen to court Miss Woodmansey; there was no secret in that. It was that he was not in the least grieved at the pain he knew his admission would cause me. And yet, I could not bear to let him know the depth of my agony. Willy was gone; Lady Vawdrey, upon whom I had counted to restore my good name, was angrier than ever; the Cannings had moved out of the house. Rey was the last to remain of all my friends.

I stood and reached out to shake his hand. "I offer my congratulations. When is the wedding to take place?"

He took my hand and shook it, though his face reddened. "Matters have not yet progressed that far. I am hopeful, however. And I am grateful that you wish to remain my friend."

"Beggars cannot be choosers," I said lightly enough.

"I understand this idiom. I wish that I did not," he said regretfully. "It pains me that a man such as you should need beg for anything."

"Thank you, my friend." As I turned to quit the room, the gnawing in my belly was so severe that I nearly felt faint. The sensation seemed to prompt the recollection of a question that remained unanswered. "Señyor Rey, I find there is something that yet troubles me. Who killed Sally, and why? And why the slashes in her lips? I should be honored if you were to accompany me in an attempt to discover the truth."

"I should like that as well. However, I find that I suddenly have many more engagements than I had prior to this past week." He came to my side and clasped me by the elbow. "Do not allow this to stop you. You must keep looking until you find the truth, whether I am there to assist or not." He looked frankly into my eyes. "Can you make me this promise?"

I realized then that I had been blessed to know such a man. "Thank you, Señyor Rey. I can and I shall." Then I turned and quit the room.

I stepped out into the square and thought on what I should do next. I was more tired than I could remember ever having felt, but the Gilberts required my presence if only for a few moments. I knew that, though Willy's burial should surely have taken place, they would still be in deepest mourning. Realizing I might be turned away, I pressed on to Gilbert House.

I rapped on the door and was asked to wait in the hall whilst Bugg determined whether or not the Gilberts were at home to me. His tread, when he returned, was brisk and strong. "Mr. and Mrs. Gilbert shall see you," he said with a bow.

I followed Bugg up the stairs and was ushered into the salon, where sat Willy's parents. They were dressed in unremitting black, especially Mr. Gilbert who had donned even a black shirt for his mourning of Willy. Their heads were bowed in sorrow, and the tears gathered in my eyes as I looked upon them. I bowed deeply and took Mrs. Gilbert's hand in mine. She, however, snatched it instantly from my grasp.

I swallowed my dismay, making allowances for her grief. "Mr. Gilbert, Mrs. Gilbert, please allow me to express my deepest sorrow for the loss of your sons," I said, choking on our mutual wretchedness. "It was my dearest wish to see Willy exonerated. I did all within my power. In point of fact, I was able to discover who took Johnny from you. Perhaps you have been informed."

Mr. Gilbert looked up. "We have."

Bewildered by his cold demeanor, I reminded myself that the man had lost both of his sons in little more than a week, and in dreadful circumstances. "I have no words to console you." My breath rattled in my throat. "I can barely console myself. I have failed to do as I promised. I blame myself entirely. I hope that one day you shall forgive me."

Silent, Mrs. Gilbert buried her face in her handkerchief.

"Come now, my love," Mr. Gilbert said. "At least he did not say 'How grateful you must be that Willy is free of his afflictions,' as have so many others."

"It is a notion that has never crossed my mind," I insisted. "It would not do to pretend he did not suffer, but his suffering could never amount to more than his love for you."

Mr. Gilbert seemed not to hear me. "To say such things is to imply that our feelings, as his mother and father, are of no account. He was our boy! We loved him! It did not matter to us that he could not walk as he ought, talk as he ought, or properly feed himself; he was still our Willy!"

I wanted nothing more than to concur, but I was restrained by bonds of shame. He had not been the same Willy to me, not until I had cause to look beyond his afflictions to the man who bore them. "I wish that I had landed upon a means to determine who was to blame from the outset," I said, my voice gurgling in my throat, "so that Willy would have been away from that place before it grew too late."

Mrs. Gilbert quit her handkerchief and looked at me. "You promised. You promised you would see him free! I shan't ever forgive you! Never!" she cried.

Mr. Gilbert put his arm around his wife's shoulders and pulled her to him. To me he said, "I think that you had better leave."

I stared at them, aghast. I had not expected them to be grateful, but I had not pictured this level of disdain. I lingered so as to find the words that would remove some of their pain, but there were none. Finally, I rendered another of my deepest bows and departed.

There was nowhere for me to go but Canning House, where my boot boy most likely fretted at my absence. He opened the door when I rapped and I stomped up the stairs, the anger of earlier that morning returned. The boot boy shrank away, and did not follow me up to my room as was his wont. This meant I had not the opportunity to ask that he bring me something to eat.

The fire yet burned in the grate. I fell into an overstuffed chair placed there for the purpose, and put my feet to the flames. I reviewed my choices and decided that the deciphering of the note from Throckmorton could wait. I took up the hat I had tossed onto the bed, and stalked out of the house and along the square until I arrived at Manwaring House. I was not sure what benefit could be had from once again interviewing Mrs. Carrick, but I could feel relatively certain that she would at least feed me.

I was soon tucking into a meat pasty and downing it with copious amounts of ale.

"I am that pleased," Mrs. Carrick said, "you have come back."

"Oh? Why is that?" I asked around a mouthful of crust soaked with mouth-watering gravy.

"I'm thinkin' I know who ' twas that killed Sally."

I replaced my tankard on the table with a thud. "Do you? Can you tell me?"

"'Twas because she was breedin'."

"Throckmorton?" Lady Clara insisted the child was her husband's, but I hoped against hope that she was wrong.

She shook her head. "He was bent on marryin' and she the same. But how could he have gotten her with child? He treated her proper-like."

This statement was evidence of nothing, as Throckmorton assumed the child to be his. "Could it not have been Huther?" I put another forkful of food in my mouth, but I did not take my eyes from her face. Her expression was grim. "Then who is it you believe to have been the father of Sally's baby?" I pressed.

"Who else?" she asked, her eyebrows raised up past her brindled hair.

"Manwaring, then."

She nodded.

"Are you certain?"

She closed her eyes and nodded again.

Lady Clara had said as much. However, I valued Mrs. Carrick's opinion on the matter, as I could hardly ask Manwaring his. "But why kill her? Why not simply have her dismissed without a character as do other debauchers?"

Mrs. Carrick shrugged. "He is not right in the head, that one. I bin thinkin' I needs to find me a new position afore he comes after me."

I stared at her, horrified, and for more than one reason. And then, quite suddenly, I understood. It wasn't her virtue for which she feared; it was her life.

I reached into my waistcoat pocket for a card and was amazed when my fingers encountered several. I pulled one out, surveyed it to ensure it bore my name, and made a mental note to praise the boot boy for his scrupulous work. "Here," I said, handing it over. "If you are in trouble, give this to anyone on the square. They shall know where to find me."

"I thank ye, m'lord." She smiled. "If ye like, I can help ye get into the house to nose about. Y'know, to learn whatever it is he does in that basement of his."

I declined; I had no wish to endanger her. Rather, I thanked her for her hospitality and, with nothing left to do, returned to Canning House. I went immediately to my room to look for the missive from Throckmorton. I tore the room apart before I finally remembered the thoroughness of the boot boy. I pulled open the drawer in the night table and there it was, carefully spread as flat as he could manage.

I took it to the chair by the fire and read it, over and over.

Still, I could not decipher what it was Throckmorton wished me to know but was too afraid to say aloud. This was the biggest mystery of all: why did he not simply tell me? Was he worried about being overheard? But if he were to kill himself, what would that matter? What would be so much worse than shooting oneself in the head? Was it myself about whom he was so concerned? Was he making me a target if he revealed aloud what he knew?

The questions multiplied as I studied the missive, line by line. The first was clear: *Meet me at Canning House.*

The second seemed a sensible follow-up: *Abide with me awhile.* ('Twas not I who took his leave so abruptly.)

Number three said: *No one shall forgive me.* Now that I knew the identity of the author, I saw the truth in this assertion.

Four: *Why did he have to die?* Did he refer to Johnny? Or himself?

Five: *An answer shall be given.* Unfortunately, not the one I yet lacked.

Six: *Regret is all I know.* I thought perhaps I should turn the paper over to Lady Vawdrey once I no longer had need of it. (I immediately thought better of it.)

Seven: *Inside is where we shall meet.* This one had proven true, but I still could not say why he wished to meet inside. He did seem compelled to look across the street from the attic room where he died. Did he wish to see what was happening at Hampton House? In the street? Did he watch for someone? He clearly feared someone, of that I was certain.

Eight: *Never deny me.* I wished that I had had the capacity to do so.

Nine: *Go now or someone shall die*. I thought this statement patently unfair. I rushed to Canning House to prevent a death, but Throckmorton never intended to leave the place alive. The notion brought a wave of despair. At times, I thought myself a coward for not wresting the gun from his hand. And yet, it seemed uncharitable to save him for the noose. The only thing I could do for him now was to discover the hidden message.

Obsessed, I read it over again. And again. There was no rhyme. There was no reason. Just nine sentences, each written one after the other. Every word was written in an even hand, every letter the same size, save the capital letters at the beginning of each sentence; they were just as they ought to be. And yet, it triggered a notion. I circled the first letter of each sentence, the result of which was a name: Manwaring.

Exceedingly early the next morning I stood outside of Manwaring House, with a dark lantern and as many of my wits as I could muster. At one point I had decided it best to forget the secret message, but the words of my friend Señyor Rey echoed in my mind and would not be denied. I glanced down the square at Hampton House; it was lighted. No doubt Rey and Miss Woodmansey, in the company of Lady Vawdrey, were on their way home from a ball.

As I turned my attention to the area steps that led down to the kitchen, a sudden gust of wind nearly blew me off my feet. With a hand to my hat and the other holding my lantern, I began to go down the stairs. Once I had descended below the level of the pavement, I slid back the shutter of the lantern to expose the light; I had no wish to go any further in the dark. Slowly and carefully I went until I arrived at the bottom where stood the kitchen entrance. Somehow Mrs. Carrick knew I would return; she opened the door for me almost before my knuckles scraped the wood.

She held a candlestick in her hand and indicated that I should shutter my lantern. I did as she asked; any woman who graced me with such delicious meat pasty deserved my ultimate trust. Slowly, we traversed the passageway that led away from the kitchen. We were headed in the opposite direction of the square, towards the mews at the back of the house. However, once the door to the mews was opened, there was a choice: go out into the area where the horses whinnied at the howling of the wind, or descend a staircase that wound down into infinite darkness. The smell that wafted up from below was stronger than that of the mews, and far more disagreeable.

Somewhat reluctantly, I followed her down the steep, narrow staircase, one hand on the rough, wooden banister and the other holding my shuttered lantern where it would not crash into the walls. By the time we reached the bottom of the stairs, my arm ached. Then she turned, putting herself between the flame of the candle and what lay beyond the landing.

"Wait until I ha' gone up and shut the door afore ye open the shutter."

"Yes, of course." I had no wish to expose Mrs. Carrick to danger. I watched her form as it went higher and higher, slowly swallowed up in the darkness, until only the flame of her candle could be seen. I heard the door open and felt the blast of air that rushed down the stairs upon its closure.

Turning towards the unseen room, I lifted my hand to reveal the light of my lantern when a light suddenly flared in my eyes.

With a yelp, I jumped back and fell hard against the stairs, my lantern flying from my grasp. The echo as it crashed, end over end, was eventually swallowed up in the darkness. Despite the commotion, I never took my eyes from the light: it was contained in a lantern very much like mine and was held aloft by Robert Manwaring.

"I must remember to thank Mrs. Carrick when next I see her. I have been yearning to make improvements on that unsightly scar!"

Slowly, I stood and studied the man before me. He looked just as he always did: perfectly handsome and perfectly sane. "You persuaded Mrs. Carrick to trap me here?" I asked in disbelief, "for the purpose of performing a surgery?"

"Whoever stitched you up did a very poor job of it," he replied.

"Regardless, there is nothing more to be done; it has healed." I eyed him warily in the case he was under the influence of a powerful narcotic.

He smiled urbanely and shook his head. "That is not so. There are people, some true surgeons and some merely enthusiasts such as myself, who are attempting to discover how to operate on the human body in order to make improvements. I believe we discussed this at the Truesdales' ball. As for myself, I am purely interested in the outer shell; how to do away with the grotesque and replace it with perfection."

"How kind of you to consider me a worthy subject," I blustered as I attempted to see what lay beyond the lantern's glow. "However, I find that I prefer not to take the risk and remain as I am."

"You think it a gamble?" Manwaring said with a bark of laughter. "I assure you, I am quite proficient."

"I rather doubt it," I said, recalling the slices to Sally's lips. The memory suffused my entire frame with sudden rage. "What of your housemaid? She wasn't improved upon; she was mutilated!"

"You wound me, Trevelin! I was not yet finished. Sadly, I was over-eager to put an end to her screaming. I never meant to put an end to her life."

"Do you mean to say you cut into her without giving her something to deaden the pain?" I thought I had known horror. I was wrong.

"She was offered brandy," he said with a stretch of his hand, "but she was very frightened, poor thing. She would not listen when I told her all would be well. Nor did a beating compel her to cooperate. Once I had begun the procedure, she still thrashed about so much that my knife slipped a few times and, well," he hesitated, "I cut the corners of her mouth. It was very unfortunate, though I have no doubt that I could have made the repair stitches virtually invisible."

"But why?" My hands curled into balls seemingly of their own accord. "What was your purpose?"

"To complete the operation, of course!" He seemed astonished. "She had too-thin lips; it was disgusting to me. I could hardly look at her!" He *tsked*. "Once I had managed to slit open each lip, I planned to insert pads of gauze contained in sausage casing and stitch them up again. Mark my words, once it all healed she would have been beautiful!"

I stared at him as I rejected every rebuke that came to mind for the sin of being wholly deficient.

He quickly tired of my silence. "As I've said, she died." He shrugged in a manner that demonstrated his perceived lack of culpability in the matter. "I left her out in the cold to preserve the body. As you know, someone stumbled upon her before I could claim her."

"You are despicable!" I cried over the thundering of my heart, and yet, I was still in such disbelief that I did not entirely perceive that I was in danger.

"You should not say such things, my lord. I had hoped that we might enjoy a civil, even collaborative, relationship. If you insist on being uncooperative, I shall be forced to take steps." He extended his arm to the side and the light of the lantern fell on a row of bone-chilling metal rods that spanned the room from wall to wall. They were fitted into the floor and ceiling much as did the bars in the window of Willy's gaol. The area had been divided up into eight small cells, some of which contained a terrified human individual.

"This here is Butterworth." Manwaring walked to the bars and held the lantern up to a man I recognized as the doorkeeper at the workhouse. He sat on a wooden chair in his cell, seething with rage. I marveled at his restraint and wondered at the reason for it.

"Well!" Manwaring said in so sanctimonious a manner that I nearly retched. "As you can see, his nose is simply repulsive. I believe I can correct it once I have determined how to control the bleeding. I must be well-practiced at it before I perform the surgery on my wife. She is a lovely woman, as I am certain you agree, but her nose is too blunt."

I turned away and heaved my most recent meal onto the floor. Throckmorton's terror had become my own. "You monster!" I said as I spit the contents of my stomach from my mouth which I wiped with the sleeve of my coat. "Your wife is one of the most beautiful women I have ever seen, yet you shall not be best pleased until you destroy her; just as you have destroyed Sally!"

"It was unfortunate, but it could not be helped," he said with a wan smile. "I am delighted that the bits of ivory I had carved for Clara were an excellent match for her teeth. Indeed, she shall thank me when I have completed all the work I have in store for her. However, she must wait until I am no longer angry with her. I was very displeased in regard to the stolen necklace and the Gilbert boy. I insisted that she put an end to that."

My stomach roiled again, but I could be glad of one thing: I had not added to Lady Clara's undeserved misery by turning her over to the constable. My thoughts went elsewhere when Manwaring shone the lantern on the next captive. It was a girl, not more than eighteen years of age. She was possessed of lovely hair and teeth but her face was covered in moles. Like Butterworth, she was too terrified to make a sound. Instead, she appealed to me for help with her eyes.

"This is Janie, one of Butterworth's friends from the workhouse. She is my next subject. I have needed to time her surgery carefully, as it shall require a great deal of fresh skin to repair the holes left behind by the moles. There are far too many of them to do otherwise," he said with another tsk.

The girl whimpered, and quick as lightning, Manwaring had his hand through the bars and had gripped her chin between his fingers. "Not a sound! Save your screaming for when the lady of the house has company. They are so very boisterous," he said, turning to me, "those guests of hers, are they not?"

The butler's mad revelations now made perfect sense, but I dared not put him in danger by mentioning them to his master.

He moved to the next cell. "This had been Sally's room. Such a pity! She had such lovely eyes. She would have been quite beautiful once I had finished with her."

"And what of Kat, Betty, and Lizzie, also from the workhouse? Are they here, as well?" I demanded. My tones were at odds with the manner in which my limbs weakened with terror.

"Mrs. Carrick has been a wonderful provider of subjects on which to experiment, hasn't she?" he said with a smile that would have been perfectly at home at Almack's.

Instantly, I despised her for what she had done until I realized she was most likely too frightened to do otherwise. "Did you get the others with child, as well?"

He looked taken aback. "Of course not! Sally was the only one pretty enough for me to approach. The others were disappointed not to receive my attentions, but it might have proved different had they survived their surgeries."

I was aghast. "They died? All of them?" I prayed that I had heard amiss.

"Yes, all of them," he said, with what seemed genuine regret. "Bleeding problems. You have no idea how much a person bleeds once you pierce them with a sharp instrument."

I rather thought I did.

The sight of my blood as it flowed from the corner of my mouth filled me with dread. I took no thought for how giddy I had become, nor was I cognizant of the fact that I was losing consciousness. The stage of my mind was obscured by ribbons of red against a white curtain. They shimmered and flowed in undulating fashion as the white grew brighter and brighter until, finally, I passed out and knew no more.

I dragged the cool air into my lungs to combat the light-headedness. How was I to know the worst was yet to come? My tormentor passed over a cell, one that contained the shadowy form of a man, and held the lantern to shine upon the next. Inside was a child, her hair long and golden, her limbs bound, and her mouth gagged. She sat on a stool in the center of the cell, her eyes downcast.

"This one has not yet learned to be still," he said. "Hence the binding. But she shall be here for quite some time, and I am confident that she shall learn."

Despite her limited ability to move, I could see that she was terrified. Something was not quite right, however. She wore a gown too ornate to have been made for a child. Slowly she lifted her head, her eyes wide with fear. It was then that I realized it was Miss Woodmansey.

"No!" I cried as I grabbed a bar in each hand and shook them frenziedly. "You must let her go! You must let *all* of them go!"

"Ah ha!" he said in triumph. "I thought you might take exception to my latest guest."

"But why? Why Miss Woodmansey?" I cried in desperation. "There is nothing to complain of, nothing that requires repair!" I looked at her; filled my vision with only her. "She is lovely! How can you not see it?" I cried as I turned to him.

He looked back, his brow raised and his smile snide; unrelenting.

"Let her go," I demanded, "and I shall tell no one what I have seen here this night!"

"Oh, my dear Trevelin! Clearly you are as addled as you are maimed. Naturally, I cannot allow you leave. I intend to keep you here indefinitely! I am glad, however, to have learned that you do not have designs on my wife, for it is clear that you are head over heels in love with Miss Woodmansey." He laughed. "If you were not, you would see for yourself that she is nothing to look at. She is a plain squab of a girl, too wide and too short."

I turned again to Miss Woodmansey and watched as the tears filled her eyes. "I fail to see how a knife could alter either," I said, genuinely perplexed. "And yet, why should you? Her size has nothing to say to it; she is charming just as she is."

"Our opinions on the matter do not agree. My hope is to successfully lengthen her legs with bone and muscle from a cadaver."

I could not take my eyes from Miss Woodmansey as she reacted to the words of her captor. Her fear was like a knife in my heart. "Manwaring," I shouted, "you are insane!"

"Not insane, Trevelin: brilliant! Every such idea was thought insane at one time or another. No, I am simply a man born before his time," he said, his voice gaining in volume and excitement, "rather like Da Vinci or Franklin of the American colonies!"

"They are absurd comparisons, both of them." I had learned the painter's view on the matter as a schoolboy. "Da Vinci believed that humans could not improve on nature, the inventions of which he said to be neither lacking nor superfluous."

Manwaring shrugged. "If that was his opinion, I can only suppose it was on account of his ignorance. How could he possibly have comprehended the notions of which I have conceived? Mankind did not possess the proper knowledge when Da Vinci walked the earth."

Only then did I perceive the depth of his derangement. I realized that I would never leave the wretched place if I did not act immediately. Looking about me, I forced myself to think. Behind Manwaring I saw the outline of a desk, placed where his captives could watch him work on his gruesome plans. "If you are as brilliant as you say, you must have some papers or charts; outlines for your surgeries."

His eyes opened wide as he smiled in delight. "Yes! Of course! I could do nothing without drawing it all out, like the builder of a house or a sculptor. There needs must be something to look at, do you see?"

"No, I do not. Perhaps if you showed me your plans for Miss Woodmansey's surgery, I might better comprehend your intentions." It required all of my forbearance to speak such atrocities.

Manwaring turned immediately to the desk and set the lantern upon it. I saw that it was a mechanical desk with a sloped surface, designed for just the sort of work of which he spoke. It was excessively disorganized, with papers scattered everywhere. As he began to sort them, I took up the lantern and smashed it into his head. He slumped onto the desk just as the captives began to shout for their release.

"Where are the keys?" I shouted.

"The top drawer!" Butterworth cried.

I found it necessary to push Manwaring's body clear of the drawer before I could pull it out. I hardly took notice of the ensuing thud as he hit the floor. "Miss Woodmansey, I shall first release this big brute so that he may protect us in the case Manwaring comes to."

"He's not dead?" Janie asked as I turned the key in the lock of Butterworth's cell.

"I do not wish to assume," I murmured as I rushed to Miss Woodmansey's cell. She had managed to stand and now clung to the metal bars. I turned the key in the lock and she fell into my arms. Tossing the key to Butterworth, I quickly untied the gag that bound her.

She opened her mouth to speak but was too overcome, and began to weep. Gently, I led her to the stool and helped her to sit. Once I had untied the ropes that bound her, I threw them to Butterworth. "Tie him up and go for the constable," I shouted as I picked her up in my arms and ran.

Chapter Sixteen

As I raced to the stairs, I heard a repeated dull thump as a man insisted, "That's for Johnny." I realized then that the unknown man in the third cell was Huther.

I ran up the staircase with Miss Woodmansey in my arms. She was as light as a feather, no burden at all. I kicked open the door at the top of the stairs and dashed down the passage to the kitchen door and out to the bottom of the area steps. I ran up those as well, Miss Woodmansey clinging to my neck so tight I was in danger of being short of air. I continued across the carriage drive and a few feet into the park in the center of the square before I stopped for breath.

I looked about, thinking on what I should do. My main concerns were the immediate health, safety, and reputation of Miss Woodmansey. As such, I could not bring her to Canning House; there was no comfort to be had for her there.

"Are you able to walk?" I asked. She nodded and I set her on her feet, then took her by the elbow and led her through the trees of the park towards Hampton House. It was slower going, but at least I was in no danger of having my breath cut off at the throat. When we gained the door, I pounded on it until a sleepy footman opened it just wide enough to peep out through the crack.

"Beggin' your pardon, sir, but it is late."

"I am Trevelin from Canning House across the square. This young lady is in need of some assistance. She is an especial friend of...of Señyor Rey. Please allow her entrance."

"Very well, sir, I shall go and inquire." He then shut the door upon us.

I grasped her by the hand and led her to the shadows at the corner of the house. "No one shall see you. Lady Vawdrey will be kind and Señyor Rey shall manage everything. I would take you to my house, but there is no one else in residence. I shall not risk your reputation."

She nodded, her eyes full of tears. "Yes, yes I understand. Thank you! Oh, thank you! I have never been so frightened in all of my life!"

I cupped her chin and lifted her gaze up to mine. "What ever happened? How did you come to be in such a place?"

"It was Mrs. Carrick," she said, gulping back tears. "Lady Clara invited my mother and I to her salon tonight. I convinced Mama that it was quite all right and perfectly respectable. It was wrong of me, but no one seemed to know what had happened to you." She dropped her gaze from mine. "I hoped you might have been invited, as well."

I thought perhaps she cared for me, even if only a little. A fire burned in my chest at the thought. "And when you did not find me there?"

"Mrs. Carrick; she was the one in that horrid wig with too much rouge on her cheeks the night we were there together..." She looked up at me and I nodded.

"She said that she had a message for me. I thought it was perhaps from you."

"But, of course," I said kindly. How else should a

272

disreputable man communicate with a proper lady? It was certainly Evelyn's way.

"I felt it strange that we had been invited, and thought perhaps you had arranged it with Lady Clara in order to see me. You did not?" she asked.

"I have been ill," I said, apologetic. Inwardly, I was ashamed that I had not so much as thought of her during my week of isolation.

"I am sorry you have been ill, but ever so glad that you are now well! I suppose it was silly of me, but I did hope for a message from you, so I told my mother I had torn a flounce and wished to repair it. Mama preferred that we depart rather than bother with the flounce. Then Mrs. Carrick said that if I wished to remain, she would arrange for me to obtain an escort home with someone very respectable. Mama looked displeased but, as there were a few ladies present with whom Mama was somewhat acquainted, she allowed me to stay."

"Mrs. Carrick deceived us both, but she was no doubt threatened with her life if she did not obey."

Miss Woodmansey nodded. "Yes, I suppose that is true. I followed her down the first set of stairs and did not know a moment of alarm. When we arrived at the ground floor, I wondered why she did not simply hand over the letter or repeat the message, whatever the case might have been. And then I realized you must have been present; in the house. So, when she led me down to the kitchen and along the passage, I assumed you waited for me in the mews. She opened a door and there were the horses and carriages. And then she opened another, and before I could speak she pushed me through and shut it behind me."

"You did not fall? Are you hurt?" I asked, alarmed.

"No, that man was there, waiting for me." This revelation proved too much and she burst into tears.

I took her in my arms and held her close. Her tear-streaked cheek fetched up against my ribs, her trembling echoing against them. She was so delicate, so much in need of my protection, it nearly undid me. We stood thus in the shadows until the footman opened the door and looked about.

"Sir!" he hissed.

We went to the door and he allowed us inside. A woman met us in the vestibule; she no doubt replaced Throckmorton as house-keeper.

"Sir, what is this?" she cried.

"This is Miss Woodmansey. She shall explain all. You must take great care of her!

"Oh, my dear!" she cried as she put her arm around Miss Woodmansey. "Of course I shall, sir! Now, be gone with you!"

I was tempted to protest my innocence in the matter, but there was not the time. "Miss Woodmansey, have the footman carry a message to your parents. Then allow this woman to tend to your needs. I shall call on you here in the morning."

She nodded, her expression dazed. I could not be certain that she understood. I gave the footman the direction of Woodmansey House, bolted out of the house, and back across the square. By the time I arrived at Manwaring House, there was nothing to be done. All was dark. I ran down the area steps and tried the kitchen door. It was locked. I could not understand how the feckless constable had been able to clear up that mess so quickly. There was nothing left for me to do but to retire for the night.

Suddenly more tired than I had ever been, I dragged myself home and rapped on the door. The boot boy opened it and followed me up the stairs to help me out of my coat. I allowed him to unwind my neck cloth, as well. He pulled the shoes from my feet and I removed my breeches before collapsing onto the bed. Finally, he blew out the candle. He crept away, quiet as a mouse, but I roused when he opened the door.

"Boy," I said. "What is your name?"

There was a short pause, and then in a small voice he said, "Jack."

"You're a good boy, Jack," I said. Then I closed my eyes and knew no more. I woke in the morning with an unexpectedly light heart. Miss Woodmansey cared for me, of that I was suddenly quite certain. It was my intention to call on her directly after I had called on Lady Clara and offered her any assistance I could render. I did not know if her husband were alive or dead, incarcerated or escaped. Neither did I know how she would react to each possibility. Nevertheless, I had been present when he met his downfall. I felt I owed it to her to answer any questions she might have about what had happened.

Short opened the door in answer to my rapping. When he saw who stood on the threshold, he smiled tremulously. "It is good to see you, my lord," he said in a voice high with pleasure and old age.

"It is good to see you as well. I trust that the screaming in this house has ceased?" I asked as I stepped inside and handed over my hat and gloves.

"Oh, indeed, sir," Short said as he helped me off with my greatcoat. "Lady Clara is in the morning room if you care to join her there."

No reply was required. I followed him up the stairs to the first floor and stepped through the doors of the sun-drenched room with some trepidation. I could not guess if I should find a grieving wife or the Lady Clara I had most recently come to know.

The table still bore the remains of breakfast, but she sat in a chair by the window, the sun illuminating the ways in which a sleepless night had ravaged her face. Her suffering incited in me a plethora of emotions: empathy with all its companions, coupled with a mild revulsion. If it had not been for her, Johnny Gilbert would not be dead, nor would Willy. I took a moment to remind myself that the true villain was her husband, and she another unwilling victim of his cruelty. Nearly everything she had done had been at his express command under threat of great harm, even death.

I sketched a bow and she turned to me. "Lord Trevelin, how good of you to call."

"Of course, how could I do otherwise?"

"Did you think me in need of comfort?"

"I cannot say. It depends on what happened after I got away. Perhaps you had better tell me."

She sighed. "Mrs. Carrick is a useful sort. She made you believe that she had gone through the door, but she merely allowed the breeze to blow out her candle as she waited at the top of the stairs. When she heard the brouhaha, she hurried to fetch me. I saw you race by with that young lady of yours."

"She is not my young lady," I began, but she put up a hand to forestall me.

"Huther explained to me what he had done. That unsavory, large fellow assisted Huther in dragging Rober…" She looked away to again take in the view from the window. "His body was removed from the premises. I expect to see neither of those gentlemen ever again. Mrs. Carrick and the girl did their best to clean up the mess, but it is of no consequence. Whatever is found below is the work of none but my husband."

The muscles of my arms and legs relaxed before I realized how taut they had been. "Then he is dead?"

She shrugged. "He shall never hurt anyone ever again."

"And the constable? What was he told?"

She looked at me in faint surprise. "No one went for the constable. What purpose would that serve?"

In truth, I had done nothing illegal, but I knew that trouble went hand-in-hand with scandal. I was vastly relieved that my name would not be associated with the death of her husband. I sank into a chair at her side. "Please accept my deepest commiseration. And yet, I cannot regret the fact that he is no longer free to hurt you." I took her hand in mind. "You are young and charming. You shall marry again."

A tear slid down her cheek as she turned away. "I do not deserve happiness, my lord. I have greatly sinned, and find I can blame only myself."

"You are not responsible for Johnny's death. That sin lies in your husband's dish."

"But it is I who threatened Throckmorton. He would never have been involved if I had not."

I could not entirely disagree. "Then I suppose I must blame myself for Throckmorton's death. I ought to have taken no thought for my own life and wrested the gun from his grasp."

She shrugged. "So that he might hang? Or worse, be taken by my husband? He died in the manner he wished to die. That he deserved death was the fault of no one but me."

"He was frightened out of his wits, and so were you. What would Manwaring have done if you did not produce the money you had lost? The card parties were his means of hiding the screams from the others. It can be no one's fault but his."

"I should have thought of another way. I should never have told him about Johnny Gilbert and what he saw," she insisted, her voice growing in volume with each sentence. "I should have been the one to suffer. I should have been the one to die."

"We none of us can know what might have happened if we had each chosen a different course." I patted her hand in mine. "I only know that we must make the best of what is left to us."

She turned to face me. "I wish to thank you, my lord, for what you have done. Goodbye." Then she drew her hand from mine and turned her gaze to the view beyond the window.

I had been dismissed, but from what? I could not say what it meant, and it was with a deep foreboding that I quit the room. When I gained the ground floor I was met by Short, who produced my things.

"You shall keep a close eye on your mistress, shall you not?" I asked him as he handed me by hat.

"I shall endeavor," he said with a deep bow.

As the door to Manwaring House shut behind me I turned my face towards Hampton House, the dwelling wherein Miss Woodmansey abided. My heart lightened again and I made my way down the pavement and through the park. When I rapped I was met by the butler, Hoagland.

"Lady Vawdrey is not at home today to visitors," he said with a bow.

"I pray that she is not ill. However, I have come to call on Miss Woodmansey."

"I shall ascertain if she is at home," Hoagland intoned. He allowed me entrance and I waited in the vestibule whilst he determined whether Miss Woodmansey wished to see me. I knew that she did.

Once he had disappeared, I sauntered down the hall to peek into the study. Señyor Rey was not therein, nor was there a fire made up in the grate. I wondered if it meant he was out or in the upstairs salon with Miss Woodmansey.

When Hoagland returned, he informed me that she would see me. For the second time that hour I was led up to the first-floor morning room. I found her standing by the fireplace and when I came through the door, she delivered a splendid curtsy. I gave her my best bow and then took her hand and kissed it tenderly.

She smiled, but I could see that she was troubled.

"I pray that you are fully recovered from the events of last night," I said.

"Mostly," she said, "though I fear that I shall never completely overcome the fear. I shall always be afraid of the dark, I do believe."

"You must give it time, my dear. In the meantime," I said, retaining possession of her hand, "there are candles, the fire in the grate, the stars in the sky, and the moon to light your way."

"You are very kind, my lord. I wonder; have you spoken with Señyor Rey?"

"No, where is he this morning? I did not see him in the study below stairs."

"After you departed," she said as she moved away, forcing me to free her hand, "Lady Vawdrey took charge of me. It was decided that he should take the message to my parents and that he should then seek rooms in a hotel. She did not think it seemly for the two of us to abide under the same roof."

I felt as if I had been slapped. "Why ever not? He is honorable, as are you!"

"Of course, but one's reputation cannot be given in exchange for convenience. You know how vicious people can be."

"Yes," I mused as I fingered my scar. "I suppose your parents shall come to fetch you soon. I am delighted to have this opportunity to speak with you first, however."

She glanced up at me from the corner of her eye through the sweet curve of her lashes. "Am I not worth the slightly longer journey to Grosvenor Square?"

"Of course you are, only…" I bit off the remainder of the sentence. This was not the moment to point out that her parents might refuse me entrance. "I am grateful that I have been allowed to speak with you in private, though I had expected Lady Vawdrey to stand over you like the virago she is."

She gave me a sad smile. "Lady Vawdrey has made her feelings about you abundantly clear. However, I asked to be allowed to speak with you in private and she agreed."

I had no need to hear what those feelings were. "Why should we care what Lady Vawdrey thinks? The woman hates me. She blames me for Throckmorton's death, and more besides. She simply resents being thwarted. That does not mean we should not do as we wish."

"You are correct, of course. I do not mean to throw away my happiness for the sake of Lady Vawdrey. However, it is not her feelings that concern me but those of my mama and papa."

"You are a clever young lady. I have no doubt that you shall prevent your parents from denying your happiness." I smiled, certain that her thoughts mirrored mine.

"I do mean to try," she said with an answering smile.

It was a beginning, but one that was still miles from what I had hoped. I could not comprehend what held her back. The night prior she had stood in the circle of my arms and now she treated me with such a measure of reserve that I began to doubt. "Come, Miss Woodmansey." I possessed myself again of her hand. "Let me into your heart. I swear that I shall never give you cause to doubt me."

"Dear Lord Trevelin," she said, her eyes more tender than I had yet seen them. "Your affection for me is not in question. Nor is mine for you, if I must say so."

She loved me! I could hardly credit it. I knelt at her tiny feet, drew her hands to my lips and kissed them with all the pent-up passion that I felt for her. "I shall care for you always," I murmured between kisses. "I shall see that you have all that you wish, that you are never hurt or lonely."

She looked into my eyes, which, with me on my knees, was not a journey so far. Her expression held an expression of extreme regret. "How? How shall you ensure that I am never lonely? How shall you convince a patroness of Almack's that I should have a voucher to their functions? How shall you ensure that my mama would come to our home? I would have *you*, yes! That *should* be enough for any woman, my lord, but not for me."

I stared at her in astonishment. "You believe that I shall be ostracized forever? It is for my reputation that you reject me? For the things I have been *said* to have done?"

She bit her lip and turned away. Her actions, however, did not obscure the tears that slipped down her cheeks.

I could see the truth of it now, as if it had happened yesterday. It was on account of Evelyn. He had not saved my life; he had taken it.

"What I cannot understand," I said to my cousin, "is why the Duke of Rutherford should wish to punish me. It was not meant to be a duel to the death; any other would have done the same. Does he hate you so much that he must take revenge on me for not allowing him to kill you?

Evelyn shook his head as if at an errant child. "He is not proud of the fact that he tore into you once you had forced him off of me. What's more," Evelyn drawled, "men are not even-tempered when it comes to their wives."

"I expect there is truth in that. Indeed, I have seen for myself," I agreed. "And yet, his wife could not have picked me out of a crowd before he made me his personal bete noir.*"*

Evelyn shrugged. "You must not regret the loss of her acquaintance. She is not worth it."

The Devil in Beauty

I could hardly credit his words. "And what of you, Eve? Was she worth the trouble you caused? When will you learn not to dally with another man's wife?"

Slowly, I picked myself up off the floor. "No, do not stir," I said when she turned her face to mine, her cheeks wet with tears. "I cannot bear to see you so distressed." I began to walk away, out of the room, to never see her again, but something made me pause. "He is a good man, your señyor," I said. "I wish you joy of him. Truly, I do." And then I left.

Later that day I found myself in the salon of Canning House, watching from the window as a carriage approached the house directly across the square. Mrs. Woodmansey exited and went to the door. I turned away; it was best not to watch her daughter make her official departure from my life. Two days later I read in the paper that the Woodmanseys had boarded ship for a holiday in Spain where Miss Desdemona Woodmansey would be married to her betrothed, Señyor Juliol Rey of Barcelona.

This news, as were my feelings, was only eclipsed by the small paragraph heralding the death of Lady Clara, wife of Mr. R. Manwaring. I was not as heartbroken as I had supposed. I did wonder how she had done it; wondered where the little muff gun had gone after they had cleared the room free of Throckmorton's demise.

That night, or perhaps early the next morning, I was wakened from a deep sleep. I could not say why, and then I heard something that made all of the hair on my head stand up on end.

"Trev!"

I recognized the voice, but to have heard it was

impossible. I sat up and peered into the darkness. Slumped in a chair in the corner of the room, his head thrown back as if dead, was the figure of a man.

"Canning!" I cried. Who else could it have been? And yet, I was full of dread that it was he, and more if it were not. I fumbled for the candlestick and lit the wick as fast as my trembling fingers would allow. The flame cast the corner into deeper shadow; I held it aloft and was able to determine that the intruder was not my last living friend.

It was Willy.

He looked very much the way he had the last time I had seen him; broken, limp, lifeless. Then, quite suddenly, he lifted his head and laughed.

I felt cold all over. "Willy? Is that…you?"

"Who else?" His grin was full and wide, just as it was before his riding accident.

"You're not dead?" I threw my feet to the floor as my entire form filled with an emotion just short of joy. (I had known hope so infrequently of late that I could scarce recall its name.)

"Of course I am dead. Has no one told you?" He still smiled and his eyes gleamed with mirth.

I sat on the edge of the bed and stared at him, unsure of what to say. Either he was merely a figment of my imagination, which rendered a reply unnecessary, or he wasn't. I could think of no suitable response for the latter.

"Come, come, Trev; don't look so dashed astounded! It twists your mouth so that it seems you are sneering at me."

"Sneering?" I shook with dismay and, I suppose, pure wonder. "Why should I sneer at you?"

Willy threw his hands, both hale, to a pair of hearty knees. "I don't know. Perhaps because I'm a spook?"

"Are you?" My voice wavered with the fearful hammering of my heart. He was dressed for riding and looked very much like himself when I knew him best. It alarmed me to no end. "You could merely be a specter in a dream," I said with a bravado I did not feel. "I am asleep and shall wake to find that this has all been a product of my imagination."

"I should not have wakened you," he said with a regretful shake of his head. "I merely wished to thank you for rescuing my name."

His name! What could that mean to him now? I wondered. I broke out in a cold sweat, sure that he had come to castigate me for my actions. "You died and I did nothing to prevent it. For what do you have to thank me?"

He sighed as one does when a child asks a question impossible to answer. "There is much to tell you, but it shall keep." He rose from his chair and strolled to the bed. I watched in amazement as his booted feet struck the floor in a brisk and even repeat.

"Willy, you are whole!"

"You begin to comprehend," he said as he reached for the blankets and drew them back.

Of their own accord, my limbs dragged me towards my pillow and he tugged the bedclothes up to my chin.

"If I fall asleep," I said in a daze, "the dream will be over, and you will be gone."

"You needn't fear, Trev. I shan't leave you."

At his words my trembling stilled, peace filled my heart, and I knew no more.

285

When I woke the next morning, the sun had made another appearance. It shone directly into my eyes; it would seem that Jack had forgotten to draw the curtains. Squinting against the onslaught of light, I considered recent events: Rey, gone; Miss Woodmansey, gone with him; Lady Clara, dead; Throckmorton, dead; Willy—dead. A heaviness settled over my heart. I endured the sorrow as I allowed my lids to open, little by little, until I stared up at the ceiling.

I lay abed and watched the sunlight dance its patterns across the plaster; it was some solace. Soon Jack would be in to start a fire and warm the room. What's more, the Cannings would eventually return to restore life to the house. For now, I would dress and start my life anew, one free of the ghosts that plagued me.

I rolled over in the direction of the chair that my imagination had filled sometime during the night. To my chagrin, it was still occupied. Digging the heels of my hands into my eyes, I groaned. "I see that I needs must set up my own establishment, after all."

"I should think so," Willy agreed with a quick survey of the room, his perfectly formed lips twisted in distaste. "This house is haunted."

The End

Trev searches for a killer with the help of a spook and a boot boy, in The Scandal in Honor--*coming soon!*

By the Same Author

Via Dunhaven Place Publishing
Lady Crenshaw's Christmas
Lord Haversham Takes Command
The Lord Who Sneered and Other Tales
Miss Armistead Makes Her Choice
O'er the River Liffey

Via Mirror Press
A Timeless Romance Anthology: Winter Collection: It Happened One Night
A Midwinter Ball: Timeless Regency Collection: Much Ado About Dancing

Via Montlake Romance
Miss Delacourt Speaks Her Mind
Miss Delacourt Has Her Day

About the Author

Award-winning, best-selling author Heidi Ashworth lives with her husband and three children in the San Francisco Bay Area. She writes sweet, traditional, Regency-era romance and mystery. *The Devil in Beauty* is the first in her Lord Trevelin Mysteries series. Look for *The Scandal in Honor*, coming soon!

Review The Devil in Beauty: http://a.co/9eu9CfM

Sign up for my newsletter at The Scribbling Divas: https://tinyurl.com/jknfanp

Facebook: https://www.facebook.com/authorheidiashworth

Find me on Amazon: https://www.amazon.com/Heidi-Ashworth/e/B001JSDUX6

Twitter:@AshworthHeidi

Website: www.HeidiAshworth.com

Blog: www.HeidiAshworth.blogspot.com

Made in the USA
San Bernardino, CA
09 November 2017